PENGUIN B

Turning Points

Since her retirement from the Melbourne Tourism Authority in 1995, Sue Calwell was recognised for her twenty years of involvement in the industry with the 'Outstanding Individual Contribution for the Australian Tourism Industry' Award in 1999.

Sue continues to be active on many boards and committees. She was the inaugural chairman of the Melbourne International Flower and Garden Show, is a director of Melbourne's premier tourist destination, The Queen Victoria Market, and is chair of the special events committee of one of the world's leading heart research facilities, The Baker Medical Research Institute. She is also the proprietor of a small retail chain, The Melbourne Sock Shop.

Sue co-authored the first two books in this series, *There's More to Life than Sex and Money* and *There's So Much More to Life than Sex and Money*, with Daniel Johnson. She lives in Melbourne with her partner Alistair and her three children.

Turning Points

EDITED BY SUE CALWELL

PENGUIN BOOKS

Penguin Books Australia Ltd
487 Maroondah Highway, PO Box 257
Ringwood, Victoria 3134, Australia
Penguin Books Ltd
Harmondsworth, Middlesex, England
Penguin Putnam Inc.
375 Hudson Street, New York, New York 10014, USA
Penguin Books Canada Limited
10 Alcorn Avenue, Toronto, Ontario, Canada M4V 3B2
Penguin Books (NZ) Ltd
Cnr Rosedale and Airborne Roads, Albany, Auckland, New Zealand
Penguin Books (South Africa) (Pty) Ltd
24 Sturdee Avenue, Rosebank, Johannesburg 2196, South Africa
Penguin Books India (P) Ltd
11, Community Centre, Panchsheel Park, New Delhi 110 017, India

First published by Penguin Books Australia Ltd 2001

1 3 5 7 9 10 8 6 4 2

Design and illustrations by Cathy Larsen, Penguin Design Studio
Cover image by Liberty of London
Typeset in 11/16 pt Sabon by Midland Typesetters, Maryborough, Victoria
Printed and bound in Australia by McPherson's Printing Group, Maryborough, Victoria

National Library of Australia
Cataloguing-in-Publication data:

Turning points

ISBN 0 14 029945 9.

1. Life change events – Case studies. 2. Courage – Case studies. 3. Friendship – Case studies. 4. Love – Case studies. I. Calwell, Sue.

158

www.penguin.com.au

To my dad, George Trevor Alfred Calwell – I wish he could have seen the wonderful people his grand-children are growing into. And to my children, who inspire me to make time for the people I love. May this book inspire others to find that time.

Contents

Hope

Courage

LOVE

SELF-ACCEPTANCE

Grief

Forgiveness

Wisdom

Inspiration

Introduction

This is the third book of stories from some amazing people who have had the desire, courage and strength to share their personal experiences with others. My own life has gone through many changes since I wrote my story in *There's More to Life than Sex and Money* and its sequel *There's So Much More to Life than Sex and Money*.

It's now six years since I took off the label plastered across my forehead that read CEO of the Melbourne Tourism Authority, an organisation that I founded and ran for twenty years. I felt that it was quite an accomplishment to survive in this high-profile position for such a length of time in an industry that was forging ahead in Australia. But once you tear off the label of the position you hold, then the discovery of who you really are begins; to quote an old saying, 'Will the real Sue Calwell please stand up?'

The readers of *There's More to Life than Sex and Money* and

There's So Much More to Life than Sex and Money will know that my co-author Daniel Johnson and I met through our children and our families became firm friends. When Daniel's young wife, Linda, died after a battle with cancer we decided to record some of life's most special experiences to help the children remember how strong those bonds were.

Our idea grew, and suddenly friends and colleagues wanted to share their stories as well. And here we are three books later. This time I have undertaken *Turning Points* solo, as Daniel returned to America and, true to his values, is loving his new life in Colorado.

And so to me. Since my departure from the corporate rat race, I was forced to face change in almost every aspect of my life. I no longer had the security of a job, my ten-year marriage had failed and I had three young children who had been accustomed to nannies, housekeepers and extended family as their primary carers. Then suddenly I was a full-time mum.

My job had been my comfort zone. It was always exciting and challenging but because of the demands and the long hours associated with the tourism and hospitality industry, I never needed to look too closely at myself or examine my lifestyle. I didn't have the time and I was simply too tired. Good excuses.

I had always resisted change in so many ways; maybe I was fearful of what it could mean. *Not* changing felt so much more secure and comfortable. We all like to have a comfort zone to feel safe in.

I discovered working outside the home was a breeze compared to the challenges of running a home and the demands of children who were then aged nine, eight and six years old. They thought it was wonderful. Mum was there to pick them up each day from school, to hear of how their day went and to participate in all aspects of their daily life.

My life revolved, and still does, around the children; I am their taxi driver to karate, chess, basketball, French lessons or whatever is on the timetable for that day. Sometimes I'm too tired to get out of the car before heading back for the next pick-up.

But this is a journey I had to make. The transition took time for me: I sometimes wonder what on earth I have done, and other days I know it is my salvation. I discovered on this journey that I must look after myself and my own needs, so I have attempted to be in control of my life and keep a balance. This is particularly relevant for me as I am a Libran and Librans need a balanced life.

The stories in this book help bring my perspective back into line and remind me of what is really important in life. I come back to re-read some stories again and again when the moment requires it. These stories show that whatever your background, wherever you live, people's lives are very similar, and the fear, the grief and the joy that we will all undergo at some time in our lives are not reserved for a select few. All the money in the world will not save us from grief, nor will it guarantee happiness.

Turning Points is an exploration of human nature. It inspires me because I see the courage that ordinary people have when their lives don't go according to plan. I see that people face change in every form and learn to live with it, and here they share their innermost strength and wisdom.

For my part, once I overcame my fear of change it was welcome in my journey. I now look forward to charge and embrace it, looking ahead and wondering what adventure life will bring next.

Sue Calwell

Acknowledgements

This book is a tribute to the people who have written letters, faxed, emailed or called to say thank you – people from all walks of life, young people and old people, who have gained something from *There's More to Life than Sex and Money* and *There's So Much More to Life than Sex and Money*. I hope *Turning Points* will also have a special place in your life.

Each time I receive a note or some feedback from a reader I am humbled by their words of thanks. I feel honoured that I could in some small way make a difference to someone's life. I believe everyone would like an opportunity to put back into our community if they can. If I have been able to do this by imploring so many people to share their own personal experiences so others can read and gain hope, then this gives me great joy.

The stories in this book are from people who have laid bare their lives: heartbreak, triumph, love, disappointment, guilt – and to all of them I express my heartfelt gratitude because you have enabled *Turning Points* to become a reality.

There are a few special friends who have kept me focused on achieving the completion of this beautiful book. They deserve uncountable thanks.

First off, Elizabeth Boydell. What can I say? She was relentless. Whenever I was down and felt it was too hard to continue trying to cajole people into writing stories for me, she gave me the confidence to keep going. She believed in me and never wavered. She also gave me a well-aimed kick in the backside when I needed it. I am so lucky to have such a friend. We shared tears and laughter, joy and sorrow as we read these stories. Elizabeth spent hours on the computer typing stories and communicating with the contributors. She was the phantom emailer. Thanks Elizabeth.

To Arthur Braithwaite, whom I have never met but who emailed me in July 2000 asking when he could expect the next book to come out. Arthur is a priest in New South Wales and used the stories from the first two books to illustrate the themes of his Sunday services. I laughed when he told me how he would apologise when people asked the name of the book he took the stories from. I assured him the next book would have a more suitable title. Arthur just seemed to know when I needed a little encouragement to keep going in my endless search for stories and he made contact with many of his friends and colleagues to ask them to contribute as well. Arthur, thank you for being so sensitive and aware, and for making contact at just the right time.

To my partner, Alistair Trimble. We have been through a lot this last year or so with many challenges. Thank you for always believing I could do it.

To my friend Glenn Nicholson, with whom I have had so many lattes while discussing and discovering what is really important in life. I have been fortunate to share your endless enthusiasm.

To all at Penguin Books: Julie Gibbs, with whom I started this journey six years ago, has never wavered in her belief that these books can make a difference in people's lives; and Kirsten Abbott, who has been the guiding hand in editing and delivering such a beautiful book.

Finally to my three children, Georgina, Victoria and Daniel, who give me unconditional love and bring me such joy every day of my life.

Friendship

Hampers on the Doorstep

SIMON MOLESWORTH

In August 1995, our then ten-year-old son Lachlan fell suddenly ill with what was initially thought to be a serious bout of influenza. Within a week or so the search for something more serious began, with encephalitis, meningitis and glandular fever being possibilities. All tests proved negative, but before our eyes over the next few months his health steadily declined until early in the New Year when his condition was so serious that he was transferred to hospital in order to be kept alive with naso-gastric feeding. He was diagnosed with chronic fatigue syndrome. Lachlan was unable to complete the final term of Grade 5 and thereafter missed years of schooling. The illness that was to follow extended over a five-year period and has still not entirely departed, although he is well down the road to recovery. Lachlan had four periods in hospital as an in-patient and at times his condition was dire. He then attended a rehabilitation hospital as an outpatient for several years.

Prior to falling so suddenly ill, Lachlan did well at school; he loved and lived life to the full. He enjoyed sports and had a zest for learning. He was popular with many friends, and at home he seemed to have more energy than the rest of us combined. He always had a project on the go and had an attitude that nothing was too hard for him. Becoming a 'log in the bed', too ill to move any part of his body, unable to feed, to talk, to read or even to listen and, worse still, unable to get effective sleep to rest, was catastrophic. A horror nightmare for anyone; but incredibly cruel for a boy always determined to seize the day – each and every day.

It was during Lachlan's illness, especially in that first horrific year, that we experienced a magnificent surge of support and love from friends and family. Almost spontaneously, people who were moved by our plight surrounded us. Many of them said, 'There but for the grace of God go I . . .' and so felt for us. It is that support that is the subject of this story.

During the worst period, my wife, Lindy, and I would take it in turns to be with Lachlan in hospital; one of us was always with him, night and day. One of us would sleep on a mattress on the floor beside his hospital bed and give comfort, which was frequently required. As dawn would break we would do a change in shift; the one in the hospital overnight would leave to return home for a shower and change while the other would take over. We would then do another change of shift mid-afternoon before the final 10 p.m. changeover for the night. During these awful weeks we frequently rendezvoused in the hospital car park or at a kerbside stop between hospital and home. For a while, this was the extent to which we overlapped. The challenges of maintaining the rest of our lives during this period, especially a family household with two younger children, are obvious.

Soon after Lachlan's hospitalisation, one of us arrived home from the hospital to find a huge basket and a couple of cardboard boxes on the step. Opening them revealed beautifully prepared meals, three courses from soup through to, say, a chocolate cake, with wine and exotic extras such as pâté, cheese and savouries. No name, no explanation; just remarkably clear labelling precisely identifying the contents of each container and the ingredients used in each of the meals. The initial surprise delivery provided meals for five days, with careful instructions for freezing, defrosting and reheating. Meticulously organised to say the least.

Now we have all heard of or read stories of kindness shown to people suffering hardship; however, once the flood has subsided or the battle is over, the kind support often trails off until eventually the people affected are left to their own devices. In our case, the most remarkable aspect of this 'meal support' was that it didn't trail off – our caring friends kept it going for months. The first box had instructions to leave the empty containers at the school office where we would find a replacement supply waiting for us. Thereafter, we knew that every Tuesday or Wednesday afternoon there was to be a changeover – empties for full.

Eventually, many months after Lachlan returned home from hospital, we asked for a letter to be published in the school's weekly newsletter. Our letter thanked the school community from the bottom of our hearts but asked the kind people to stop. We were overwhelmed with their continuing generosity and felt we couldn't allow it to continue with our moral indebtedness growing daily to those who were continuing to be so kind.

To this day, we do not know all of those who were behind these wonderful acts of kindness. We know that there had to be quite a number of people involved preparing meals and we know that it required excellent organisational skills to coordinate. We do know that those involved included teachers at the school, as one of our younger children overheard two people talking about the hampers just at the moment when a question was asked: 'Is next week the teachers' week with the Molesworths' meals?'

After the cessation of the meal deliveries, as the months merged into years, people continually offered support; they wrote letters suggesting treatments of which they had read or heard; visited; sent cards and cheery balloons; and dropped off gifts, such as an occasional box of chocolates. One family even maintained for years a regular supply of children's comics and a monthly garden magazine for us. If we had ever had doubt about the capacity of the human spirit to be kind and generous, it was completely cast aside after our experiences with Lachlan's illness. It renewed our faith in there being a deep-seated goodness in our fellow humans. All too often, we read of cruelties, of unkind or unthinking acts, and no doubt such things constantly occur, but our experience during adversity has been a good one and truly deserves to be told. For all of those who showed us such kindness, we will forever have warmth in our hearts.

My Life in Jail

PHYLLIS CRAWCOUR

This is a funny subject to write about, but one that's very relevant to me now.

I am an inmate at Deer Park Women's Prison. I couldn't understand how twelve perfect strangers who'd viewed me for only a short time could hold my future in their hands and ultimately have me sentenced to three years in jail. None of it made any sense to me and my faith in the justice system quickly disappeared.

Once brought to my new home many dilemmas and obstacles faced me. At sixty years of age I was entering into virgin territory, and I wondered who and what was I going to be the target of?

How was I going to face separation from the man I dearly loved and had shared my life with for forty-two years? I knew nothing about jail politics and the pecking order in there. Could I fit in? I was terrified and traumatised, so much so that I became withdrawn and depressed, isolating myself in my cell.

Initially I wanted to die but the thought of my husband and three sons who loved me made me realise how unreasonable and selfish I was being.

The turning point came four months after being imprisoned. I was being badgered daily by one of the heavies for being stuck up and unsociable. Even when I tried sitting with her and watching television, I was accused of being a lazy bitch who just sat around all day doing nothing! Every day I put up with the ridicule and provocation until one day I answered her back.

The fully fledged verbal fight that ensued soon looked to develop into a physical brawl as she approached me with her clenched fists. I asked her to stop for a moment so I could take my glasses off. This struck her as funny and as she roared with laughter she said, 'For an old girl you've got real guts for taking me on.'

She was the 'Bea Smith' of the institution, and I found out that no one had ever answered her back before. From that day on she became my mentor, teaching me about jail life and how to cope with the loss of freedom.

I picked myself, and my attitude, up and enrolled in full-time education, taking on computers, woodwork, horticulture, drama, creative writing and art. On getting to know the principal and the drug counsellor at the education department, I mentioned that I had been a personal assistant and secretary for fourteen years. They were looking for someone to help in the office and before long I was organising both of them. As each day arrived it brought new challenges and fulfillment to me.

Each day I grew emotionally and mentally. I was actually taking time to find out who I really was. I became a mother to the girls, my co-inmates, and dried their tears and hugged them. Mostly I just listened, and occasionally gave what advice I felt I could, but only if asked. This led to me being appointed peer group support worker, helping the new arrivals to settle in and steering them through the traumatic first few weeks.

In many ways (and this may sound strange) jail has been good for me. It has given me time to explore my inner self. I have seen the other side of the result of criminal activities – angry and lost souls who can only find comfort in needles or tablets. It has shown me that jail does not rehabilitate these poor girls, who are on that terrible treadmill of forever returning to this place.

The amount of drugs readily available here is amazing, and the ways and means by which the girls get their supplies in is nothing short of brilliant. It's just a pity they don't use their brains to create a better life for themselves. I see mothers and children sobbing when it comes to the end of a visit – they do really care – but the power of heroin over their lives is fundamentally their first priority.

In the strangest places you come across God's magic

One of my goals when I leave here is to pass on some of the qualities I have learned about myself to other newly released girls. I hope to work in some sort of voluntary capacity to put something constructive back into life.

I have learned that there are always two sides to every coin. I've enjoyed the good life with a husband, children, friends and world travel, and now I've endured the loss of freedom and separation from those I love. I know now that I was selfish and pray that that streak has forever disappeared.

When I leave here, my husband and I will both be sixty-six. Our retirement years will have extra meaning for us both and point us in a new direction in our lives. I pray that God will give us good health and many more years together.

In the strangest places you come across God's magic. One evening I was sitting outside and saw the most magnificent cloud formations. As they passed overhead I realised that if there had been no clouds in my life I could have continued to be shallow and selfish and would never have known how dearly I am loved and supported.

The Art of Success

LES TWENTYMAN

Have you ever wondered what it is that makes someone a success? Is it by kicking the deciding goal in a tense AFL Grand Final? Is it by becoming a captain of industry and then engineering a company take-over that leaves 500 long-term employees out of a job, all in the name of global best practice? Is it by winning an Olympic gold medal, with John and Janette Howard sitting in the crowd cheering you on?

Let me tell you what I think makes you a success. I think you are a success when you are written off as worthless, and you come back and prove your denigrators wrong. You are a success when you are officially declared a nuisance and an outcast, and you bounce back and achieve more than most of your knockers ever dreamt about. In short, you are a success when you make something from nothing, when you turn a negative into a positive.

Danny was seventeen years old when I first met him. I was working for Sunshine Council then and, with a colleague Jim

Markovski, came across this young bloke who was under police notice for 'wilful damage' to public property. Back then Danny was what some people would describe as a 'graffiti artist' and others would call a 'vandal'. He loved painting things, and, in the absence of canvas and art paper, he did his paintings anywhere he could, on trains, on walls, on the sides of bridges and buildings. For that was Danny's studio, he had no other. His paintings started appearing all over the western suburbs. If you have travelled through Footscray or Sunshine over the past ten years you would have seen them. By one of those weird coincidences that make life bearable, one of his pieces accidentally formed the background to a Toyota television commercial I was filmed in some years ago.

I'm not sure what it is about graffiti, but it manages to upset a lot of people. Despite the fact that a large percentage of the urban skyline is now covered with advertising hoardings of far less artistic merit than much of the graffiti you come across, many otherwise sensible people just lose their composure at the thought of it. Just the other day the entire Year 12 component of a Melbourne suburban secondary college was suspended, en masse, because a message, innocuous and totally inoffensive, was painted on the school roof. The sort of unjust collective punishment, generally the last resort of cowards, which they'd never dare try on adults.

Danny is one of the more gifted artists I have ever met. That, of course, cut no ice with the law and order system, and he ended up in all kinds of strife. Buildings and walls and trains are sacred, you see, at least until either the developers come along and knock them down or the government privatises them. They even locked him up for a while, because they didn't know what to do with him. Around the time Jim and I met him, he was facing court again. We had Rob Stary, one of Melbourne's better criminal barristers, defending him, and we decided to let Danny's artwork speak for itself.

There are some magistrates around, of course, who would have locked Danny away, on the grounds that it wasn't his first time. Lots of magistrates aren't very imaginative. But we were lucky. Julian Fitzgerald was sitting on the bench that day and we handed him a portfolio of Danny's artistic work. He spent several minutes looking through it, and then announced that he was deeply impressed. Jim and I both spoke on his behalf, and proposed that, with funding from the Twentieth Man Fund, Danny be enrolled in a fine arts course.

Danny has hardly looked back in the ten years since. His story attracted the notice of the television world, and 'Today Tonight' in Melbourne has featured two stories on him. He now has his own company, with people working for him, and is in constant demand because of the recognised quality of his work. He has done several display paintings at High Point West shopping centre, and is regularly invited to speak to students, including those hoping to pursue a similar career. He remains grateful to Jim and me for the direction we sent him in, and has been kind enough to state publicly, on more than one occasion, 'But for these two blokes, my life would have ended up very differently.'

Danny is getting married soon to his best mate, Ivanka. Ivanka completes his success story. They are not asking many people to the wedding. After all, the reception is at the Sheraton, at over $100 a head. But they asked Jim and me to come along. I have had some great moments recently. I had a book published. I took part in the Olympic Torch Relay. But nothing will give me more pleasure and satisfaction than to be a part of Danny and Ivanka's wedding day. For that will be the day that Danny, the nuisance, the outcast, the vandal, completes his comeback. That will be the day that Danny will know the real meaning of success.

Ion's Story: Defection, Rowing and a New Life

SUE CHAPMAN-POPA

Ion, my husband, had been asked to contribute to one of Sue Calwell's books on several occasions.

At Anglesea, Sue begged him again for the gazillionth time, as she had a deadline looming. I asked Ion if he would do it and he gave his usual reply, 'Nah.' I was curious as to why he felt this way. I thought he had learned many life lessons at a pretty young age, and that someone might identify with him or find something in his story consoling if ever faced with any or all of 'the smorgasbord of situations' he found himself in after he decided to defect at twenty-one years of age, disillusioned with communism, from Romania, while participating in their national team at an international rowing regatta in Mannheim, West Germany, in 1978.

Today we went for a walk in the hot Melbourne summer and talked about Sue's book for the last time. It's as a result of this that I decided to write his story for him.

I finally realised just before we set out why he didn't want to put his thoughts down on paper. He really doesn't want to remember, especially the bad bits. If he did, he would remember being interrogated and interviewed by a US intelligence agency at length, after requesting political asylum in Munich, to see if he had any secrets to divulge or if there was any espionage he could take part in. He would remember having two 24/7 bodyguards for the first six months 'while the dust settled', unable to inform his family he was okay. He would remember the pain he caused them, especially his parents, because they thought for those six months that he was dead. He would remember trying to convince Vasille and Ilinca that it was him on the phone, not some sicko torturing them, pretending to be their son.

Then there was the betrayal of his co-defector who made secret plans to go to the USA without informing him, after the two of them had endured so much together. Ion had assumed they were going to stick together no matter what. God knows that there had been plenty of time to tell him of his plans.

He would recall the traumatic silent rejection of certain German locals, the ones who particularly disliked *gastarbeiters* (foreign workers), who when hearing Ion speak Romanian, acted as if he were a leper; they couldn't get away from him fast enough.

He would remember the homesickness of knowing he could never go back. He was AWOL from his time in the Romanian National Service, which would surely mean imprisonment just like his father had endured as a Russian POW in Siberia during World War II: five years of hard labour, eating the soles of his shoes and drinking urine because he was starving and thirsty.

He would remember the anguish of asking himself every minute of every hour of every day if he would do it again, 'Knowing what I know now, would I?'

Ion resolved in those early days that he would not seek too much emotional security in the Romanian community, because he realised there was no going back and that he had to integrate fully into whatever community he was in. It was the only way that he would move forward and make a real go of wherever he ended up. It was during these darkest moments that special people and special moments came shining through.

There was the German teacher Herr Edzell who taught all the *gastarbeiters* in the town. He was a sports fanatic and he and his wife invited Ion and his co-defector into their home on several occasions, and even though they couldn't communicate, the Romanians could feel the warmth of their welcome.

There were the bohemian-arty-radical friends of Ion's French–Australian girlfriend, Isabelle, who lived in Paris. Isabelle and her friends supported and cared for him when he moved to Paris to be with her and then looked out for him when he moved to Melbourne after he and Isabelle had gone their separate ways two weeks after Ion's arrival in Australia.

There was the great feeling of living healthily again, giving up the smokes, losing some kilos and starting to train regularly at Mercantile Rowing Club and then at Banks Rowing Club. Ion couldn't speak any English but he knew how to row. This routine gave his day structure; it made his stressed-out young body relax.

After Ion got fit, strong and seriously into rowing again, he met Reinhold Batschi who at the time was the new head coach of Australian rowing. He was also a Romanian, also a defector, who went on to became coach of the two Australian Olympic teams (1984 and 1988) of which Ion was a member. (They won bronze in '84.) Reinhold was the coach of the crew in 1983, when they won bronze at the World Championships in Germany, and in 1986 when they won gold at the World Championships, the Commonwealth Games and the European Championships. Reinhold understood Ion's past and was there with him in the present during his most triumphant moments as an oarsman.

The most special person, though, was Ted Sorani. The Italian–Romanian life member of Mercantile Rowing Club who was suspicious at first of Ion – he thought he was a spy. Ted avoided Ion. Ion thought he had misunderstood the other rowers who were pointing at Ted saying something about him being Romanian. Ion would approach him and Ted would only speak English. Finally, when Ted was convinced that Ion was not a spy he spoke to him in Romanian. Then Ion was invited to Ted's house for a barbecue. He was introduced to Ted's lovely wife, Cenza, and their four kids. It was soon after this that Ion was invited by the whole Sorani family to live with them. He stayed for more than a year, rent-free. Ted found Ion a job and gave him the biggest gift of all, the sense of belonging. With that came the strength within Ion that he knew he was going to make it. Ted and his family became Ion's anchor, and in many ways they still are, twenty-two years later.

Ion and I have two children, our daughter, Rosie, and our son, Ted. His best friend is Daniel (Sue Calwell's son). We were all together at Anglesea this summer, at Ted's house.

The Pillbox Hat

ANONYMOUS

Twenty years ago, I drove a cab for a living. It was a cowboy's life, a life for someone who wanted no boss. What I didn't realise was that it was also a ministry. Because I drove the night shift, my cab became a moving confessional. Passengers climbed in, sat behind me in total anonymity and told me about their lives. I encountered people whose lives amazed me, ennobled me, made me laugh, and weep. But none touched me more than that of a woman I picked up late one night.

I responded to a call from a small block of flats in a quiet part of town. I assumed I was being sent to pick up some partygoers, someone who had just had a fight with a lover, or a worker heading to an early shift. When I arrived at 2.30 a.m., the building was dark except for a single light in a ground floor window. Under these circumstances, many drivers would just honk once or twice, wait a minute, then drive away. But I had seen too many impoverished people who depended on taxis as their only means of transportation. Unless a situation smelled of danger, I always went to the door. This passenger might be someone who needed my assistance, I reasoned to myself. So I walked to the door and knocked.

'Just a minute,' answered a frail, elderly voice. I could hear something being dragged across the floor. After a long pause, the door opened. A small woman in her eighties stood before me. She was wearing a print dress and a pillbox hat with a veil pinned on it, like somebody out of a 1940s movie. By her side was a small nylon suitcase. The apartment looked as if no one had lived in it for years. All the furniture was covered with sheets. There were no clocks on the walls, no knick-knacks or utensils on the counters. In the corner was a cardboard box filled with photos and glassware.

I took the suitcase to the cab, then returned to assist the woman. She took my arm and we walked slowly toward the curb. She kept thanking me for my kindness.

'It's nothing,' I told her. 'I just try to treat my passengers the way I would want my mother treated.'

'Oh, you're such a good boy,' she said.

When we got in the cab, she gave me an address, then asked, 'Could you drive through downtown?'

'It's not the shortest way,' I answered quickly.

'Oh, I don't mind,' she said. 'I'm in no hurry. I'm on my way to a hospice.'

I looked in the rear-view mirror. Her eyes were glistening.

'I don't have any family left,' she continued. 'The doctor says I don't have very long.'

I quietly reached over and shut off the meter.

'Which route would you like me to take?' I asked.

For the next two hours, we drove through the city. She showed me the building where she had once worked as an elevator operator. We drove through the neighbourhood where she and her husband had lived when they were newlyweds. She had me pull up in front of a furniture warehouse that had once been a ballroom where she had gone dancing as a girl. Sometimes she'd ask me to slow in front of a particular building or corner and would sit staring into the darkness, saying nothing.

As the first hint of sun was creasing the horizon, she suddenly said, 'I'm tired. Let's go now.'

We drove in silence to the address she had given me. It was a low building, like a small convalescent home, with a driveway that passed under a portico. Two orderlies came out to the cab as soon as we pulled up. They were solicitous and intent, watching her every move. They must have been expecting her. I opened the trunk and took the small suitcase to the door. The woman was already seated in a wheelchair.

Great moments often catch us unaware

'How much do I owe you?' she asked, reaching into her purse.

'Nothing,' I said.

'You have to make a living,' she answered.

'There are other passengers,' I responded.

Almost without thinking, I bent and gave her a hug. She held onto me tightly.

'You gave an old woman a little moment of joy,' she said.

I squeezed her hand, then walked into the dim morning light. Behind me, a door shut. It was the sound of the closing of a life.

I didn't pick up any more passengers that shift. I drove aimlessly, lost in thought. For the rest of that day I could hardly talk. What if that woman had gotten an angry driver or one who was impatient to end his shift? What if I had refused to take the run, or had honked once, then driven away? On a quick review, I don't think that I have done very many more important things in my life.

We're conditioned to think that our lives revolve around great moments. But great moments often catch us unaware – beautifully wrapped in what others may consider small ones.

A Chance Meeting

MARY FRYDENLUND

Many years ago in about 1967 I worked at the Oslo Telephone Exchange and Public Phone Booths in Norway. One morning when I arrived at work, two girls were sleeping on the hard wooden benches next to their backpacks. It turned out that they were Australians travelling around the world. They had arrived in Oslo late in the evening, and the youth hostel where they had booked a room was closed, and they had nowhere to stay the night.

One of the girls wanted to book a phone call to Australia, as it was her father's birthday. She told us that she only wanted to speak for three minutes, and asked us to cut the call after three minutes. The call came through and the girl talked to her father for a long time as the operator forgot to cut the call. When she came out she was charged for fifteen minutes, as the manager said she must have known that she had been talking for longer than intended. The girl got very upset, as she didn't have the amount of money charged, and the manager said she would take the girl's watch as payment. The girl cried and was very frustrated, tired and angry.

During all this I felt very sorry for her and telephoned the main boss at the telephone company and told him the whole sad story. He told us to let her pay for three minutes and forget the rest.

When things had settled down I asked the two girls to leave their luggage with me, and enjoy Oslo for a few hours and come back when I had finished work. Then they could come home with me, have a bath, wash some clothes and have a couple of good nights' sleep.

We spent a few nice days together. One day we went to the beach, and we talked a lot about Australia. I had been fascinated by Australia since reading some of Neville Shute's books, and my favourite book at the time was *A Town Like Alice*. The girls left Oslo to continue their travels, and a few months later one of them sent me a letter thanking me for her stay with me.

For thirty-three years we have written every Christmas, keeping in touch, telling about our families and how and what we have been doing.

I had a hard year in 1998, and one day as I went on one of my therapeutic cross-country skiing trips I decided that in the year 2000 I would go to Australia. In January 2000 my dream came true. My husband and I travelled to Melbourne to watch the Australian Open tennis tournament. I had called my friend to tell her I was on my way, and she very kindly offered me accommodation, but as there were two more in our party we arranged to stay in a hotel.

On our first evening in Melbourne my friend picked us up from the hotel and took us around town and to see the area where she lived. We connected at once and I spent the evening with her and her family. We had a lovely meal together. It was exciting to meet her family and get an update on Sue's life. Sue made my stay fantastic. We talked a lot, renewed our friendship, and enjoyed each other's company.

Sue's husband, Alistair, arranged for us to go to Kooyong, as it was my husband's big dream to play tennis there. We played tennis, and afterwards we had a drink on the Goolagong Terrace. As we sat there Evonne Goolagong Cawley passed us, and we had our photograph taken with her. That really was the highlight of our perfect day. We are planning to go back to Melbourne next year, to watch the tennis again and we hope to meet Sue and her family once more.

Have you guessed which Sue I am talking about? My friend is Sue Calwell, and she has asked me to tell our story to you. Don't be afraid to stretch your hand and heart out to a stranger in trouble. It might turn out to be a friendship for the rest of your life.

And last I will quote an old Norwegian saying (from the Viking period):

If you have a friend you believe in, visit him often, as bushes and long grass will grow on the road that is not wandered upon.

Havamal

Golden Girls

LEON WEIGARD

The world's greatest sportsperson in the lead-up to the 1972 Olympic Games in Munich was the sixteen-year-old blonde Sydney schoolgirl, Shane Gould. She held every freestyle world record from 100 to 800 metres and was tipped as a potential winner of four or five gold medals.

The swimming events are scheduled in the first week of the Olympic program – this allows the focus to move to the main stadium during the second week for the athletics, the finish of the marathon and the closing ceremony. Such a schedule leaves the swimmers as prime subjects for the world's media during those 'find a story, any story' days prior to the opening ceremony – and it's a real media bunfight.

The media descended on Shane the minute she arrived at the Olympic Village – just like paparazzi around royalty. They were relentless, and the constant flash of cameras, intrusive microphones, phone calls, television interviews and autograph hunters must have been overwhelming for the youngster. Officials were at their wits end – they just could not contain the flood of media representatives from every corner of the world. Everyone wanted Shane.

Meanwhile the rest of our swim team simply enjoyed village life, their training sessions, a stroll into Munich and any other activities completely unhindered. Beverley Whitfield was part of this team – she was two years older than Shane and also had blonde hair. She saw the problem and proposed the most effective plan. They simply swapped ID badges; Shane Gould became Bev Whitfield and Bev Whitfield became Shane Gould.

All the international media knew was that Shane Gould was a young blonde Aussie – and that's who they got. Bev gave her own time up to be Shane, she posed for photos and did interviews while Shane went about the business of training, resting and doing whatever it was that allowed her to go on to win three gold medals.

Strangely, this story of Bev and Shane had not been broken by the Australian media, who must have decided to keep quiet about it. But everyone on the Australian team knew about it and admired her for it.

Bev's event was the backstroke and she was rated an outside chance of making the 200 metre final. As everyone on the team knew of her kindness and how much extra activity she had taken on in the build-up to her race, we were all thrilled that she achieved her major goal – a place in the final.

On the big day, the finalists are introduced. Bev gave a happy, almost casual wave to the crowd and soon they were off! For 100 metres she was competitive. Go Bev! The third, usually the killer lap for strugglers, was taken in her stride and then, within the shadows of the post, she produced a mighty surge and came in first, winning gold for herself and Australia.

Now that was a heart-warming moment. The Aussie team exploded with joy and toasted her victory until all hours. Bev Whitfield's name will be forever listed among that elitist of groups – the Gold Medallists.

Note

Sadly Bev died a year or so ago and missed the accolades that were belatedly bestowed on our former champions.

The Invisible Touch

NATASHA OBEROI

My grandfather, Rai Bahadur M.S. Oberoi, is the founder of the Oberoi Group of Hotels and a much-loved icon in the hotel industry. He turned 102 this year and even though there are a million stories about him, this one in particular touches my heart.

My grandfather's long-time friend and companion, who is in her seventies, visits him twice a day. She comes for lunch and again in the evening. My grandfather is most reluctant to leave his estate and has not done so for two years. It is no wonder that his butler was absolutely dumbfounded when one day last year he asked for his car and chauffeur.

The butler went into complete panic and after much deliberation decided he had better phone my father, who was in a meeting. My father was quite taken aback at first and inquired as to where my grandfather wanted to go.

He was informed that my grandfather's companion was in bed

with the 'flu and had not visited him for a couple of days, and so he had wanted to visit her. My father smiled and said that if he wanted the car, he should be given the car.

I am told that he dressed in a suit, not forgetting his waistcoat and pocket watch, and got in the car and spent a few hours visiting his friend.

Often it is the small things that cost no money but mean so much.

Making a Difference

JOHN WILLIAMS

I have been travelling to China on business since 1996, and became a sponsor of a Chinese child through World Vision in 1998. At the end of a business trip in December 2000, I joined a study tour of Yongsheng, a declared poverty county in the north-west corner of Yunnan province, where my sponsor child lives.

I met the WV staff and the ten other project sponsors who were joining the study tour in Kunming. Our trip was to take us to seven schools in the county, some of them high in the mountains at 3400 metres. The Yongsheng county is populated mainly by minority groups, the largest group being the Yi.

I had written several times to my sponsor child, Li Qin Bao, a ten-year-old girl in Grade 4. We corresponded in Pinyin, which is an alphabetic transliteration of Chinese characters used by school children. From Li Qin's letters it seemed that she was quite bright, and I had the most recent photo of her to help me recognise her.

On the first day in the mountains we visited two schools, Shui Ping and Gantangzi. On the second day we were to visit schools at Manpo, Daan, Guangniulang, Guangmei and Zili. Li Qin (which means 'beautiful' and 'diligent') was at Guangmei school.

We were full of anticipation as we arrived at the first school, Shui Ping, where there were two sponsored children. This initial meeting gave us all mixed emotions. The children were wonderful, playful, laughing, and waving at us. But their condition was a shock. They were filthy, poorly dressed, many of them clearly unwell. The school buildings were derelict. Some children walk more than two hours each way to school. Others, who live even further away, stay in the school dormitory, which is terribly cramped, with double bunks, two children sleeping in each bunk, which is only a board with a light blanket covering. This school is one which WV has not rebuilt as yet, but where they provide financial support for teachers' wages and school materials.

The encounter made us realise the material poverty of these people. To see their abundant gratitude for having received so little from us was both a delight and an embarrassment.

We moved from Shui Ping to Gantangzi. Here some of the villagers invited us into their homes, which are very basic, built of mud, and used as storehouses for their crops and meat, with an open wood fire on the floor. It was intriguing talking with these farmers through our interpreter. They had the same concerns and hopes as parents in Australia – the importance of education for their children; the need for development to provide jobs; the fear of insecurity; the hope of an improved lifestyle.

Our journey continued the next day and at every school we visited I began to realise that the meeting between sponsors and their children was having a big emotional impact on both the sponsor and the child. So much so, that I was starting to wonder if these meetings were a good idea. To send money to WV for a sponsored program is wonderful, but to meet your sponsor child in person, and see how little they have, and how much more they need, is distressing. The approach of WV is to use the major part of sponsor funds to improve the economy of the county, and only a small amount goes to pay for the education of the sponsored child.

Finally we arrived at Guangmei, where I was to meet Li Qin. I had completely reassessed my expectation of this meeting by now, but as soon as we drove into Guangmei and I saw the school my spirits lifted. The school was nestled into the side of a hill with a spectacular outlook to the mountain range and gorge. There was a long pathway leading down to the school, and lined up on each side of this pathway were all the school children. Across the gateway to the school was a yellow banner, saying, 'Welcome to you, our dear sponsors, and to the World Vision Workers!' I was enthralled. And being the only sponsor with a child at this school, I was asked to lead the way for the ten other sponsors and the five WV staff.

As I walked down the path, all the children applauded and I applauded with them; this was truly an unexpected honour. I looked at both sides of the line of children as I walked into the school quadrangle, but I couldn't see Li Qin.

After we had all entered the quadrangle, the children began a 'conga line' dance, snaking their way around the quadrangle and singing. It was a beautiful welcome. Two of the WV staff, Elizabeth and Minnie, asked if I could see Li Qin amongst all these children. At the very moment they asked me, I saw her! She was looking directly at me and smiling; I recognised her immediately. I replied,

'Yes, that's Li Qin, right there, in the red jacket.' 'Are you sure?' they asked, 'Yes, I'm certain, that's Li Qin!' They were amazed and so was I. In the swirling movement of children, I recognised her so surely.

The dance continued, and as it did, something danced in me. I wanted to join Li Qin in the school dance. 'Was it okay?' I asked Elizabeth. 'I suppose so,' she said hesitantly. I moved along the line of dancers, found her, and a teacher let me into the line. I joined the line with my hands on Li Qin's shoulders. It was an unimagined gift to meet 'my child' in this way.

After the dance, the children sang several songs for us, and then I was introduced to Li Qin and her father, and spent a wonderful half-hour chatting with them. I gave them the small gifts I had brought: calendars of Sydney and of Australian animals, colourful silk scarves for Li Qin and her younger sister, and some sweets for her family.

What bridges can be built between people of the world

All too soon, it was time to leave. My meeting with Li Qin had been beautiful beyond any expectation. During our talk together, she had been a little shy, but relaxed and seemingly quite confident. There was a moment when she looked directly into my eyes, held my gaze for several seconds and smiled. It was a sacred moment, an encounter of the beautiful kind. We left the school, and Li Qin with her father came to the top of the pathway to wave us goodbye. We both called out 'zai jian' (see you again), and we will!

What bridges can be built between people of the world when we reach out with a helping hand? It doesn't take much to help lift a community out of poverty, and when we meet at a personal level, without the walls of affluence, culture and race between us, we meet as fathers and daughters, mothers and sons, brothers and sisters.

I started this China trip as a businessman and child sponsor. I returned to Australia strongly supportive of the mission of World Vision, and emotionally connected to the Yi Chinese, and to a beautiful, bright girl from Guangmei, called Li Qin Bao.

Christmas Cards

MATTHEW DENNE

Since leaving school, life had thrown up so many twists and turns, and I had had no time to sit back and reflect on what was happening. With university and all the social activity it entails alongside part-time jobs, and then full-time jobs, there was not really any time to spare. It was the kind of lifestyle where you only realise how testing it can be when you are living it.

Existing in this manner, you lose touch with the important things in life. Sometimes you even forget about these important things all together. Here I was growing up so quickly from the once timid little schoolboy to a person who seemingly had his finger in too many pies for his own good.

They say the best things in life are free. I suppose that's because you can't put a value on them. Friends are the perfect example of this. I realised that I had been living the life that looked after me, myself, and I, and with everything that was going on in my life,

I had neglected those people for whom I had once always had time.

Christmas was just around the corner. To this day I don't know what prompted me to do it, but I bought a packet of Christmas cards and retrieved my old address book. If self-centredness was anything to go by, my address book was the perfect symbol with its dust-covered exterior. Looking over the names inside took me back to those times when the best things in life *were* free, and writing in those cards brought this theory into reality. The words just flowed; I had so much to say because I had never taken the time to say them. Perhaps it was the time of year, or something else, but I felt so invigorated and rejuvenated as a result of this writing therapy.

I wouldn't for a moment blame anyone for not replying to my long-overdue attempts to fill in many years. But what is it about the male human species that we are always inclined to keep an eye on past flames? Sure enough, the cards sent out represented my now non-existent love-life.

Spending another night trying for a hat-trick of solitaire victories, the usual silence was broken by the phone ringing. 'Is Matthew there?' the female voice at the other end of the line inquired. The life brought out in me by the Christmas card episode repeated itself. 'Andrea, how are you going?' was my instant response. Andrea was indeed one of my old flames and we hadn't spoken for ages. As you would expect, the conversation began tentatively, particularly from my end. But gradually the words started to flow as they had many years before. There is no need to detail what we spoke about but except to say that sleep deprivation was the only reason we decided to end the conversation early the next morning.

Every generation seems to have its corny pastimes and 'catching up for coffee' was this one. Andrea and I arranged to meet and before our rendezvous I must have spent more time in front of the mirror than we spent on the phone that night. But there was no need for fancy clothes or other superficial efforts that I had become accustomed to. She was so natural and I suppose that made me lose my awkwardness. We just sat and talked as though our lives depended on it. But this was the beautiful irony of it all. The feeling of being on borrowed time had long passed. I was living life again and it was through this simple yet ever-so-rewarding reunification of two people that had brought it all about.

Andrea and I had a very involved relationship at one point in time, but ever since this whirlwind 'catching up for coffee', she has become the sister I never had. The U-turn my life took in those few days I owe all to her. I got many other replies from other people as a result of that Christmas card mail out. I have learnt to find time for those in my life whom I should never neglect or put behind my own ego. Maybe I will never be famous or solve all the world's problems but I know that when the sun begins to set on my life in the hopefully distant future, I will be able to look back on these precious moments with contentment and a complete feeling of satisfaction.

The Tramp

YVONNE CHOLMONDELEY

What a day. The rain poured down relentlessly. It was a good chance for my husband to go into town to pay the bills and to catch up with some of the other local farmers who would be there exchanging news and, of course, talking about the weather.

It wouldn't have been any fun for our two young children, so I opted to stay with them at home in the warmth of our cozy farm kitchen. While they used their imagination with pencils and paper, I prepared a large pot of vegetable soup. In those days, fifty years ago, we always used the heat of the coal range to keep a hotpot of stew or soup cooking, as well as a kettle continually on the boil, just in case an unexpected visitor dropped by.

The rain never let up. Around midday there was a knock on the back door. When I opened it there was a man standing there, dripping wet. He was obviously a tramp. In a very cultured voice, he asked if he could chop some wood in return for a meal. The chopping block was out in the open, so that was out of the question. Besides, he only had one hand; the other was a double metal claw.

A little surprised, I heard myself inviting him in. He hung his coat in the scullery, then came into the living room to sit with the children at the table. As I filled their bowls with soup, he spoke very gently to them and they in turn showed no apprehension about his missing hand. What beautiful manners and respect those two children and the man were sharing. Unfortunately, the man wouldn't stay for long, he wanted his solitude on the road. It was such a brief stay.

After that I always kept an eye out for him, but he never came back. Sometimes I ask myself,

Who was that man with the well-spoken voice?
Was he a tramp by deed or by choice?
Or was he an angel in disguise
Testing our ability to love, not despise.

Vintage Windfall

GORDON LINDSAY

I used to invite Laurie Rofe to lunch often. The reasons were many. He had been very kind to me. I enjoyed his company and we were friends. As a young man, he had introduced me to the Vintage Sports Car Club of Australia and its members. He had even travelled to Adelaide with me to buy a 1934 3-litre Lagonda and followed me home in his own car in case of mishaps on the journey. But most of all, I invited him to lunch often because he owned a 1935 4.5-litre Lagonda Rapide, which he used to drive to meet me.

Now, for the uninitiated, the Lagonda Rapide is a very desirable motorcar indeed. Bulldog Drummond had one, and he claimed that it 'had the legs of any car in England'. Who would argue with that? It has a top speed of over 100 miles per hour and a sister car won the Le Mans twenty-four-hour race in 1935. And yet it also managed to masquerade successfully as a comfortable four-seater touring car. It is extraordinarily good looking, rather like Bulldog

Drummond himself. It has a long bonnet, a proud, badged radiator and magnificent sweeping mudguards.

Whilst Laurie tucked in to lunch, I used to sneak outside, walk around his car and hope that I would be treated to a spin, which was invariably the case.

One Saturday morning, glancing through the 'vintage' columns of the used car section of the *Age*, looking at cars that I could not afford, I was amazed and somewhat alarmed to see that Laurie had put his Rapide up for sale. The alarm was due to the sum asked, which was quite outside my reach, short of selling the family home. This course of action crossed my mind, but I thought it best to ring Laurie first to make sure that it wasn't a misprint.

It appeared that Laurie needed the money and no, it wasn't a misprint. I decided to make interested noises while wondering what I could sell without my wife noticing. I kept up the pretence over the weekend and did a lot of sums.

I was a partner in a small engineering business at the time and the previous year we had done very well. The result was that we had paid a lot of provisional tax. The following year was not so good financially and quite unexpectedly, on the Monday morning, I received a rebate cheque from the Australian Tax Office for exactly the amount that Laurie was asking for the Rapide.

We have been together now for twenty-five years.

Sweet Dreams

BRENDA DIMMITT

I think it was my stomach that brought us together. Nurses are invariably on the scrounge for something sweet to eat on a busy shift, and I was no exception. Gwen was a patient in the re-admission ward of the Spinal Injury Unit at Melbourne's Austin Hospital. She was a paraplegic and had been confined to a wheelchair since the 1950s, then aged in her early thirties. She had maintained a very independent lifestyle and was still managing well, more than thirty years on. Gwen had been admitted for a short spell to resolve a skin problem, which is one of the perils patients come up against when disabled.

Renowned for her generous nature, Gwen always had a supply of sweets in a drawer or a dessert from her meal tray that she had put aside for some needy nurse. When offered to me on one occasion I displayed such relish and enthusiasm, which gave her an equal measure of delight, that an instant appreciation of pleasures shared sparked a friendship between us. Despite the age difference of about twenty years, there was an immediate empathy between us. It was just lovely to talk together and listen to each other's views on current affairs, politics or personal events in our lives. I don't ever remember being at odds with one another. Instead we eagerly shared our own thoughts and opinions on all manner. It was one of those friendships you feel totally safe in.

Whenever I had moments to spare at work, I would join Gwen in a game of Scrabble or cards at her bedside. She was always so warm and welcoming in her manner whenever I entered the room. A more selfless, generous person I am yet to meet, for Gwen would be just as delighted if you won the game of Scrabble or played your cards well. Our talents at these games were evenly matched, so it was never a foregone conclusion who would be the victor. But there was also a very strong and determined side to Gwen's personality, fiercely proud and always honourable. I greatly admired these qualities.

After Gwen left the hospital for home again, we kept in close touch. I would often go for lunch at her place where she would cook me a delicious roast and I would bring her a French vanilla slice, which she loved. She spoilt me rotten with all the little thoughtful gifts and gestures she bestowed upon me over the years that followed. During those visits I usually cut her hair, to save her time and money, or got out in the little back garden and tidied up while Gwen looked on with pleasure and helped wherever she could. Although one is a bit limited from a wheelchair, we found ways of sharing the task. Later, we would settle down to our favourite games once more and while away the rest of the afternoon. They were joyous times together.

It was the winter of 1988, not an exceptionally cold one really, but Gwen found those months trying and had difficulty keeping warm. This was the first sign that all was not well. There appeared to be symptoms of a bladder infection but nothing was conclusive. Gwen was simply not 'sparking' in her usual way and felt frustrated with herself. It was around this time that I had a dream one night that moved me deeply. I can visualise it still. I came into a room and there was Gwen coming towards me with outstretched arms ready to embrace me. She wore a graceful, long white dress and I remember thinking, 'Gwen is walking! Why doesn't she do that all the time?' She looked so happy to see me and I felt such a sense of love through the whole experience. I related this dream to Gwen, when next we spoke, and she thought how wonderful it sounded, but we both wondered at its meaning.

She was eventually admitted to hospital for further treatment, as coping at home was getting beyond her. Also, there was bleeding present from the bladder, which was of real concern. Shortly after this, the doctors reached their diagnosis. Gwen had inoperable cancer of the bladder and had about four months to live. The news was like an arrow to my heart and I wept when I was told. After eight years, our friendship was to be concluded. When I went to Gwen, who was fully informed of her condition, she said, 'Now we know what that dream was telling us.' She accepted her fate without complaint or bitterness and it was a time when we grew even closer. We talked openly about our expectation of life after death – that it is leaving one level of existence for another. 'I promise if there is any way I can communicate with you after I've gone, I will,' she told me with great conviction.

To watch her body deteriorate was emotionally painful but her spirit was always strong and joyful. I was with her as much as I could be and we valued every moment. It was only during the last few days that she drifted between consciousness and a hallucinatory state. I would sit by the bed holding her hand or stroking her face. She would 'come to' briefly and look at me with such loving intensity and say, 'I love you, Pet,' then drift away again. This is my last memory of her before she died.

It was some months later when I had another of those incredible dreams that fill me with warmth and love. Gwen was there with me, looking so well and happy, and we talked in the way we had always enjoyed. I woke feeling elated. The next day, after working an evening shift on the spinal ward, I gave the 'handover' report to a special friend of mine who was doing the night shifts. She had also become close to Gwen in the latter months, and so I related my dream to her. I wondered what was wrong for a moment as she went white, then red and exclaimed, 'I was all set to tell you! Last night, when I was down the end of the ward where it is dark and quiet, I had this overwhelming feeling of a presence just behind me. It really scared me at first, but then it suddenly came into my mind that it was Gwen and she seemed to be asking where you were. Without words I was saying, "She's not here, Gwen. She is at home." Then the feeling was gone.' It was around this same time at night that I had my dream about Gwen.

I shall always deem it a great honour to have known Gwen in my lifetime. She not only touched my heart, but that of many others amongst hospital staff and patients. Gwen also had a loving family, which included three cherished grandchildren. All would agree, she was a true lady and inspirational in her courage and strength of character.

Hope

One Sunny Day

RAY BEATTY

Horror can strike at the most unexpected place and time, like on a warm, sunny August afternoon, just after lunch, when a little white Honda motored up the Calder Highway, taking my wife, Helga, with five-year-old Justine and three-year-old Maxim on holiday to Mildura.

Perfect day, perfect conditions. Suddenly a front-wheel strut buckled. The car swerved and rolled three times. Crushed metal, smashed glass, and then silence.

Minutes passed, then Helga regained consciousness and dragged herself out of the wreck. She thought Justine was dead, and saw Maxim in his safety seat, his head smashed and bleeding. She pulled him out, wrapped a cloth around his head and limped, weeping, along the highway where you could see from horizon to horizon in the brilliant sunshine. But there was no traffic, no movement. Another minute and sound came from the car. Justine pulled herself out, with barely a scratch, and ran to her relieved and grieving mother.

Eventually a car came past and they were taken to hospital. Maxim's head had smashed like a hard-boiled egg that's been dropped on the floor. They worked to relieve pressure and remove blood, but he needed specialist care. He was too critical to risk an air ambulance so they sent him by road ambulance all the way to the Royal Children's Hospital in Melbourne.

That day I was at work, taking aspirin for a massive headache that had suddenly hit me at 2 o'clock. By late afternoon I was about to go home when I received the call from the hospital. The news was devastating, and I was told the ambulance would not arrive till late that night.

It was past midnight when they wheeled him in, straight to theatre where a top neurosurgeon waited. I joined Helga and Justine in the gallop along the corridor. 'Hold on, Max, we'll soon fix you up,' reassured a nurse. A small voice came out from under the mass of bandages: 'It's not Max, it's Maxim.' There was hope!

For hours they laboured, picking bone splinters out of his brain, reshaping the skull, stitching the ripped scalp. It was morning by the time he was taken to the neurology ward, his head swathed like an Egyptian mummy.

For two days we waited for him to wake. As we stretched our legs around the ward we saw the other children. Four were in comas, the longest of which had been going on for two years. Their parents and relatives diligently visited every day, cleaning them, moving their limbs, reading into ears that did not hear – or did they? We took up reading to our patient, too.

Others in the ward had suffered degrees of brain damage. Some were conscious but looked out of unseeing eyes. There were growing, beautiful children with the brains of infants, no longer able to feed or clean themselves. Others were physically crippled by the destruction of the brain: twisted bodies, uncoordinated limbs, contorted faces. We looked at our sleeping baby, head in a turban, eyes blackened and swollen, face bruised, and we prayed (we who scarcely knew how), and we wept.

Finally he did wake up, confused and in pain. Helga, Justine and I, we sat next to his cot, we took turns and did shifts so that he would never be alone. And we talked to him, talked and talked.

It soon became apparent that he had lost at least a year – he was now at the stage of a two-year-old. But we firmly believed – instinctively – that his brain could be rebuilt. We kept talking and read to him, played with puzzling toys and showed him lots of colour and pictures.

A few weeks later, out of the hospital, we continued the 'Save Maxim' campaign. Helga taught him to read before he reached school. I read stories and poems. Justine sang songs. We rummaged the libraries and bookshops for help: *Teach Your Baby to Read*, *Dr Spock*, any books on early childhood development, anything that could give us clues. Little Justine was both our pupil and Maxim's teacher, enlisted to the rescue task.

We were warned to beware of epilepsy, so day and night we anxiously watched his behaviour (for the next fifteen years), because we were told fits could happen right into his adolescence.

After two or three years of solid recovery and no more symptoms we finally relaxed a little. He seemed normal, was obviously intelligent, had a quick wit and sense of humour. He could remember the things he learned at school. We felt we had won a hard-fought battle, the price was great but the reward was huge.

Maxim is now twenty-four. The only after-effects are a blind eye, which looks quite normal, and under his hair a jigsaw puzzle of scars testifying to his Humpty-Dumpty head.

This year he graduated from Melbourne University with a Bachelor of Economics and a Bachelor of Arts in languages. He speaks and writes fluent Japanese, and a couple of years ago took himself to the Sorbonne to learn French.

Helga and I parted over a decade ago, and are both happily married again. But we can always take pride in the fact that when a real, devastating crisis hit we were able to face it with a united strength far greater than our individual selves. Even in these times of uncertain relationships, never underestimate the power of commitment to a cause greater than yourselves.

Reaching Out

Ari Badaines

Outside the sun was warm and high over the rolling hills of farmland in southwest England. Inside, thirty people sat on cushions in a circle, their fifth day of a week-long personal growth group.

Participants had wept deeply over painful childhood experiences, grieved for recently ended relationships and raged against their demons; but one man, Yoakes, sat unmoved, untouched, rarely speaking. He was best described as round and soft and isolated.

As leader of this group, my heart went out to him from the first. I imagined Yoakes had experienced a lonely childhood, probably bullied by other kids, and had been friendless through all of his approximately thirty-four years.

Our group, it seemed, was a final attempt to reverse this historical pattern of isolation and withdrawal – some spark, some hope still yearned and believed, but as yet neither he nor the group had done anything to support that hope.

My concern grew as the hours passed and I could think of nothing useful to suggest to him.

In the evening session the light of day began its slow surrender to the night, casting long shadows in the room. In the centre of the room a woman was reliving the all-to-early death of her mother when she was a young child. Through her sobs she begged her mother not to die condemning her as a child to long years ahead of pain and isolation, as her father would soon marry a woman who would reject her. All eyes, many filled with tears, were riveted on this intense scene.

As moved as I was by what was happening in the centre of the room, I was distracted when I glanced at Yoakes. There in his left eye a small tear was forming – the first sign I had seen of any emotion.

He knew I had noticed, but he did not look away. Then I noticed his left hand move ever so slightly from its resting place on his knee. Slowly, slowly, slowly, he slid it to his left, stopping mid-way. I nodded almost imperceptibly, but willed him with all my heart to keep going.

His hand continued its arc, finally touching the hand of the woman sitting next to him. She opened her hand, gently enveloping his, and I watched his tears brim over, falling freely, but without shame or embarrassment.

Nothing was said that evening and in the two remaining days Yoakes continued slowly to reach out for connection, and in turn, others reached out to him.

I never saw him again, but I still like to think that what he began that day has continued, so that his inextinguishable yearning for contact has been met.

Walk Away

JILL LOVETT

In early 1997, my marriage of thirty-eight years ended. I used to believe that no matter how difficult my marriage might be, it was my duty to hang in there and make it work. This is the story of how I came to realise that marriage for life is not always possible.

My husband, John (not his real name), and I were married in 1959. John seemed to share my dreams in every way. We were young, full of optimism and keen to create a happier family than those of our somewhat dysfunctional backgrounds. By 1975 we had six children, four sons and two daughters.

The following year John had a heart attack. He did recover physically but emotionally he was a changed man. When he returned home from the hospital, my life and the lives of our children were never the same again. The trauma of the heart attack had released all the unresolved conflicts from his unhappy childhood, and these now began to manifest in sudden bouts of explosive rage, verbal abuse, and even physical violence towards me.

Over the next twenty years we endured the wrath and unpredictable moods of this once-loving man. On numerous occasions I was forced out of our home in the middle of the night with no money and nowhere to go, or sometimes when we were driving I would be dumped out of the car and left on the roadside because I had upset him in some way. Other times he would take me to the Salvation Army Women's Refuge and leave me there on my own for weeks at a time so I could 'learn how to be a proper wife and mother', as he termed it.

People wonder why I didn't leave. The reasons were simple. I had no money, nowhere to go and six children who needed me.

It was just a week after our thirty-eighth wedding anniversary (our children had all left home) when I walked nervously into my husband's office.

'I've come to tell you that I'm leaving home,' I announced, my voice quavering slightly. John looked at me blankly, speechless for the first time in his life. Finally he spoke in the usual gruff tone he reserved for me, 'Look, Jill, I don't have time for this rubbish right now. I know that you are deliberately trying to sabotage my work.' I turned and walked away, certain that it was indeed time to go.

During those early weeks and months I moved through life with a strange inner strength, but I missed my old home with a pain that was almost physical. My counsellor, a Uniting Church minister, wisely summed up my situation. 'You may be wandering in the wilderness like the children of Israel,' he remarked, 'but you can't go back to Egypt because it is still the same place of bondage. Your husband hasn't changed and doesn't want to.' I knew he was right and I kept on looking towards the Promised Land.

Looking back on those early days on my own, I am still amazed at how I managed to survive. I registered with Centrelink, found a place to rent, and finally moved, with the pitifully small amount of furniture I was allowed piled up in my son's trailer, to my new home. I knew I was doing the right thing, particularly when I found a small verse stuck on the rangehood over the stove in my new kitchen: *The eyes of the Lord are over the righteous and his ears are open unto their prayers.* (1 Peter 3:12) Tears came to my eyes at these words of comfort left behind by the previous tenant.

Of course, there were the protracted legal and property settlements, which revealed to my shock that my husband and I were penniless. All those years while I had scrimped to make ends meet, John had been borrowing hundreds of thousands of dollars using our home as collateral to raise money for his business and for development schemes that were going to make us 'millionaires'. All his loans now had to be paid out. The legal saga finally ended when I received a piece of paper announcing I was divorced.

Recently I reviewed my situation: sixty-one years old, a divorced grandmother of ten, able to work only part-time because of my pension, no home and no money to buy one. Despite the wonderful support and encouragement I received from all my children, my housing problem hung over my head like a dark cloud, what else to do but pray?

Then I remembered that one of my sons and his wife owned a small cottage that had been rented out for some years by a young couple and their children. Mustering my courage I emailed him asking if there was any possibility I might rent it. The answer came back a few hours later. The cottage amazingly would become available for rent in a few weeks time at a substantially cheaper rent and I could stay there indefinitely. However, I was doomed to disappointment again. The cottage turned out to be unsuitable for my needs, being extremely dilapidated and in an inaccessible position. I was forced to move to the rented villa where I am today.

If I were to meet another woman today going through the sort of marriage I endured for so long, I would tell her gently that it is not really a Christian act to prop up a dead and destructive marriage.

I have not yet reached the Promised Land – maybe I never will on this earth – but I do know that God is leading me, step by step, towards self-respect, dignity and the freedom to be the person he created me to be.

Ten Years On

STEVE DUFFY

1991 | The first time I mentioned to a doctor my concern about a lump in my groin he told me not to worry about it, so I didn't.

1992 | It was still there and I thought I could feel a small lump in my armpit. Even the surgeon was surprised how much I bled when he took out the tombola-sized nut. ('Thin blood,' he said.) A week's wait for the pathology report. Next, an appointment with an oncologist. I wasn't that worried; it hadn't really occurred to me that oncologists only see people with cancer. 'You have a 50 per cent chance of death in ten years,' he said.

I felt like the victim of a baseball bat attack. Adele and I clung together in disbelief. Tears, shock and a hollow, hollow feeling in the stomach. Hey, two pre-school boys might lose their father. My partner of twelve years might lose her man. And you know what? It was one of the best things that has ever happened to me.

1992–1994 | In the first weeks after diagnosis of non-Hodgkin's lymphoma, Adele and I conceived our third son, and I prepared myself for CHOP chemotherapy. Friends offered solace and support like a lens coming into focus. My dear friends organised a fundraiser to help financially while I would be undergoing treatment. What a wonderful day that was, a celebration of life and love. Then came the blood tests, scans, more biopsies, bone marrow sample and all the poking and prodding. Mainstream society denies pain and death through a subterfuge of pity, ignorance and supposed invulnerability. Without filling in an application form, I had been fully inducted into a secret society. I suppose I'd never really thought about having my life threatened, not to mention death. Now I was thinking about it quite a lot.

'Why me?' This was one of the many questions I had to face. I was in freefall. I had to find a parachute if I was to survive this. Just as my friends were so supportive, especially those who had been through some crisis themselves, I had to find the resources within myself to make my future. I began to read about the power of the mind, the power of positive thought. I read tales of hope and very serious attitude. My mind was opening to ideas that weren't mainstream. One's mind, like a parachute, works best when it is open. I found a therapist I could talk to. I was introduced to the strangeness of reiki. A friend in similar circumstances found a guru. For fitness and health I began walking. While walking I listened to tapes that I had recorded, inspirational music interspersed with self-motivating statements and messages – sort of like self-hypnosis.

So now it was off to the Chemo Casino. Play those games. Go for the jackpot: intravenous poisons; steroids; something to make the white blood cell count go up; interferon for something else; and, of course, the endless blood tests. It's not until you get inside the

Chemo Casino that you realise you are one of the machines, waiting for your own eyes to light up. Seven months of treatment. Much longer to recover from the treatment. As my hair fell out and my skin turned grey, my two brothers shaved their heads in empathy. Adele's belly swelled in pregnancy as she raised two young sons and nursed me. She was awe-inspiring. William Armando Sorani Duffy was born two days before my last dose of CHOP chemotherapy.

I took the positives from all of these things: Adele's strength, William's new life, my other two sons, Jack and Max, the *simpatico* behaviour of others who had had hard knocks and come through, the support of friends. Writers such as Ainslie Meares and Bernie Siegel enlightened and expanded my view. I was walking and thinking my way to health. The flash of confronting death need not be blinding but illuminating: a lantern to expose the power of the mind and the strength of the soul. I could not lie down and accept the prognosis. Nothing could be lost by trying to take control. 'Victim' is not a word I use to describe myself.

Don't get me wrong, it is not all beer and skittles once you've (as John Wayne said) 'licked the big C'. The terror calls in often. But I take strength from my wrestles with doubt and depression. I must be ever watchful of the trap of negative thought.

2000 | It's coming up for ten years and I'm fine. This whole experience has made me a stronger and, I think, a happier person.

P.S. I've always found it interesting that the oncologist used the negative spin in his prognosis; that is 50 per cent chance of death is not quite the same thing as 50 per cent chance of life!

To Climb a Mountain

CAROL ROJO

I always loved walking and walked most nights after work. I also bush walked regularly, and it was my dream to trek in the Himalayas. One Sunday morning I decided to go for a long walk.

When I returned, a little fatigued, my husband and my brother were ready to go out. We had organised to visit my father, who was ill in hospital. My brother called his little Jack Russell to him; she was just a pup and typically very disobedient. She wouldn't go to him. I was standing behind the car and decided to kneel down and call her. At the same time, my husband started the car. I thought he knew I was there.

It all happened very quickly, with the car reversing over me. I heard my neck crack and felt the excruciating pain in my arms immediately. I screamed in pain. Panicking, my husband moved the car and phoned for an ambulance. I just wanted the pain to go. The ambulance officers put a neck brace on me and gave me some pethidine, which helped a little. I was taken to the nearest hospital where they did X-rays.

I lay there waiting, not able to move my neck and in a lot of pain. I thought about my arms and legs – everything flashed before me. Eventually they came and told me that I was to be flown by helicopter to the Austin Hospital. This was a fine way of getting a helicopter ride.

My husband had the long five-hour drive to the Austin and I remember feeling worried – it would be the longest drive of his life.

After many tests I was wheeled into the theatre at 12.30 a.m. on Monday morning. I woke in intensive care with John standing next to me crying. I couldn't move or talk; I was on morphine and wasn't feeling much pain. I wanted him to know that everything was going to be all right, so with my swollen hands I managed to write 'I love you' on a piece of scrap paper. It was barely tangible, but to this day he still has that note.

After intensive care you progress down to ward and then to a rehabilitation centre. On my first day at rehab I was determined to go for a walk with my husband and daughter. I was very wobbly, but I walked. At first, just a few steps exhausted me, but I continued this routine every day and twelve months down the track with physio and rehabilitation I have made incredible progress.

I am back at work part-time and every day I make sure I walk. My husband and I have had a long and rich journey where the experience has strengthened and changed our lives forever. I still dream of my Himalaya trek and will achieve this when I am stronger.

Back on Track

JAMES HORSMAN

Life was sweet until I was fourteen years old. Mum and Dad were always there with my brother and me. They came to every baseball and rugby game I played and no matter what trouble I got into at school they were always there for me.

Then, one day, Mum asked me if my stereo worked. I asked her, 'Why?' Her reply was, 'Your Dad's moving out, so we need your stereo for the lounge room.'

After that life went bad.

I started using hard-core drugs because it kept my mind off what was going on at home. Dad wasn't there any more and I couldn't handle it. I was too afraid to stay straight because it hurt too much that the family wasn't the same and never would be the same.

I stayed bent on tripping for two years. During that time I saw a lot of things that I hope no one else ever has to see. For example, I saw two mates on a train track dead; I saw one of them actually get hit by the train and I couldn't do anything to help. I have also seen four people die from overdoses with the needle still in their arm.

I was always 'ripped' at work because I hated it but managed to be straight for baseball training in the evenings.

It makes you wonder why you would want to do this when there is such a risk of dying from taking drugs. But when I tried to stop using drugs I couldn't. Dad didn't come back, and it is so hard to give up when you do it every day, like I did. And it was so easy to get my hands on drugs. No matter what I wanted, I knew someone who could get them for me.

During this time I was diagnosed with Attention Deficit Disorder (ADD), and a shrink told me that the drugs made me violent. When I drank I was a happy drunk, until someone upset me and then I had a very short fuse. One time I was on speed and drinking at the same time when a guy said the wrong thing, so I beat him up with a trolley pole until the cops came and dragged me off him. I was charged with assault and received a five-year good behaviour bond. Even this didn't make me snap out of it.

When I was about sixteen and a half, I started to listen to a family friend called Duncan Rogers. He invited me for a holiday to his small country town and I went. It was fun, so I asked if I could stay on and work on a farm as it was something I had always wanted to do. I worked for three months on a local farm. For the first few weeks I was trashed every day, as my brother would send up a quart a week and I would smoke about one gram a day.

One day I was talking to Duncan about school. I still don't quite know how it happened, but the next day he rang up a place called BRACE, a literacy testing place, and booked me in for a test. My score was really bad so we decided to look at going back to school. I needed help. Duncan arranged a meeting at the local high school with the principal. At my old high school I never actually went to any classes as I was always wagging with my mates.

Now I'm studying Maths, English and Metal and Agricultural Studies at a TAFE college in the next town. I also have a daily literacy tutor session at the high school and now I can read and write better. In the beginning Duncan was always there for me, to help with my homework or any problem that I was having. He supported me just like my Dad had done.

My future looks positive and I hope to have a fulfilling life. I owe it to my Mum and Dad for supporting me, but I mainly owe it to Duncan, who sadly died two months ago of a heart attack. He was, and still is, my inspiration. If it weren't for Duncan, I would probably still be on drugs. I have been straight for one and a half years now. This is my life story so far.

Don't Give up Your Dreams

ELIZABETH FINLAY

Most of us have dreams when we are growing up. My dream was to train hard enough in my track and field events to take me to the 1968 Mexico Olympics. I was a sprinter and a Queensland schoolgirl champion at fourteen.

Unfortunately, due to the health of my father, my dreams had to be put on hold and I started working at age fifteen. Life went on. I married and had two daughters. I still enjoyed being active and my exercise routine, like that of many young mums, was a trip to the gym. Every now and then, that feeling of missing my dreams would nag me, but all I could do was brush it aside as something that was now beyond my reach.

Two weeks after I turned forty I was diagnosed with a 20 centimetre tumour covering my right ovary and appendix. Major surgery followed, and I was told that I had a rare form of cancer that stems from the appendix and creates many small mucous-forming tumours in the abdominal region.

This sort of news makes you realise how fragile life is. The treatment for this cancer was not chemotherapy; it was a complicated wash of special chemicals pumped into my body at ongoing intervals. My doctors told me that one of the best ways to fight the illness was with the help of a good diet and plenty of exercise.

This was a great reason to go back to my sport and try to fulfil my dream. Of course, the age factor and fitness standard came into it now. I decided to try to track down my old Queensland coach Bernie Hogan, who turned out to be still involved in training and competing at the age of seventy-three. He enlightened me about the Veterans Athletics Association and encouraged me to think seriously about joining this body of athletes who compete right up there until they are in their nineties.

The only problem was that Bernie lived in Queensland and I had now lived in Victoria for more than twenty years, but Bernie set about finding me a coach in Melbourne.

Roy Foley was the best thing that happened in my life. He was seventy-eight years old when I joined his training camp. He worked me patiently, starting with a couple of hours every afternoon, then as I progressed without injury he told me he could have me ready for the World Games in Japan in two years. He also said I was the right muscle group for the pentathlon, an event that covers five disciplines for Veteran women: 200 metres, 800 metres, javelin, discus and shot-put. On top of training for that event, he decided that I should compete in the hammer throw and the individual 100 metres as well. That was exactly the goal I was looking for and decided to go full bore and pray my health would hold out. I threw myself into training.

My first competition was a local Victorian meet only a few

months after I started out. The fear when I knelt down on my starting blocks to compete in my first 100 metres in twenty-six years was overwhelming, but it was all washed away when I won the event. I was lucky enough to go on and win my pentathlon that day also. I was totally hooked and felt fourteen again.

I competed in the Australian Championships six months on and came fourth in the pentathlon, which made me want to try even harder to reach my goal. This time I was determined not to let my dream pass me by. In 1993, just before the World Games in Japan, I took time off to complete one of my cancer treatments and then pulled a hamstring after going back into training too hard.

It was a major setback but I decided that after all the other pain my body had put me through, a muscle was not going to hold me back. Again Roy patiently worked with me and repaired me enough to be accepted into the Australian relay team at the tenth World Veterans Championships in Miyazaki, Japan.

At last there I was, twenty-eight years after my dream began, marching in my Australian uniform at the opening ceremony of an international athletics meet.

My relay team went on to win a silver medal. As I stood on that podium with the rest of my team, I could only thank God for giving me the challenge I needed to see that you must never give up your dream.

The Pleasures in Life

MERLIE CLAYTON

Our lives were changed by a single phone call on the night of 2 August 1990. We had just finished dinner when the phone rang. I handed it to my husband, Barry, then I watched the colour fade from his face, his words suspended in mid-sentence. He leant forward and laid his head in his hands.

'They've closed the place. I've been retrenched.' His anguish was evident as he asked between sobs, 'What are we going to tell the kids? I've never been out of work, dumped on the scrap heap.' I remember how angry I felt. I remember thinking that this was the worst thing that could happen to us. I was wrong.

Three weeks later our son was dead. He was killed in an accident. We never got the chance to say goodbye. I remember wondering at the time whether I had the strength to get the family through all the heartache.

Slowly we have rebuilt our lives. The bond of love my children have woven has given us the strength and courage to pick up the pieces. I have also found comfort in my religion, although at times I cannot pray because I feel so empty. Somehow I've managed to cope, thanks to the support of wonderful family and friends.

Our lives have changed dramatically. With less income, we have had to become thrifty and it is amazing what a little bit of innovation and creativity can do. I have learnt countless ways to use mince meat; the old Hills Hoist now supports beans; we grow our own vegies; and we bake our own bread and biscuits. Home Brand groceries have become trendy and free tastings in supermarkets are not to be missed. Thanks to the local library we keep up with the latest books and magazines. We enter lots of competitions – someone has to win – and it gives us something to dream about. An ordinary meal can be made special when eaten by candlelight. Use the best tablecloth, the prettiest china, your crystal glasses.

We came up with giving gifts of love. It's a challenge to see who gives the most unusual gift of love. My grandchildren loved the smooth flat rock wrapped in tissue paper. The card read, 'Mystical Magical Rock – when you are lonely or sad hold me in your hand and remember how special and loved you are.'

Family unity has become more important than wealth or material things. There is time for me to write and for my husband to draw. Perhaps, if he had not been retrenched, he would not have discovered his talent for drawing.

Looking back as we pass the ten-year mark, we have a lot to be grateful for, things that used to be important have been replaced by new values.

And while we will never recover from the loss of our youngest son, the world is still a beautiful place. The expensive holidays and dining out have vanished from our lives, but we still have our sense of humour.

Take time to stop and smell the flowers

Look around at Nature's beauty – the setting sun, the blue skies, the budding flowers. Take time to stop and smell the flowers. But most of all never, never give up.

When We Change, the World will Change

CHARLIE HOGG

I was just seventeen years old and in my final year at school when I travelled to Canberra to the Australian Universities Festival. I was with a group of friends, all eager to explore the new experiences we would find. It was the time of the Vietnam War and it was the first time that television brought the horror of war into our lounge rooms. I had very strong anti-war feelings and was a regular at the peace marches protesting against Australian involvement.

There was to be a peace march during the festival. When we all assembled on campus there was a great sense of camaraderie among the marchers. We linked arms and sang John Lennon's 'Give Peace a Chance' and chanted slogans till our voices became hoarse. A huge contingent of federal police stood sternly just off campus, with arms folded, silently observing.

Just as we marched off campus towards our destination of Parliament House a few overexcited demonstrators challenged the police.

Suddenly all hell broke loose. The police charged and we ran for our lives towards the university as the feds (as the demonstrators called them) could not arrest us on campus. I was pretty fast and hit the campus like a rugby player diving over the try line. However, many were arrested. I noticed one of my friends being marched to a bus by a police officer. I thought I should go and see where they were taking him. I tentatively approached and asked the officer what was happening to him. He grabbed my arm and said, 'You're coming too.'

Once the bus was full we were driven to the federal police headquarters and marched into the already overcrowded cells. We were all arrested but it didn't seem to dampen the enthusiasm; the singing and the chanting continued. I was allowed to ring my father to see if he wouldn't mind sending the $50 to get me out.

As the night wore on, the singing and chanting died down and a conversation began. I shared a cell with many of Australia's student and peace movement leaders. Their words were very emotional, very angry. Some were proposing violent responses to the day's actions. I sat quietly in my corner and listened. It became so clear to me that here we were marching for peace and yet we were so angry, aggressive, full of blame and even hatred. We were such a peaceless group of people! How could such a group create a more peaceful world?

It was only then that I really began to look hard at my own state of mind, my attitudes and how I had contributed to a more peaceless world. It was a bit of a shock. I was so committed to stopping the war in Vietnam, no doubt a worthy cause, and yet often I declared war in my own home, or even in my own mind. I felt a hypocrite. I was preaching to others about the sins of war and violence and anger but there it was in me . . . perhaps in a more subtle form, but it was there.

My whole approach to change was turned upside down. From the outside-in approach I took up the inside-out approach: when *we* change, the world will change. So began my spiritual journey.

I spent some years wandering around the world living in various religious and spiritual communities. I spent time with Sikhs, Buddhists, Taoists, Jains, Hindus, Muslims, Christians, Yogis and more. Finally I began to meditate. It was an extraordinary experience to observe that by using just my thoughts I could transform the feeling in my mind, and that then had a flow-on effect on my attitudes and actions.

Now I begin every day of my life with an hour of meditation. It is my favourite time. It's been like an inner research project to understand myself and how I become peaceless, but also to understand how I can create and sustain peace in my life. Not just when I meditate, but more importantly in my relationships and work.

So peace has a different meaning for me now.

Courage

Your Aim Should Exceed Your Grasp

SUSIE MARONEY

My story starts when I was born, I guess. My twin brother and I were premature and spent a few years struggling with various problems, including asthma. Our mum started us in swimming lessons at the age of three to help strengthen our lungs. From these lessons I progressed to competitive swimming. I reached the top ten of my age group at the Nationals but always found these competitions nerve-wracking. My coach kept putting me in longer races as he found the longer the race, the better I seemed to perform.

At the age of fourteen my coach entered me in a 16-kilometre swim at Manly Dam and I ended up coming second to the current world champion at the time. We were all surprised. It was the next year at the age of fifteen when I arrived at Dover to swim the English Channel that I reached a sort of 'turning point'. It was the day after I had successfully swum across to France and we were relaxing on the beach when we saw another swimmer being carried over the pebbles towards the water. She was being carried because she had no legs. They had been amputated mid-thigh.

Before she came into view I had thought to myself, 'Well, that's it.' I had achieved my goal and now I could get on with my life. As we finally found out this girl's history I began to really think about goals and dreams and challenges. The girl was from Germany and at the age of three she had fallen off her father's tractor on their farm. The tractor rolled over and cut off her legs. She spent the next year in hospital and the years thereafter dreaming of a challenge for herself. She finally settled on the English Channel because she thought if she could do that then she could do anything. Only approximately 600 people have successfully swum the Channel out of 9000 attempts so it was quite a challenge.

Over the next few days we watched her train up and down the harbour until finally she started her swim. After seventeen hours and only 500 metres off the coast of France she was pulled out – the weather had turned and she was exhausted.

When I heard this, and then heard that she was going to return the next year and attempt the swim again (the next year she made it in twenty-one hours), I thought to myself that life itself is full of challenges and goals and that you don't just stop at the first one and congratulate yourself and that's it.

My mum used to say, 'Your aim should exceed your grasp,' which is true. I returned the next year also and did a double Channel crossing and then sat down and thought of the next goal – Cuba to the United States. And so my career has gone on with different challenges and different dreams.

After I swam the double crossing, an ex-headmaster who lived in Dover gave me this poem by Sir Walter Scott, which I have kept since. It just about sums it all up.

Far better it is
to dare mighty things,
to win glorious triumphs,
even though checked by failure
than to take rank with those poor spirits
who never enjoy much
nor suffer much
because they live in the grey twilight
that knows neither victory nor defeat.

Road to Recovery

ANN DAVIS

My daughter Carey had been on the run for two years, unable to come to terms with the gang rape that shattered her life a month after she turned thirteen. She ran and I followed, rescuing her from one potentially dangerous situation after another. So when the phone rang late that Monday night, I immediately anticipated more bad news.

It was Carey but, to my relief and delight, she had good news. 'I've been back at school for three weeks. I didn't tell you before because I wanted to make sure that it would work out okay.'

'Carey, that's wonderful. How did it happen?'

'Well . . .' For the next few minutes she filled me in. She'd been to see the headmaster at Manly High School and told him about her life: the rape; the beating she'd later received from her assailants for turning them in to the police; running away; dealing with Youth and Community Services; her attempts to live with several relatives; attending four high schools in two years trying to finish her education and dropping out each time; her life on the streets of Sydney; her futile attempt to return home; and the fact that she was now living in a rented house with five other young people all determined to break the homelessness cycle.

From what she said the headmaster seemed fantastic. He arranged enrolment, uniforms, bus passes and spread the word to his staff that as Carey had approached him because she wanted to finish school they were to give her any additional help she needed.

I had tears in my eyes by the time she had finished. 'That's terrific. What made you suddenly wake up to yourself?' I couldn't help the question. In spite of the pain and sympathy I felt on her behalf, she'd led me a wild chase since the rape. Carey was, naturally, traumatised after this episode and we had worked hard to make her feel safe within the family. Carey had been beginning to relax, comforted by the fact that I dropped her off and picked her up from school each day, that I was protecting her, as promised, from a chance encounter with one of her rapists. All four were out on bail and living in the same country town in which we lived. Then, one horrible day, a teacher implied she'd probably 'asked for it'. Unable to handle the unreasonable guilt, which even adults who have been assaulted feel, Carey ran.

That night on the phone, she told me she was sick of not belonging, that she wanted to come home, but couldn't ever again live in the same town as her attackers. I knew how hard it had been for her to come and give evidence at the trials. Only one of the boys pleaded guilty. In spite of his confession, the other three were convinced that they could somehow evade justice. They were wrong, but no jail time or detention in a juvenile centre would ever make up for what they had done to my daughter, and subsequently, my family.

I'd been mulling over plans to move house and bring Carey home. I made an instant decision and said, 'I have good news too.'

The discussion that followed was filled with happy plans, a yearning for better times. She confided that she wanted to go to university so she could train to 'help other kids like me'. I've never felt such pride in one of my children. After living with four sisters, Carey was lonely and homesick and we were both excited by the prospect of a 'normal' life. We were also both physically and emotionally exhausted from the traumas of the past two years.

'When will you shift? When will you come to Sydney?' She needed reassurance and I gave it. 'As soon as your sister finishes her Higher School Certificate, I promise. We'll all be together for Christmas. I'm so proud of you, Carey. I'll come to Sydney for a few days soon and we'll look at different suburbs to see where we want to live. I love you, little girl. Work hard.'

We finished the call full of hope. I replaced the receiver and started to shake. Having Carey home was not going to be easy. She'd been too long away from the discipline of family life. She had also made a conscious decision the night of her assault never again to lose control of her own actions, her own life. It would be difficult. There would be arguments and dissension, but with hard work and lots of love, it would be possible. When I told the other girls of my conversation with Carey they were one hundred percent supportive of the scheme. Their sister had triumphed over incredible obstacles and appeared to be recovering. They all agreed she deserved our love and support.

The fact that Carey suffered a massive asthma attack and died one week after that phone call in no way diminishes her bravery or her ambition to reclaim her life. In fact, it left the rest of us with a legacy of pride and respect for her that eventually helped to ease the pain of losing her.

Slides of Courage

Dr Vacy Vlazna

Courage, that glorious mystery of human nature, has multiple expressions. To get a deeper understanding of this characteristic, it might be helpful to examine it carefully under a microscope. Let's imagine East Timor is the microscope under which we can acutely view courage. Here are two slides of courage.

Slide 1. Dr Kevin Baker

Dr Kevin Baker is an anaesthetist at Liverpool hospital in Sydney's west. He and his wife, Liz Glynn, a nurse, made many visits to East Timor during Indonesian occupation, conducting voluntary clinics with over 200 patients a day.

In April and May 1999, I accompanied Kevin to Timor to set up a scholarship program for Timorese University students. However, as the militia ruled Timor, our efforts became focused on setting up an emergency operating theatre. Motael Clinic, run by the Carmelite nuns, was (and still is now) a maternity clinic, but during that time it became a makeshift hospital for independence supporters, as these patients deteriorated rapidly or died if sent to the Indonesian military hospital. Kevin had scrounged the equipment for the theatre from a private hospital in Sydney that was closing down and luckily it arrived just before the bloodshed of the Liquica and Carrascalao massacres.

Dr Dan Murphy, an outspoken American, was running a general clinic at Motael. Kevin was setting up the theatre and also assisting in operations with a Médecin du Monde doctor, Willy Rouen, who was operating under a reading lamp. During this period, when Foreign Affairs had pulled out its staff and warned people not to go to East Timor, Kevin worked tirelessly in clinics at Don Bosco and Motael. He also took great risks attending to wounded or ill Falintil (Timorese resistance army) soldiers who were smuggled from the mountains to secret places in Dili. All these meetings were clandestine and each time Kevin could have easily been walking into a trap. Dili was a place where misplaced trust was lethal.

During the referendum, Kevin and Liz returned again to East Timor and conducted clinics at the Don Bosco School. On 6 August 2000 they were virtually prisoners in the besieged capital until they were evacuated to Darwin the next day. They had to leave behind their valiant Timorese interpreter, Sanches, who is now in Sydney studying English language while living with his Australian 'parents', Kevin and Liz.

Slide 2. Australian journalists

One night in May 1999, David Shea from SBS ran into the Turismo Hotel announcing that Aniceto Guterras's house had been surrounded by militia. Aniceto was the head of Yayasan Hak, a

Timorese human rights non-governmental organisation (NGO). Two dilapidated blue taxis were quickly filled with twelve journalists, including John Martinkus, Jason South, Mark Dodd, Nick Farrow, Geoff Thompson and Terry MacDonald, plus Kevin with his medical bag, and off they charged into the darkness.

The guys weren't going for a story. They were going to help Aniceto. It occurred to me that I was seeing the Aussie spirit of comradeship symbolised by Gallipoli tinged with the same courage that fired the young Balibo journalists in 1975 to seek truth of the Indonesian invasion in the heart of danger. After a couple of tense hours, they returned. Kevin said it was a combination of high drama and the keystone cops. As it happened, three taxis arrived at Aniceto's home, and there was a Mexican standoff between journalists and militia, all of whom nervously chain-smoked, so much so that Kevin said you could only see the little lights from the cigarettes flaring through the clouds of smoke.

During the negotiations Aniceto escaped and went into hiding. Mission accomplished. Since then, I have a deep respect for journalists in 'war' zones. They are a unique species. When there is gunfire, normal folk head in the opposite direction, but they head towards trouble. One freelance journalist, John Martinkus, who had a price on his head, stayed in Timor for nearly two years, 1998–2000, and was one of the journalists who refused to leave the United Nations headquarters compound when the UN was preparing to abandon the mission. He returned to Timor with Interfet. John is highly respected amongst his colleagues, not just for bravery but for the integrity of his stories.

Let's look closer at the slides. What is the source of the courage in Kevin and Liz, in John Martinkus, and the other journalists? A courage that endured life-threatening situations.

The answer lies, in part, in an overwhelming love for the Timorcse and the innocent trust they placed in any foreigner who may (or may not) have helped them. Keep in mind Timor had been closed to foreigners for about fifteen years and only the massacre at Santa Cruz opened it to the world. Also, the answer lies in part in a fierce sense of justice for a gentle people unjustly persecuted. But, mainly, the source lies in the daily courage of the Timorese who faced brutality for twenty-five years. In Timor there was always someone whose bravery surpassed that of another. Thousands of slides. Hundreds of thousands of Timorese with a personal experience of courage. In Timor, courage was commonplace.

Witness the referendum. The Timorese people, en masse, mainly illiterate farming people, lined up to vote before the UNAMET staff even got to the polling places at 5.30 a.m.! They knew the repercussions, and were prepared to sacrifice everything for freedom. Unimaginable courage. My soul kneels humbly before Timorese courage; a testimony to the magnificence of the human spirit.

Robes to Dish Rags

COLLEEN MELDRUM

Life is such an interesting journey and the twists and turns that fate has in store never cease to amaze me. I wonder if we knew what was around the next corner we would survive as well as we do. My life, like everyone else's, has been filled with ups and downs but luckily mainly ups.

I was born in Tasmania and had a very happy childhood growing up on a farm with very loving parents and one brother. I learned at an early age that I was adopted, which never caused me a moment's concern until I had children of my own and, needing a background medical history, felt I should try and find my birth mother. However, that's another story.

I married and had two children but sadly my marriage didn't last. Then I met and married Richard, my present husband, twenty years ago, taking on four stepchildren to make us a family of six.

We have had a fascinating voyage melding two families together, a voyage that at times was difficult and at other times very amusing but never, never dull. Suddenly my life became hectic with looking after a large family, with Richard's work in local government and his business, which often took him overseas, and with our involvement in charity.

It seemed we were always hopping on and off planes travelling the world, staying in beautiful hotels in exotic locations, dining at great restaurants, and meeting fascinating people. All in all we led a diverse and busy life. There were charity functions, first nights, balls, luncheons and dinners to attend, and at the same time we were looking after six children, overseeing their homework, keeping the peace, gardening and looking after our lovely house and garden at Portsea.

Then Richard became Lord Mayor of Melbourne, a job that we both took on with relish and fervour. It was a great honour indeed. We both worked long hours and literally devoted our lives to the city we loved. We tried to be all things to all people, giving everything we had to a job we felt privileged to have been given. However, as Charles Dickens so eloquently put it, 'They were the best of times and they were the worst of times.' No matter what we did or how much we tried there was always someone ready to criticise, belittle and pull us down. Damned if we did and damned if we didn't! The armchair critics were ever ready to find fault while never prepared to find out the real facts. However, we survived the term having had a wonderfully interesting and, I think, successful year.

Sadly the job had taken its toll on Richard's architectural practice; the building industry was at its lowest and we were faced with losing a lot of money, with bankruptcy. We lost our house in the city and our house at Portsea. Richard sold his magnificent collection of books; we sold our art and anything else that would raise some funds. My heart was saddened to see Richard lose so much of what he had worked so hard to achieve, to see a man who had given so much and been so generous throughout his life have so much taken away.

Well, the critics had a field day. 'They must have money stashed away!' The reality was we didn't. We were flat broke. During this traumatic period I never once felt sorry for myself. I felt lucky that I had achieved so much; that I had a wonderful family; that I had been able to travel; that I had had a beautiful house and that I had, with my own hands, built a beautiful garden. I believed that we had shared our home with so many people over the years, hopefully giving joy to a lot of people as well as to our family. I truly felt I had been most fortunate in my trip through life and this was just another chapter I had to deal with.

What to do? I hadn't been employed for over twenty years. I had no skills to speak of, and knew nothing about computers or anything else that an employer would require for that matter. What is more, I was well over thirty-five. However, I knew that I could either sink or swim and I certainly was not prepared to sink. The one skill I knew I had was as an experienced home manager. I could wash, iron, clean windows, scrub floors, drive, shop and garden. In fact I could do any chore to assist in the smooth running of a house.

My daughter decided at that time she needed to take a new direction. She was a trained nurse by profession but felt a change was in order and so together we set up a little business called 'Home Runners'. Off we set with mop and bucket in hand. The idea of a former Lady Mayoress as a cleaning lady gave us plenty of publicity in the first few weeks via the media. I was interviewed for magazines, radio, television and newspapers. Because of this publicity we were able to get quite a lot of clients and we worked very hard physically and arrived home at night too exhausted to eat. However,

I knew I would survive and that somehow I would eventually be able to regain a reasonable way of life.

During this time I don't think I ever lost my sense of humour. I didn't ever feel degraded: I felt worthwhile and skilled at what I was doing. Certainly the first-night invitations disappeared, the invitations to lunch became fewer and cottage pie cooked by my husband never tasted so good. For someone who could barely boil water when I met him, he could now cook a mean, if humble, meal to be enjoyed after a long day.

Did all this change me? In some ways it certainly did. My values have changed. I have discovered it is unimportant to be on the 'A' list. I have discovered what true friends really mean and that acquaintances are just that. I have discovered what joy two dogs can bring standing wagging their tails, so pleased to see you arrive home. I have discovered I can do a lot of things I would never have believed I could. I have discovered that what you put into life you get back threefold. I have discovered Dimmeys. I have discovered computers and how to use them. In fact my discovery course has been exciting, exhilarating and rewarding. I now believe I can cope with anything life has planned for me. My children have been the greatest support and inspiration for me during this time, and with their love and caring I have been able to grow and move on.

I no longer clean houses for a living, due to all sorts of reasons, and I have a wonderful job with a charity that I first helped when I was Lady Mayoress. It just shows what goes around comes around.

There were times when I felt I wouldn't make it but they were few and far between. It certainly hasn't been easy, but when I look around there are so many people coping with much greater heartache than we had. We have remained in good health and good spirits, and most of all we have learned so much from our journey.

•

Avril's Smile

BARRY EVERINGHAM

It has been said many times that the family who prays together stays together. Be that as it may. In our case we found that the family who suffers together is strengthened.

In July 1987, Avril Everingham, my wife, was diagnosed with cancer. It was a bolt from the blue, and we immediately gathered around to support her. The children were usually at boarding school but this happened during the mid-term holiday.

Those who know Avril will agree she is unsinkable. Always smiling, always ready with a kind word, always giving the benefit of the doubt, and this time, typically, she kept her suspicions quiet until they were confirmed. One Sunday she had been gardening, her usual form of relaxing. She had come in before dark and had a soaking bath. We were later told she had noticed an indentation in the left breast, prodded it, and felt a searing pain. The next day she went to her local GP, the following day she was sitting in front of a cancer specialist and the day after that was in hospital being prepared for the removal of the offending breast.

Our children, Dougal, then seventeen, and Nancy, sixteen, were told. They were relaxed – well as relaxed as they could be. Having been raised to expect the best out of life, they didn't panic. Their rationale was simple – nothing would happen to Mum.

Dougal had a schoolmate staying with us and, together with Nancy and me, they were waiting at the hospital when a very pale and listless version of the woman we all loved was wheeled back to her flower-filled room after the operation. When she saw the kids her face lit up – she knew she was in safe hands.

And she was. Nancy did the things girls usually do; she rubbed oil and cream on her mother's face, arms and hands. The boys sat on the end of the bed and chatted about whatever boys chat about when they make a hospital visit.

How was father during all of this? To be honest he didn't travel all that well. He went through the 'poor me' syndrome. What if she dies? What will I do? Can I take her place with the kids?

I must admit alcohol somewhat dimmed the misery, but along the way it caused the other people most concerned misery of their own. That's a story for another day – as it is only recently that I got to know exactly what I was like.

Avril's recovery was remarkable and her doctor was really very impressed. At the time she became ill, Avril was organising functions for the Victoria State Opera. She had on her plate all the details for a forthcoming fundraising ball to be held two weeks up the track on the stage in the State Theatre in the Victoria Arts Centre complex.

I think her illness threw the organising committee into a tail-spin – but they didn't know just how tough Avril could be. The day before she was due to be released from hospital I went to see her and found a committee meeting going on around her bed! 'Oh, can you come back later,' she said. 'I'm busy now.'

It wasn't long before she had hold of the reigns and life took on its usual pattern. But two years later, her old foe returned, this time in the sternum – not the best of places to get cancer.

She had radiotherapy to get rid of that invasion. This time Nancy was abroad studying and we felt there was no necessity for her to return home. Dougal was a tower of strength and I had taken (what passed at the time for) control of myself.

Much later when Avril and I were living in New York, Avril came back to Australia to see the family. When Nancy met her at Tullamarine, Avril looked so ill she took her to her doctor who sent her to hospital. She was diagnosed with cancer in her spine.

I was due back on a visit and was met by a very distressed Nancy who this time believed her mother was dying. After I had spoken to the doctor and seen Avril I came to the same conclusion. Dougal has his mother's genes – he needed more convincing. 'Mum will be okay,' he confided in me.

Well, Mum is okay now. She still has regular treatment but her life is normal. This she owes to her iron will, her absolute determination to be around for those she loves and her love for life, with all its ups and downs.

And as for me? Well, I'm still around too – for Avril and the children and a sweet, adorable grandchild. If Avril could find the strength to be here – why would any of us not be here for her?

Ched Towns: Tribute to a Fine Man

BARRY MARKOFF

Ched Towns passed away on 20 January 2000. An inspiration to those he came in contact with, Ched fell to one of the challenges he could not conquer, the mountain of Mera Peak. Despite being blind, no challenge was too great for Ched. Whether parachuting out of a plane from over 5000 metres, trekking in Nepal or competing in triathlons, including the Hawaiian Ironman, Ched conquered all. Ched's inspirational presentations have touched the hearts and souls of tens of thousands of people, not only in Australia but also all around the world.

Ched led a passionate life that turned from anger and frustration to excitement and passion. He grew up in a tough working-class area of Penrith, west of Sydney, loving rugby league and with a dream of playing for the Penrith Panthers. Things, however, started to go astray as his eyesight deteriorated, and his night vision in particular becoming very limited. Ched recalled how he used to hang around the lights at the training grounds so that he could at least see a little bit and as a result was nicknamed 'The Moth'. When his eyesight became too bad he finished up consulting a specialist who shattered his dreams by telling him that he was suffering from retinis pigmentosa, a condition that eventually led to him going blind.

Ched became angry and frustrated at the world. Aged eighteen and able to enter licensed premises, but still too proud to admit he had virtually nil vision, Ched would get into scrap after scrap. He was a big man with huge hands, and he, in his own words, 'just swung at everything'. He demolished chairs, tables, along with a few opponents, but always copped the worst of it, especially when the fight continued in the car park, where he didn't have the 'luxury' of being in a confined space. As his wife, Judy, commented, 'There was many a time I had to pick Ched up from either the hospital or the police station.'

The next ten years saw Ched go downhill as he started to lose his self-esteem; he felt he was useless to society. His feelings of frustration and anger were further enhanced by not being able to hold down a regular job because of his sight problem.

The turning point in Ched's life was a trip to England for a radical, although ultimately unsuccessful, bee-sting treatment to cure his condition. He and five other blind people went to London with a woman who claimed to be able to cure blindness with a treatment program that involved being stung by dozens of bees, day after day. Ched was willing to do anything to get his sight back, and towards the end of the treatment he was enduring eighty bee stings per day on his forehead and neck. Photos taken of Ched at this time show him looking like the elephant man!

Sick of being confined to their quarters for days on end in London, Ched organised daily outings for the group, searching for and finding new adventures further and further afield in the streets of London. Ched used to say what an amusing sight it must have been – six blind people in a line, one hand on the shoulder in front of them, meandering through London, not seeing a thing. They even went on the feared London underground, standing in a line hoping and praying that when the train stopped, the door would be in front of them. When it wasn't of course, it was every man for himself, and they felt their way along the train to find the door, doing a roll call of names once they were settled. They eventually had to give this adventure away for two reasons. They didn't know where they were heading, and they were leaving too many of their group on the platform.

The experiment and six months away from his family made Ched realise that his blindness was not going to change. On his return to Australia he was a changed man. With a new attitude, he accepted his blindness and was happy to live life as a visually impaired person. He threw himself into sport and adventure with no challenge too great. Ched competed in the 1988 Seoul Paralympics in the discus and javelin, and in 1997 he won silver at the world triathlon championships.

He waterskied and played golf, he had a scuba diving licence, and in 1997 he kayaked from Australia to New Guinea. Ched also competed in numerous triathlons, became the first blind man to free-fall 4000 metres in 1992 and loved to go water rafting.

Ched kept setting himself goals; his last one was to climb Mt Everest and thus become the first visually impaired person to scale the world's highest peak at 8850 metres. He had done the preparation by either running, swimming, riding or doing weights for six to ten hours per day, six to seven days a week. Climbing Mera Peak was just one step towards his ultimate goal of Everest. Unfortunately

Ched's life ended there, but you can rest assured, it would have been with a smile on his face as he flirted with adventure when his life ended.

Ched's final days on this earth were how he would have wanted them to be. Apart from climbing Mera Peak in early to mid-January, Ched was also one of about eighty people who clawed their way up the cold, jagged shoulder of Mt Kosciuszko on New Year's Eve to celebrate the millennium dawn at the highest point in Australia. Ched, his daughter, Carlie, and her boyfriend, Aaron, got there first. 'They found a rock right at the top,' recalls Ched's son, Kane. 'Dad had really high standards . . . Do it right, be the best. He wanted them to be the highest people in the country and they were.'

One year prior to his death Ched had spoken to his wife and soul mate, Judy, and their two children. He mentioned that if anything happened to him they were not to be upset because they had all had the best life that any family could have ever had together. Ched considered he had a magnificent life filled with wonderful adventures and experiences and supported by the best family, friends and acquaintances anybody could ever have.

Ched Towns was one of the most remarkable men that I have ever met. People like Ched cannot be relaced, but it is important that his messages about life are handed from person to person and generation to generation. Ched Towns – sadly missed but never to be forgotten.

The Hidden Handicap

OLGA TOMIC

How excited were you when the doctor said 'positive'?

Pre-natal classes were a breeze and prepared me for everything – except giving birth to a handicapped child.

A physical handicap is visible and can be quite devastating to the parents in the immediate time after the birth and for some time afterwards. However, the 'hidden handicap', Attention Deficit Disorder (ADD/ADHD), can be recognisable around eighteen months after your child is born.

Having a previous child helps you to compare the progress of children, even though the professionals say not to compare. I used it as a guide, and thank God I did.

My first-born was a girl, a beautiful blue-eyed blonde. Restless as ever, she charmed the people around her but drove her parents crazy. She never slept, loved to scream and threw the most effective tantrums. Oh, she was manipulative from the start, but she was our first and I adored her.

By the time she was two we had a little addition to our clan, Jason. Our family was complete with this perfect baby boy. He was quite the opposite from our little girl; he slept when put down, he drank his milk when prompted, he smiled, and he made all the right noises for the cutest, most adorable baby. That is where it ended.

Welcome to my medical nightmare. Jason was twelve months old, a sick little boy with a raging temperature, typical gastroenteritis symptoms and a glowing red face. I took him to the local doctor who referred us to a paediatrician. Jason had burst both eardrums with all his screaming. He was hospitalised for four days, and cared for by the staff and myself.

Following that, and a failed marriage, life went on. I was expecting Jason, at two years, to be able to say 'Mum' or respond when I called him, but nothing happened except a grunt or scream here and there. The paediatrician suggested a visit to the Ear, Nose and Throat (ENT) surgeon. Jason had glue ear. His burst eardrums had been forgotten about after his bout of gastroenteritis and had left him clearly deaf. An operation later that week began his long haul to recovering some of his hearing.

On our final visit to the ENT surgeon he suggested a visit to a child developmental paediatrician. The surgeon was the first to pick up on the deeper problem with Jason.

Dr Anne was wonderful. She diagnosed ADD/ADHD and immediately prescribed him with drugs to slow his hyperactivity. This improved things slightly but we became aware that if this medication was not given in the right quantity for body weight it had an adverse effect. Wow! What an effect. Let's climb some walls. Let's dangle out of high windows, perhaps run in front of an on-coming car, or even take a closer look at that train track but, gees, no one told me a train was coming.

At around this time, Jason's psychological assessment showed that as a four-year-old child he had the mental capacity of a two-and-a-half-year-old. I was lost. I had nowhere to turn and no support.

By this stage, Jason was unbearable, demanding, loud and hyperactive. He was always having accidents and had had every part of his face stitched back on. Yes, even his mouth was stitched back on when we found out that curtain rods could not hold the weight of a child.

Jason needed specialist care. He needed to be in an area with better facilities that catered for children with problems. He began to have speech therapy and occupational therapy on a weekly basis, and after an early intervention assessment was offered two mornings per week of one-to-one care during kindergarten classes. The rest of the time he was violent, disruptive and rude, but the paediatrician was reluctant to offer further medication. Instead they offered behavioural management on a weekly basis.

I was taught how to manage this hyperactive, tantrum-throwing child who loved to kick, punch, scream and abuse others. I was told to ignore him, give him controlled time out and reward him for good behaviour. Theoretically, it was wonderful. However, what do you do in the supermarket halfway through your grocery shopping when out comes an almighty scream? 'I want this! I want that! Now, now, now! I hate you, Mum! Go away.' I was told to calmly take my child and walk on.

When Jason was six-and-a-half he began school. Once again I struck a brick wall. Another assessment was pending for assistance in the school. By this stage, I resented the public service and was also starting to resent the medical service.

Jason was offered 7.6 hours of assistance. These hours were quickly used up in the school ground during recess, as otherwise there was no one to look after him in case he ran out of the yard.

During class he was once again loud and disruptive. They heard him not only in the classroom but throughout the whole school. My daughter, who attended the same school, came home every night and said, 'Mum, Jason did this, or Jason did that.' 'Jason spent the whole time in the corner.' 'We heard him all day.' One child in particular used to hit Jason. For one term, I put up with this treatment until Jason came home with a huge haematoma on his head. I asked what had happened. Jason, my daughter and several other children told me that this boy had hit Jason over the head with a cricket bat.

The school failed to inform me. Once again, they thought I would remain silent. Instead, I went to the school and demanded answers. They told me the usual thing. The matter was being dealt with and the other boy's parents had been notified. I was not happy. I walked out and went straight to the local police station and lodged a formal complaint. I asked them to prosecute the principal of the school for negligence. Finally, the boy was expelled and I removed not only my son but also my daughter from that school.

Jason moved to small special school that had specialised teachers and all the therapists special children need. They were absolutely wonderful, although caring for Jason at home was still very difficult.

At one point I started showing signs of a nervous breakdown. I was told to do something, but what? Since Jason started at his new school, he has seen three speech therapists, two occupational therapists, four psychologists, one ENT surgeon, six paediatricians and one psychiatrist. It has been a long hard haul, one mainly of superficial compassion and sympathy. I have been told on more than one occasion to go home and cope. Over the years many doctors tried many drugs in an effort to make Jason's behaviour more manageable. I can't tell you the cocktails of drugs he has been on for most of his thirteen years.

The human services eventually saw how bad he was and instructed me to take him to a respite home. He now lives there with three other children his own age. There are three adult carers who look after these children and I might say they do a wonderful job. He is not far away from me and still attends the same school.

Jason speaks with us each day and stays with us each Wednesday night. He visits his father each alternate weekend and stays overnight. We all get on so much better and we look forward to seeing each other. The time now is quality time and not angry time.

I would like to thank all my friends who helped me over the years and put up with Jason's nagging and violent behaviour when they visited. God only knows why they came back for a second visit. They are my dearest friends.

No Knead for Success

CAROL BATES

When my two sons were born I wanted them to have the best possible diet so I decided the way to do this was to make everything myself. From soups and casseroles to muesli, biscuits, ice cream and cordial and anything else I could think of, I made it all. I also taught myself to bake bread and never for one moment did I imagine the effect this small accomplishment would have on our lives.

The commercial aspect of my bread making began in such a small way. One day my son took some of my freshly baked bread to school and a teacher asked me if I would make bread for her each time I baked. I did so and in no time at all I was hauling basket loads of fresh, hot bread up to the school, sometimes twice weekly, and each time I would gain new customers. My house was filled with bowls of dough rising on every available surface.

I would have continued to do this had not fate intervened in the shape of a car accident that left me with a back injury immobilising me for seven miserable months. I lay in pain throughout the winter in Red Hill where the fog kept rolling in and the rain dripped sullenly from the trees day after day. I had a great deal of time to reflect and thought about all the missed opportunities. My husband and I had always opted for safety and security, and although we dreamt of working together in our own business the time never seemed quite right. Those dreams were shattered now anyway because I really didn't think I would be able to walk again, let alone run a business.

Fortunately we found a wonderful chiropractor who was able to help me and I was given a second chance. This time I wasn't going to waste a moment of it. Ken resigned from the bank, we took out a lease on a new shop in Red Hill South on the Mornington Peninsula and, without consulting or discussing it with anyone, we opened a shop called All Things Natural. We stocked only the very best of natural foods and I, naturally, made the bread.

We had so much faith in our idea that it never really occurred to us that it could fail. The population of Red Hill was only 600, we were miles from anywhere and the concept of natural organic foods was practically unheard of at this time. We were considered either foolhardy or extremely far-sighted, depending on whom you spoke to, especially as we had a mortgage, a personal loan and two small children to support. We were ecstatic when we took $500 in our first week of trading – we could pay our bills and buy food and that was all that mattered. Money was never our prime motivation; we just wanted to work together, earn enough to live off and enjoy our boys. Our values have never altered. We worked extremely hard but we loved our business and our customers, and our shop was always full of laughter. We were very happy.

I had started out making bread for the shop but I just couldn't keep up with the demand so I hit upon the idea of teaching. My first class was with six local women and from that day on we haven't been without a class in twenty years. Someone suggested we put our ingredients into a kit to sell after the class. This also proved to be a great idea and our kits now sell throughout Australia.

Our business went from strength to strength and I was asked to write a book on my 'No Knead' method of bread making. To my absolute astonishment and delight it became a best seller, selling over 150 000 copies. Our next decision was to buy Stoneground Flour Milling because we felt we should have control over our supplies. We moved to larger premises but the milling became too much for Ken and we had to subcontract it out. When we bought our own premises we felt we had it all. Little did we realise that our next decision could see us losing everything we had worked for for the last fifteen years.

The day a 'franchising consultant' walked into our lives was, in a way, the day we lost control of our business. He was so enthusiastic about our business. He felt it was just perfect for franchising, and assured us that we would have complete control over every aspect, that it was the ideal way for a small business with a great idea to expand and, best of all, allow for a better distribution of our products, which had always been a problem. There were very few people to seek advice from on franchising and, looking back, I think we were under the misconception that he was there to help us make a decision rather than buy his services. As we have learnt to our cost, franchising is very risky, particularly in Australia. I think if people knew what had happened to us no one would dream of franchising their idea. One day I would like to write a book entitled *Never, Never Franchise* – I'm sure it would be a best-seller.

Our contracts turned out to be not worth the paper they were written on, as incidentally are most franchise contracts. We were given the most appalling legal advice by so-called 'franchise lawyers'. Once again we thought we were in the hands of experts but they saw us as a honey pot to dip into at will. So after founding a business that had brought us nothing but goodwill and happiness, we were faced with a nightmare. It was absolutely no consolation to find that others had struck exactly the same problems; in fact it was infuriating to think we hadn't been either aware or informed of just what could go wrong. The lies, the betrayal and the threats ended up making me ill and we tasted the frustration and misery of other people controlling our lives.

It always seems to take some sort of crisis to point us in another direction. During these years of upheaval, Ken and I began to develop a property in the beautiful Yarra Valley. We found that the shifting of rocks, digging, weeding, planting and planning were an ideal antidote to all the stress we were under. Somehow when you're putting huge rocks in place with the aid of a crowbar and a small front-end loader, the mind must concentrate on the task at hand if you don't want to be crushed. Fortunately we were able to harness the energy we might well have wasted in being angry, bitter or frustrated and use it in a positive way to achieve the most amazing outcome.

We have created a paradise of lakes, fountains, garden rooms, tranquil vistas and a haven for wildlife. We have been able to put the same passion and energy that drove our business into something else that we love and will eventually be able to share with others.

Our problems are being resolved and our business continues to grow in an entirely unexpected and exciting direction. If perseverance and dedication to hard work count for anything, we will succeed in the end.

Struck Down

JAN MCGUINNESS

'You've got a virus and will be out of action for the rest of the week,' announced the young locum in response to the fact that I was aching all over and couldn't move.

Bedridden for three days! As the working mother of a sixteen-month-old baby girl, illness was something I couldn't be doing with. There was simply no time for it in my frantic life. I was annoyed and impatient with myself and with him. As it turned out I had plenty of time to contemplate my reaction and many other things over the next year. That's how long I was out of action.

The locum was too inexperienced to recognise my nasty flu as the paralysing Guillian Barre syndrome, a condition so rare that it afflicts about one in every 100 000 people. One day and serious deterioration later I was on my way to hospital.

Guillian Barre hit me like an instant dose of multiple sclerosis. One day I was walking around feeling a bit stiff and sore. The next

I was aching all over and unable to visit the bathroom without help. Within three days I couldn't move at all from the neck down.

The syndrome is triggered by a mild or subliminal infection that causes the immune system to attack rather than defend the body. This can take days, as in my case, or several weeks. It can wrack you with pain or be pain free. You can take months or years to recover.

I'd never heard of it or its effects. One day I was immersed in work and plans. The next I was a prisoner of my inert body and my world was on hold. The prognosis was terrifying. At worst I could be paralysed, or recovering for over a year, ending up permanently on crutches or in a wheelchair. At best, I could take months to recover and be fully restored. I focused exclusively on the latter possibility, encouraged by the generality that the faster the onset of Guillian Barre, the faster the recovery from it.

Meanwhile, there was much to deal with. The pain was so intense that pethidine injections meant to offer eight hours of relief worked for about sixty minutes on me. Breathing was a big issue and had to be constantly monitored; as the peripheral nervous system breaks down, your breathing can be suppressed. People have died in circumstances where the condition went unrecognised. One day my breathing failed and I finished up in intensive care with a tracheotomy.

The whole experience was like a descent into hell. I felt like I'd fallen through a hole in reality and onto the end of a pitchfork in one of the lower levels of a Hieronymus Bosch painting. Above all, I'd resigned from my job to be with my daughter and I now saw that precious time with her drifting away.

After six weeks the paralysis began wearing off and I was removed from intensive care. Then commenced many months of intensive physiotherapy and learning to walk again.

First I learned to roll like a baby, then to sit up and to stand. Standing was agony as the blood rushed into my immobile limbs, and I couldn't do it unaided. I forced myself to spend torturous half-hours in the standing frame, a Dickensian wrack into which I was strapped while lying on the floor and then lifted upright. I'd try to read a book as tears streamed down my face but I was determined because it hastened my recovery. I'd already beaten the record by weaning myself off the respirator in intensive care so that I could get up to the ward and on with physiotherapy.

But some of my fellow sufferers – there were five of us including a ten-year-old boy and an eighty-year-old grandmother – had different attitudes. One in particular was making a meal of it. Her husband came daily to feed her and dance attention and she showed few signs of recovery despite being in physiotherapy much longer than the rest of us. Perhaps the woman had never been paid much attention before and actually enjoyed being doted upon.

Although I could have done without it, the experience was illuminating. The reactions of family and friends taught me as much about them as it did about myself. An aunt who visited me in intensive care didn't return once she realised that the end of the unit was sectioned off for AIDS patients.

On the other hand people I hadn't worked with for years rallied round and raised enough money to keep me in weekly deliveries of Kevin O'Neill flowers. I'd often wished for a regular source of floral tributes and joked about being thin and forced to eat my way back to health. Sometimes you get what you want but not in the way you wanted it.

As the long-term patient of the hospital, I was constantly reminded that without my health I had nothing. If I ever got it back there were things I was determined to do differently.

In fact I did fully recover, but Guillian Barre took a year out of my life and the opportunity to have more children. Its impact was like a meat cleaver through my existence. There was before Guillian Barre and there was after, which I approached with fresh insights and the belief that I'd been given a second chance. Without rushing into anything I made some important and lasting changes in my personal life. At work I learnt to slow down and to accept that I wasn't indispensable.

Although it was immensely harrowing and painful, I don't consider Guillian Barre the worst thing that has ever happened to me because it taught me so much and because it proved that for whatever reason, I could endure.

It did take me years to overcome the shock of discovering that one's predictable, everyday existence can be shattered in an instant. While this no longer keeps me awake at night, complacency has no part in my make-up.

When the High Bar Falls

BRENDAN GULLIFER

How quickly things change. My epiphany did not involve death or terminal illness. It involved the Sydney Olympics. The company I worked for went into liquidation the day before the opening ceremony. The Olympics were to have been our graduation, the platform on which we thrust ourselves into the next stage of global operation. We would bring the world's press to the world's press. Using the Internet and digital printers we would send global editions of newspapers from more than twenty countries down the wires to make them available at the main press centre and other outlets around Sydney in hard copy, in real time.

It was a brilliant idea and had worked elsewhere. Our newspaper delivery system had become standard fare at major high-tech conferences and exhibitions. Check into more than 200 hotels across America and the latest edition of your hometown European newspaper would be delivered to your room. Check out kiosks at JFK

Airport, the United Nations, Central Station and major book stores across London and Europe and you would see point of sale material for our company and snazzy sales racks with newspapers from around the world. Our growth was tremendous. We went from six employees to seventy with operations in fourteen cities in a matter of months.

The trade and business press covered us, and CNN and CNBC included updates in television reports that went worldwide. Newspaper publishers who at first scoffed at our ideas began to jostle to come aboard. The idea of their publication being available in the world's greatest cities made them dance like children in the snow. We offered them the dream of the new millennium – become global with us, and do it with the push of a button. We planned to go beyond hotels and retail outlets, to be on cruiseships and airlines, and in far-flung tourist resorts such as Bali, Penang, the Caribbean and Broome. Wherever the wealthy and mobile congregated, we would be there to give them what was previously unavailable – the latest edition of their hometown newspaper. And the smart money men of Wall Street dumping US$1 million a month to keep us up and running said our target was to be in thirty cities by 2001.

In hindsight, my history with the company was just as rushed. Following a casual meeting in the company's Manhattan head office last year, I had gone from being a part-time consultant to managing director for this part of the world with offices in Melbourne and Sydney, a national sales and marketing director and a team on assignment here from the US.

I worked at a frenzied pace. Sixteen-hour days were not unusual. Not a week went past when I wasn't on a plane (one time in March I made three interstate trips in six days). A weekly 6 a.m. conference call with New York grew to twice weekly and sometimes there would be three of these calls in less than six days (with regular calls on Saturday mornings). And frequently they were long. More than ninety minutes was not uncommon. Even now, I don't know what sense I made in those early hours. I would sit in my lounge room through the winter and wave the kids off to school as the endless talk of strategy and logistics and advertising and public relations continued down the transpacific lines with my American colleagues, wired and sipping Starbucks late in their day.

And somehow, perhaps through some subliminal process that operated in those earlier hours, I became an evangelist for our technology. I would speak about globalisation and distance and family and friends; of how our hometown daily newspaper is the one habit we leave behind when we travel far from home; about how the more high-tech we become, the more high-touch we demand to be; and that for airlines and hotels and companies to supply their most important clients with their latest edition of their hometown newspaper was the most effective weapon in the corporate armoury to win and keep new clients.

I spoke of Geoffrey Blainey's *Tyranny of Distance*, and how our technology was beating this. We weren't just changing the newspaper business. We were changing the world. In one speech just before the Games, I pointed to the Aboriginal photos hanging on the walls of the hospitality room, lively and moving shots of outback indigenous families caught at various times throughout the day. And I said how our product reflected similar emotions of homes left behind and familiar routines changed. At the time, I admitted it was a 'long bow' but thought it clever. In hindsight, it seems ridiculous.

The Sydney 2000 Games were to be our next beachhead. With fifty newspapers in our network, journalists and VIPs would be gobsmacked to receive same-day editions of their hometown newspaper over breakfast. Our penetration was superlative. More than thirty major Sydney hotels, luxury yachts moored in the Harbour, hospitality rooms at the airport and at Homebush Stadium, the world's biggest television studio at the Olympic International Broadcast Centre, the Main Press Centre, the Media Village, the Olympic Village – we left no stone unturned. Athletes from Europe, Asia and America could compete and then hours later see how the press at home reported their performance.

The call came through on my mobile at 6 a.m., the day before the opening ceremony. It was the chief executive officer. Our venture capital backers in the USA had pulled the plug. No more funds, no more company. A plea to advance bridging finance to create time to find another investor was flatly declined. It was a policy decision, they said, a strategic move away from the dot.com sector. Suddenly, seventy of us were out of work. Our small world-changing technoship had run aground – suddenly, inelegantly and at the worst possible time.

But there was an additional instruction from head office. Our Olympic operation had been prepaid – the rental of huge digital print machines and the fitout of a factory at Sydney Olympic Park had already been accounted for. By drastically reducing our operations, we could supply newspapers to only visiting journalists. So no hotels, no VIPs, no luxury cruiseships. Only the international press. Our print staff walked off the job, having heard of our problems. It was up to our small team of executive colleagues to run the site at Homebush – six of us to work an operation that originally had a staff of more than eighteen.

The next two weeks passed in a dream-like state. Nights were spent in conference calls with the USA, beginning at 11 p.m. (9 a.m. New York time) and often extending until 3 or 4 a.m. as we tried to manage our unravelling mission. During the day my colleagues and I received hundreds of calls from hotels and Olympic sponsors asking where their newspapers were. 'Sorry, we've gone into liquidation.' It all sounded so lame. And then our small world-weary band made the daily treck out to Sydney Olympic Park before dawn (seventy-five minutes by bus and train from the house we had rented in Glebe) to begin printing that day's editions. Coming home in the late afternoon, walking through the crowds at Circular Quay and around the city, feeling as divorced from the festivities as *ET* – no sleep, no job and no future. It was a strange juxtaposition.

The only certainty life presents is uncertainty

It's taken more than a month to wind up Australian operations, to pay out creditors and close things down. And future Olympics will never have the same meaning for me. A book I borrowed from the library said that you are never unemployed, you are only ever a *consultant*. But I've been a consultant before, and I am now definitely unemployed. It won't last forever, I know. I've had some interesting offers, which I am mulling over. But I now believe that the only certainty life presents is uncertainty, that strange bedfellow of change. Expect the unexpected and you won't be disappointed.

Love

New Beginnings

CAROLINE WARD

I fell in love. I had always known it would happen – always. And I had waited. I was almost thirty, Michael was forty-three. As soon as I saw him there was a voice in my head that said as clear as anything, 'This is the man you're going to marry.' It took four years before we finally got together, but once we did, that was it. Nothing and no one could come between us. 'You can trust me implicitly, Caroline. I will never let you down.' He said those words to me after our first night out. I can still hear them. I knew it was true, he never would. And he didn't.

It was about five months into our relationship that Michael started experiencing pain in his upper back. Lung cancer. Terminal they told us. How long? We didn't ask and we didn't want to know.

After the initial devastation, the well of sorrow at being about to lose each other after waiting so long, we were given a gift in disguise. My mother Joan rang the day after all the tests were finalised.

'What's the news?' she asked.

'The worst you can imagine,' I replied.

A long pause.

'So . . . new beginnings.'

New beginnings! Was she mad? It was the end. I don't remember what happened next but when I got off the phone Michael asked me what was wrong. I told him what Mum had said. He jumped off the bed and went into his study. He came back with a book titled *Self Hypnosis*. It was the beginning of something very new for both of us.

We had both been serious party players in the entertainment industry, and during the next five months our lives changed dramatically. No drugs – cigarettes, alcohol or recreational. No meat. No sugar. No chilli. No mushrooms. I had to learn to cook all over again. Gone were the days of going to bed at four in the morning. We were getting up at four and walking and meditating. A veil was lifted and a beautiful world came into view. While the cancer was spreading, Michael was healthier than he could ever remember being.

One typical Sydney Sunday we were walking through the harbourside park near our house in Balmain and out of nowhere a summer storm hit. We ran to the closest shelter, a disused ferry wharf. Laughing and dripping wet yet warm, we were very, very happy. He stopped and just looked at me for the longest time.

'So, do you wanna get married?' That voice of four years earlier echoed through time.

I smiled from my heart. 'Of course I do.'

That was December. On 15 February I turned thirty; on the seventeenth we were married. I think it was pretty hard for the small group of thirty we invited. Michael had lost quite a bit of weight and while he still looked gorgeous, when I look back, it was clear that his life force was ebbing away. At the time, I didn't notice. We were happy and we had a beautiful day.

We went to my dad's apartment on one of the Queensland islands and it was there that I came to see that the battle we had been fighting was moving into an all-out war. Michael was losing the strength to live, imperceptibly, and I denied it totally.

When we got back things were a bit more difficult. Side effects from the only medication he was on were taking their toll. Things were happening in his body over which he had no control. He was frightened. At one stage we were booked to go to Melbourne to attend the Gawler Foundation five-day retreat for people with life-threatening diseases. Michael didn't want to go, telling me the night before our flight. I got so angry. I hadn't been that angry with him ever. I told him I was going with or without him. I think my reaction was partly due to my denial of what stage he was in and partly because I felt there was something crucial I needed to learn while we were at the retreat. In the end we went. It wasn't a pleasant experience. Michael really didn't want to be there and somehow we had a tension, an edge between us a lot of the time. But I got what I went for.

In the session that Ian Gawler took for the carers, I can only remember one thing that he said but that's the thing that made all the difference. 'Never give up on anyone. Always believe it's possible for them to get well . . . and if you happen to be with someone as they are moving on, it can be the greatest privilege. You have to give them permission to leave, and you can be of great help to them in this.'

Ten days after we got back, Jacob the doctor was at the house. He was there most days so it wasn't unusual, but this day was the day I finally woke up. I realised that it was nearly time, that Michael would die and that I couldn't stop it happening.

I managed to leave the house and make it to our dear friend Judy's place where I broke down absolutely and completely. With deep physical pain in my chest and a heart overwhelmed with sorrow, I sobbed uncontrollably. Jude helped me to her meditation room. Through the tears and the pain and the sorrow, I felt myself surrender my need to control. It was my only choice. I had hit 'rock-bottom' as they say in AA.

From some place deep inside I let go and in my letting go I challenged God. 'God, I don't know who you are or what you do for a living, but I can't do this any more. You have to do it. It's too hard.'

At that very moment the darkness of my sorrow turned to light. The pain completely vanished, the sobbing stopped. I was awash with the light of a love I had never known. Then I was gently held in a cocoon of peace, a peace I had not ever experienced. At that point it was as if my intellect opened and the voice was very clear, as clear as it had been that first day Michael and I met.

'You don't own this soul. It is as if you are two actors coming together to play a scene. It is not your job to worry about the next scene, it will be whatever it is. You just have to play this one the best you can, and the method for that is to find the joy in every moment.'

I knew that this was true. This understanding was my salvation. I was able to return home and talk to Michael about the future. I was ready to give him my permission to go. I sat on the edge of the bed but was somehow watching from outside myself.

'It is as if we are on a journey and there is only one road to take us wherever we're heading. At some point there is a fork in the road. One road is marked for your moving on and the other is your recovery. But the road to get there is the same. We have to find the joy in every moment and then if you do move on, it will be with dignity and grace, and I will be left with wonderful memories. If you stay, it will be an extraordinary foundation for our future life together.'

We just looked into each others' eyes. I think he was so thankful to finally be allowed to do what he needed to do. The next ten days were remarkable. We did commit to finding the joy in every moment. And God, that exquisite presence that lifted me from the darkness of my pain, just became stronger and stronger. Our home was overflowing with the light of love and joy and peace. It was palpable. And it was preparing Michael to leave.

On 17 April, exactly two months after we'd been married, Michael died. At about sunrise a tumour burst in his brain, flooding him with toxins. He was delirious. I was frightened. Somehow it passed. He became lucid around mid-morning but he was in a lot of pain for the first time. He had made it this far without taking anything stronger than Panadeine Forte, but now he needed oxygen and when Jacob arrived he gave him his first shot of morphine.

That session with Ian Gawler came back. This was it . . . this was the privilege and the opportunity to help him move on. Zoe, a healer with whom Michael had been doing some work, had taught me a meditation that would help Michael leave when it was time. It was time.

In the silence we were so connected and yet so free

I relieved Jacob and lay down beside my husband on our bed in that lovely room amid the treetops. Helping him onto his side, I began. Gently nuzzled in behind him, I stroked him and began the meditation. He took his last breath, I knew that. There was an incredible silence as the soul, my friend and my love prepared to move on, doing so with exquisite grace and pure dignity. I could feel the energy being drawn upwards. In moments I could tell he had gathered himself fully and was ready. He held. And in the holding and in the silence we were so connected and yet so free. God had given us that. The beauty of that moment will stay forever etched in my being. It was up to me. The final permission. It really was time now.

'Fly my love . . .' and he was gone. And the silence was supreme.

Michael had given me a new life, he had taught me about health, love and joy. He had given me back to God. I would be fine. And he had healed so many things for himself and had been carried forward on the wings of such beauty that I know his new life, wherever it is, is also just fine.

A Blessed Life

ARTHUR BRAITHWAITE

The more weddings I've been fortunate to preside over the last few years, the more convinced I've become that weddings are monumental occasions in the lives of those undertaking them. I'm also convinced that couples who value the deeper importance of the occasion are more likely to look on them as lifelong commitments.

At the same time I'm not sure that all church ministers see it like this. Some give the impression that weddings are unavoidable extras, which have to be fitted in between other more important religious appointments.

I am a minister and recently I had cause to wonder whether baptisms could make the same lasting impression. I had just baptised a baby girl and afterwards we adjourned to the family's house to celebrate. I found myself in conversation with a fellow guest who recalled a baptism he'd been to a few years before. 'It was all over in ten minutes,' he remarked. Upon which I found myself unexpectedly being thanked for 'doing a good service', as it were, by way of contrast!

Baptisms, called christenings in some churches, don't often come my way, though I can understand they may well take on a measure of routine if a minister in a parish found himself having to conduct them every week. I am an 'Order' priest and not attached to a parish but, rather, have chaplaincy duties in schools and organisations.

The parents of the baby girl had become friends of mine after I had administered their wedding two years before. It was natural that they would come with the request for me to be the minister at the baptism of Amara. Of course I accepted. They chose a church a few suburbs away because, as is often the case these days with people having more freedom to choose, they liked the look of it.

More surprising was the fact that they said they were expecting eighty or ninety people to attend, not only family and relatives, but also friends and neighbours. I may not get to many baptisms, but I considered that had to be an unusually high number for a christening gathering. This was the first thought that was to lead to Amara's baptism becoming, for all those present, a singularly personal and memorable occasion.

What a pity, I thought to myself, that we can't preserve the occasion for Amara to look back on later. Yes, there would be photographs and, yes, there would be memories and stories to tell. But wouldn't it be wonderful if everybody there could record their thoughts and feelings.

So began a search of the city, a search for a baptism book in which everybody present could write a thought. Religious shops had never heard of the idea, and stationers couldn't produce anything elegant enough. Finally, at a boutique printing outlet I found the exact thing: a hard cover, square signature book, with patterned pages and decorative edging, with a smiling sun on the cover, and 'Forever' scribbled across the top.

Before offering grace at the backyard lunchtime party, I got everyone's attention by announcing that all present were invited to write something in this book. They could tell how they felt, what the day was like for them, or they could offer Amara a wish or a prayer. The word 'Forever' had to appear somewhere in what they wrote. The book would be kept for Amara and given to her as a teenager.

The idea seemed to win the approval of all present. We planned it so that the first pages were reserved for parents, godparents and both lots of grandparents. These pages would be doubles, one for a photo and the other for writing. One grandfather had died four years before, but grandma said she could write what he would have said! At the very front of the book we pasted in a copy of the service and a photo of the baptism.

Between mouthfuls of roast chicken and salad, that book went the rounds of the gathering, and by the end of the afternoon it had every page covered. I knew, indeed everyone knew, we had done something refreshing, something inspiring.

Dear Amara, Forever may you find happiness in all of life's changes. Forever may you have fun and enjoyment in anything you choose to do.

Dear Amara, Welcome to the shores of the Smiths. When you read this many years from now, you will know the love of your mum and dad is unsurpassed. It will help you become a wonderful lady forever.

. . . Life brings lots of happiness mixed with some tough moments. Your parents and friends will always be there to remind you of the good times forever.

Amara, the sweetness of a little child, such as you, brings heaven very near, for only God could give a gift as definitely dear. You have chosen well in selecting Alan and Alaina as your parents. They will give you unconditional love forever.

With its bright, decorative cover, the book already had a teenager look about it. Now its contents give a page after page affirmation that this teenager is known and wanted. Amara will know that she has a heritage, a legacy from a lot of people, many of them doubtlessly no longer alive to tell her that themselves. Yes, the day will come when Amara will be presented with proof that she was welcomed into this world and she will see that it was a special day for all involved.

Cyber Love

David Palumbo

I was a workaholic. I neglected my wife and son. I got divorced.

After my divorce I moved to Las Vegas where I started a paint contracting company. I still worked seven days a week and had little or no time for family, friends or myself. I was told how much of an 'ass' I was becoming. Making a conscious decision to get what I really wanted in life, I set out to find a woman who would be my friend, lover, supporter, advisor – everything. I wanted the family I had previously lost.

I posted my vital statistics with Match.com, an Internet company. Why not? I could save time. Time is what I had wasted so foolishly in the past. Among the letters I received came a very special one from Anne in Australia. Having been to Australia eighteen months earlier, I was interested.

Anne came to America for our first meeting. I met her at the airport and a light went off in my head as soon as I caught sight of her. My first look at Anne was from behind. Not bad, but the front view was even better. I remember thinking she must like me as well because we hugged and kissed and held hands as we proceeded to the baggage collection. I think we were both secretly relieved and pleasantly surprised.

Anne and I continued to visit each other over the next year and a half. We knew the day would come when a decision had to be made, so finally we decided that I would move to Australia and we would get married. She had two children, Kim, thirteen, and Bobby, eleven. I was so excited; I was going to have a new family, Anne the kids and myself.

Anne brought Kim to America for my last few weeks in the country. We shared the last night of the twentieth century and the first morning of the twenty-first century together. We couldn't have been happier. On 26 January 2000 we boarded Qantas flight 100 and arrived in Australia fifteen hours later.

Shortly after arriving I realised that Anne was living the same life I had been living before I met her. She was a single mother running a business with her partner Robert. She was neglecting family, friends and herself. She was a workaholic. Kim and Bobby were left to their own devices a lot and led quite independent lives. Coming from a 'family first' mindset, I wanted our family to work. I organised activities and set out some rules, thinking that would bring us closer together as a family. Wrong. They drove us further apart. To my surprise Anne didn't like the changes either. She had been single for the past eleven years, dating only a few times since leaving her husband. Anne had become her own decision-maker and breadwinner. She didn't need anyone making changes for her or her kids. Before long we were fighting and falling apart. How could this be?

Imagine for a moment: you move to a foreign country to be with the woman you love; you sell your business; you leave your friends, family and your way of life; you work day and night to set up a new business; you have no friends, no transportation and no place to go even if you had; your fiancée has little spare time and often arrives home from work and immediately changes into her pyjamas so you know you are not leaving the house that night. Yes, I was losing control.

Anne gave me the financial support I needed but not her love, emotional support, loyalty and belief in me or us. She even told me once 'David, you have not proven yourself to me.' Anne asked me to leave several times but I wouldn't go. Call me stubborn, but something (maybe love) told me not to leave. I was sure we could work this out. There were times when we looked into each other's eyes and without a word spoken knew we were bonded for life.

I began to analyse myself and our situation. I was a time bomb with the conflicting emotions of love and pride. 'I am the man. I am always right.' What to do? Stay and risk hating each other or leave, letting us heal?

'Anne, I am leaving. We can't make it here. There are too many negative influences. You need to see me as I am and not as you want me to be.' She agreed, 'When are you leaving?'

Hurt and confused is the only way to describe how I felt. As I was making arrangements to return to America it occurred to me that maybe Anne was just reacting to what I had said and that that wasn't how she truly felt. We had so much history together – our fantastic trips around America and Australia, all those wonderful times that neither of us would ever forget. I knew I had to give us one last try before getting on the next plane to America and never seeing Anne again.

'Anne, I am leaving but I want you to come with me. We love

each other and you know we belong together. Let's give ourselves another chance in America, away from what has gone wrong here.'

Just then I could see a small dent in Anne's armour. She was hesitant, but she wanted to believe what I was saying. We talked and talked and finally Anne agreed to give us another chance, but this time in America. We agreed that the children will stay in Australia. Anne will travel back and forth every three months to be with her family. I will return often to visit the few good friends I have made here. I do love Australia and will miss the country and the people. Anne and I may retire here when that time comes.

Over the past month nothing has happened to change our plans; in fact Anne seems more excited as each day passes, as do I.

If you have come away with any new opinions about Internet dating I hope they are positive. Remember, relationships are made or destroyed by people . . . period. This Internet story has turned into a love story with a very happy ending – Anne has agreed to marry me in Las Vegas some time in 2001.

The Sound of Music

JULIE ANTHONY

Being a farmer is a tough way to make a living, especially in the Mallee. Eleven inches of rain per year . . . Not on your Nellie! It's more like every third year; one step forward and two steps back.

As a child I was pretty much oblivious to all this. All we kids in the district knew was that we had space to roam, fresh air and plenty of imagination to create any scenario we wanted. There were five in my class and thirty in total at the school, just like a big family. I loved it; I never wanted to leave.

I loved driving the tractor and helping Dad prepare the soil for crops to be planted. I used to ride on the back of the combine, pushing the seed and the super phosphate through the stars so that they wouldn't get blocked. Yes, a farmer's life for me! I even had a working knowledge of the 32-volt lighting plant, which we relied on for our power. Dad made sure I knew a bit about most things on the farm, including wool classing, and Mum made sure I could cook and sew and clean house properly. I was a regular Wonder Woman.

Did I hear you say 'what about singing'? Well, while I was doing all of the aforementioned, I sang. So did Mum and Dad and my brother, Steve – very Von Trapp, and perfect preparation for when I did the stage version of *The Sound of Music* many years later. I belted out songs as I drove the tractor so the neighbours always knew who was behind the wheel; and so it went on.

People would comment to Mum and Dad, 'Julie's got a pretty good voice for a kid her age, maybe you should do something about it.' Like what? No performing arts school here, no singing or music teachers. Oh, one teacher came to town and taught piano, and there was a kid who could just manage to play a very slow, four-fingered version of the *Blue Danube*.

I think the comments were starting to get through to Mum and Dad, confirming what they had known all along. I was a natural singer, and maybe something should be done to nurture this talent – but what and how?

The moment that changed my life was not heralded by a trumpet fanfare. Instead it was the result of a chance meeting in the main street of a country town between my dad and one of the members of the local band, who was bemoaning the fact that their singer had left town that day, and they had a gig that night!

There is a lovely saying 'do the good you know' and my dad did that instinctively. 'Julie is always singing around the place, she must know enough songs to help you out. I'll bring her up tonight.' It was as simple as that.

Later Mum and Dad took me to Adelaide to enter a talent contest, which I won. This started the family down the path of moving from their much loved life on the farm to Sydney to pursue my career. They established themselves in the inner western suburbs and Dad got a job, and went from the life of being a farmer to working in the security industry to support the family. They all had to adapt to a very different life.

So when Julie Lush drove out of the farm at Galga on her way to Sydney to trust her luck at singing, Julie Anthony was born, and the rest you know. Julie Lush has always balanced Julie Anthony. My farm days and the happy-go-lucky, two-feet-on-the-ground attitude have always been with me in showbusiness, and it has worked like a charm.

I will always be grateful to my parents, Les and Betty Lush, who changed their lives completely so that I could follow my dream.

Joseph's Story

MARY ANNE HARTLEY

'It may not be foetal distress. I think there could be a problem with the baby's heart.'

As a lawyer who specialised in medical negligence, I was well aware that the read-out on the foetal heart monitor was worrying so I readily agreed to an emergency Caesarean section to expedite delivery. When I came out of the general anaesthetic, there was my handsome, big baby boy, Joseph. He seemed perfect in every way: he was a strong, confident snuggler and immediately got on with the business of breastfeeding. I was besotted.

While we were still in hospital, the doctors checked Joseph's heart and said he had a kind of arrhythmia that would almost certainly resolve in the next few weeks. It was nothing to worry about. To me, this fitted with his robust, healthy physique. I did notice some white patches on his skin, but the paediatrician assured me these were perfectly normal.

When Joseph was just a few months old, I noticed some strange transitory movements in his body not long after his second vaccination. His little eyeballs would roll back into his head ever so briefly and he would jerk a little. Another medical check-up indicated that, sure enough, there was something wrong. These movements indicated that he was having infantile spasms, which are like baby epilepsy.

Joseph was admitted to the Children's Hospital for a brain scan, and after a harrowing day waiting for someone to tell me the results, the paediatrician finally came to see me late in the afternoon. He tried to tell me that he could not give me an answer to Joseph's condition until he had consulted with a further specialist. I mustered my meagre cross-examination skills and within twenty minutes I had the news – Joseph had a genetic condition called Tuberous Sclerosis.

Having consulted numerous medical dictionaries, neurology textbooks and knowledgeable friends, I discovered that TS is a disorder of the laying down of tissue, and raises the possibility of tumours occurring throughout the body. Joseph's heart problem turned out to be a benign tumour, which thankfully has had no ongoing effects, and the innocuous white patches that I had noticed on his skin were also part of the condition.

Ten years on, Joseph has a range of skin tumours – a few brown patches and little raised red spots all around his nose and on his cheeks. Unfortunately, these are getting more obvious and he is noticing them, but I am told that different kinds of laser treatment over the next few years will make the problem less obvious. When Joseph noticed the red spots on his face at the age of nine, he was very receptive to the explanation that everyone's skin grows in a slightly different way and that's the way his skin happens to grow.

But there is something more about TS. In many cases, it is

accompanied by severe epilepsy, intellectual disability, anti-social behaviour and autism. Worst of all, it is impossible to predict its effects from infancy. It's a case of wait and see.

We worried for a while about what Joseph would become. But then it dawned on me that just as I had no means of predicting how my bright older daughter would turn out, the same applied to Joseph. So I have learned to simply accept each child and what happens to them. The only danger in my approach is that I may not be sufficiently demanding of Joseph, but his marvellous school, Port Phillip Specialist School, seems to make up for any deficiency of mine.

Joseph has introduced us to the world of special schools and disabled children. He has learned to read, write, count and to barrack for Collingwood Football Club. He is comfortable with himself and confident of his abilities, qualities I have tried to instill in both my children. His autism makes him a little unsocial at times, but generally he is well mannered and easy to be with. Happily, none of the symptoms of TS appears to have affected, in any way, his belief that he is my big beautiful boy.

Not only has he brought great joy and amusement to our lives, but he has brought us down to earth. A family comprising a dentist, a lawyer and a blonde, blue-eyed, bright girl had every prospect of being elitist and intellectually arrogant. We believe that Joseph has helped us to be more humane and sensitive, and hopefully better contributors to our community.

Mick

Professor John Funder

Newman College, at the top of Swanston Street in the University of Melbourne, is a triumph of Walter Burley Griffin design, even if the Barrabool sandstone needs constant attention. In the late 1950s the students segregated in binary mode, a warp of hearties ('jockstrappers' or JS) and a woof of aesthetes (FI, where the 'I' stands for intellectuals). The prototypic JS was from the bush, and interested in football and racehorses. His FI opposite sometimes read novels, and talked about philosophy and religion. Common ground included an obsession with college food, and indistinguishable academic results.

Into this divide in 1961 came the Reverend Michael Scott, SJ, MA (Dublin), as rector, to a slightly puzzled welcome from both sides. He was direct, not bookish and had a labrador called Jake, which endeared him to the JS. He was passionate not about philosophy or physics, the subject of his Masters, but about modern art in general, and contemporary religious art and architecture in particular. FI and

JS alike were equally innocent of interest or even prejudice in these areas: to a JS it seemed harmless, and to an FI sort of quaint.

And so he transformed two small downstairs rooms into an oratory, altar and benches of rough-hewn bridge timber, where he said mass each morning. He bought pictures, commissioned pictures, was given pictures. He gutted the unused biology laboratory, and set it up as a gallery. Predatory Toorak ladies would invite themselves for a guided tour: with infinite care Mick would say to me, 'You know so-and-so. I wonder whether you would accompany us this afternoon, as I might be called away.' Rock solid defence, rare ease and grace. My father, who had briefly been in the Jesuit novitiate with him, said one of the most graceful things he had ever seen was Mick Scott swimming.

In the December of 1964, my last year in College, Kathleen and I were married in the Newman chapel. We set up house, and she went on with psychology, and I with medicine. We moved from tiny flat to small flat to modest house, all in the then very mixed suburb of East Melbourne, where Anna and Hugh were born. One of our wedding presents was a year's subscription to the *New Yorker* and there, among early Updike and Pauline Kael, were stories by the Irish author Mary Lavin, which we read among napkins and thesis drafts.

And then the bombshell: Mick Scott is going to leave the Jesuits, leave the priesthood. He's put in his papers to Rome, he's off on retreat. I went to see him when he got back to Newman, in transit, and he showed me a series of books. In order, the dedications ran: 'For M', 'For M.S.', 'For Michael', 'For Michael Scott'. They were Mary Lavin's books, from the 1950s onwards. He told me, simply, that he was going to live in Ireland, and that he and the widowed Mary were to be married.

They had been students together in Dublin in the thirties and had fallen in love. He doubted his vocation, took counsel, prayed and finally decided to return to Australia. Mary married a lawyer, and they had three daughters. She wrote short stories and novels, oblique and elegant and very Irish, and sent him copies. After her husband died the dam broke; 'Michael Scott' was the clarion call, and he responded. Both JS and FI viewed his decision with slightly puzzled acceptance: it probably comes of all that arty stuff, but good luck to him.

In May 1970 we flew out to San Francisco, the long way round. Many of our contemporaries had already taken off overseas, after discharging their bonds as teachers, doing their articles as lawyers or residence as doctors: many evenings were spent at Station Pier, at one end of ever straightening streamers. There was no way we were going straight to San Francisco, where I was not due until 5 July; Europe, and High Culture, called.

So in London we hired an abominable Bedford Motor Home, Trabant to the timeless VW Kombi and discovered at Calais that everything was on the wrong side of the road. After about two days we revised our itinerary to exclude Spain and Greece and Scandinavia, and possibly Morocco. Flat out at 40 mph on the autoroute/autostrada/autobahn, we went from Paris through Provence to Genoa and Florence and Rome, then up the Brenner Pass through Austria and Switzerland across England to Holyhead. From Holyhead the ferry to Dunloghaire, across the bay from Dublin.

Kathleen's antecedents were Brennans and Rogans, and so we wanted to see the parish records in villages to the north of Dublin and just outside Kilkenny. From Dunloghaire we trundled into the local caravan park: 'Jist take what you'd be needing for the children,' said the lady in the kiosk, 'and you can fix me up later.'

I phoned Mick and Mary, living in County Meath an hour away. 'Could we come and see you tomorrow?' 'We'd be delighted,' Mary said, sight unseen. Kathleen had suggested three o'clock in the afternoon: 'If it's clearly not a goer,' she said, 'we'll have a quick cup of tea and leave them in peace.'

And so we parked outside the manor house, and went in. Tea, and cake, a thousand questions, gales of laughter: lemon barley for the kids, and talk. There are people I know who can talk under wet cement: Mary Lavin could talk under set cement. How lovely to meet you, Michael has told me so much about you. I don't know what we've got, but you must stay for dinner. A chicken, six onions, counterintuitively no potatoes, baked apples, bread and cheese, wine from the van. The children were fed first, then went down demurely. Inside, round the table, torrents of talk, great gales of laughter.

Around midnight Kathleen and I staggered off to the 'double bed' in the van, commodious enough for a pair of anorexic dwarfs. At 6 a.m. the children wanted milk, and I tiptoed into the kitchen. There was Mick, in slippers and apron, washing up. His eyebrows, always owlish, jerked upwards: she talked to me until two o'clock. I've never seen a happier man.

Jennifer is Home

WAL MAGGS

Some lives are special, unusual and filled with mystery. This is the case with Jennifer, our eldest daughter.

Jennifer was born on 21 March 1960. I took Beth, my wife, to the maternity section of the local hospital, and, as the custom was at the time, I was sent home to await the news. I answered the phone and was told that Beth had given birth to a girl.

'Congratulations! You have a daughter.' There was a pause, and then, in a different tone: 'There is, however, an abnormality.' Being a first-time father, I wondered what an abnormality was. Dreadful images passed through my mind. The nurse continued: 'Your daughter has a cleft palate.'

I was allowed next day to visit my wife. She was only twenty-one, young and beautiful, and like me struggling to come to terms with this shattering news. Jennifer couldn't feed. She had no sucking ability. After trial and error, the nurses began feeding her by spoon.

But as Jennifer swallowed, the milk would run out her nose. The battle had only begun.

As time went by, we grew mystified. Jennifer didn't seem to hear us. She didn't look at us, nor show any interest in us. We took her to a specialist. He tested her and found that it wasn't a hearing problem. She was autistic, profoundly autistic, as it turned out.

Jennifer developed abnormal behaviour. For example, she never learned to speak. She rocked back and forth for hours on end. She hardly slept. As she grew, she became obsessive about objects in the home. If it was a broom, she played with it day and night. If it was locked away, she stood in front of the cupboard and screamed for hours on end. She had a prodigious memory. If we took her to a relative's home, she knew exactly where the broom or another object was from her last visit, and began a relentless screaming until it was given to her.

Jennifer demanded our constant attention. She was a fast runner for her age, and abnormally strong. If we took our eyes off her, she was off. One day Beth found her hanging by her fingertips from an outside window ledge. It was a dangerous drop to the concrete path below.

Jennifer had surgery on her cleft palate. The operation was partially successful. Later in life, a further operation corrected the problem.

Beth and I and our other two daughters, Judith and Paula, were becoming exhausted. Our lives revolved around Jennifer. To get some sleep, we took all the furniture out of her bedroom, lay a mattress on the floor, and in winter left an electric wall heater on. We took the doorknob off the inside, and closed her door. We slept lightly. We could hear her rocking back and forth, banging her head against the door, sometimes crying.

Shopping proved difficult. I couldn't help because of work. Beth used to walk to the shopping centre, with Jennifer and the other two girls (the youngest in a pram and Jennifer in a harness). Jennifer would grab at everything in the shopping aisles. Once, Beth was distracted and Jennifer was gone.

The family reached crisis point. Our health was suffering. We were living a stressful life, often deprived of sleep. I knew deep down that this couldn't continue. But what was the alternative? We loved Jennifer dearly. We managed to get a respite break for a week or two. But this proved difficult to arrange for a child like Jennifer. The pressure and tension mounted. We were faced with a dilemma: Jennifer or the family. We needed permanent care for Jennifer.

By this time Beth was pregnant with our next child. We were told of a government home at Newcastle. When we visited, the nurse-in-charge said: 'I'm sorry. You do have a big problem, but there are just no vacancies.' As we were shown around, another nurse quietly told us: 'The only way to have Jennifer admitted is to arrange a short respite holiday here, and then refuse to take her home.' Admission by default.

This was what we did. It was one of the saddest days of our lives. When we returned, our home was quiet, but we missed Jennifer desperately. Our hearts were broken. Jennifer was five, going on six years old.

For the next thirty-two years we travelled the long journey by car every four or five weeks from Sydney to Newcastle in the beginning, then later to Stockton, when Jennifer moved. Travelling to see Jennifer became part of our lives. In all that time we were never really sure if Jennifer recognised us. At first we used to visit as a whole family until, bit by bit, the other girls got married and Jim, our youngest, moved into a place of his own.

When Jennifer turned twenty-one, we put on a birthday party for the ward. It was a party like no other. We sang 'Happy Birthday', blew out the candles, and then put cake, drinks and sweets in front of Jennifer and the others.

Soon there was cake and ice cream everywhere. They all ate quickly, using hands to push cake into mouths, unconcerned about table manners. But didn't they enjoy themselves! The tables and floors were a mess. But the nurses were used to this and soon afterwards all was back to normal.

Jennifer lived till she was thirty-seven years of age. We received a phone call one day. Jennifer had choked to death. She had put too much food into her mouth, which was normal enough, but on this occasion it was small pieces of sausage. Some had lodged in her lungs and throat, and, despite the best efforts of the staff, she collapsed. A doctor was called, but she died. Jennifer now rests near us in a small country cemetery. Under her name are the words: 'A special child'. The gum trees cradle her with their soft shadow.

Jennifer is home.

Living Two Lives

ELLEN GREEN

I feel as though my life has been on hold for the past seven years.

It was exactly seven years ago that I decided to travel overseas for three weeks. I realised that if I didn't go, then I would be grounded for quite some time. I had become increasingly aware that my husband Russ wasn't coping with the simple everyday things he'd always been able to do so well. So, it was then or not for a long time. Before I left I carefully wrote out all instructions for using the gas hotplates, the microwave, the washing machine and the answering machine – even how to change the channels on the television. It was an anxious time and all this was a year before the diagnosis of Alzheimer's. Instinctively, though, I knew.

The following year Russ had an operation for a benign bowel tumour. The anaesthetic sent him completely off the planet. Afterwards the surgeon suggested to me that I had a case of Alzheimer's to deal with. This was subsequently confirmed at the memory clinic, and my life hasn't been the same since that time.

The early stages of this difficult condition were a little easier on me but harder on Russ as he struggled so hard to hang on to what he knew while never really admitting that anything was wrong. 'I'm okay. I get by!' was his catch-phrase.

Life at home became more and more difficult. There was the endless sorting of papers and tidying of drawers, never wanting to go out anywhere or have a holiday. Then came the paranoia. I came home from a meeting one day to be greeted by a house in disarray, axes, an iron bar, bricks lined up near the front door. His explanation? Murderers were coming to get him. He had even warned the poor new young neighbour over the road of the assassination attempt. I knew that I couldn't risk leaving Russ alone any more so I paid for carers to come and mind him whenever I had to go out. When I was with him it was like living two lives, his and mine. I had forgotten what a good night's sleep was like.

Three years ago I placed Russ in respite care for the first time. It was so hard. How would I feel if someone did that to me! I cried all the way home. However, when I picked him up after the respite it was just as if he'd never been away at all. I realised that we needed help and for the next year we managed with a combination of carers who came into the home to mind Russ, day-care that gave me breathing space for a day and residential respite for longer times. During this time I tried not to give up any of my interests as I sensed how important that was to my sanity and to making me a better carer.

Two years ago I visited a clairvoyant. This was something I'd not done before but I felt I wanted some guidance. I was clutching at straws. She told me that Russ would be in permanent care within two months and she described the place exactly. As I didn't have his name down anywhere yet I was a little sceptical, but within two months I had found a place answering her description and had a phone call offering Russ a place. The shock was incredible. I had to make an instant decision.

I know now that it was the best thing for us both even though it was so hard at the time. It has been an enormous adjustment for me. I have been through the guilt, the loneliness, the relief and the grieving and I've also had to learn to live on my own for the first time in my life. It was also hard trying to justify my decision to Russ's family and friends.

Nearly two years after placement, Russ is now in a nursing home, having deteriorated so quickly. I am slowly coming to accept that I have to get on with my life. I can do no more for him than I am already doing. He has expert care twenty-four hours a day and lots of great activity programs, although he can no longer participate in them. He seems happy. He shows me no real affection. He doesn't communicate. He can't concentrate at all.

There has been a period of intense and painful grieving to experience. There has been a double grieving; a grieving for my husband and grieving for the relationship I used to have with my step-children. I am managing my life by trying to keep things in perspective. I meditate. I still need my spiritual nurturing and I have addressed my mental, physical, social and emotional needs also.

Life can be a tremendous experience

I now have the courage to live, to really live and not just exist. I am now travelling on my own journey for the first time in my life.

I have regained the freedom that I surrendered to look after Russ. I have learned so much about myself in the process. I have found out that I have shown enormous courage to undertake such an adventure, that I am enterprising and have a great amount of common sense and nous, and most importantly that I like my own company. I have found that all this has been developing my inner strength. I doubt that I would have experienced this had things been different and Alzheimer's had not entered my life.

This is the beginning of the rest of my life. It is possible to transform crises into opportunities and to lean on that inner strength that we all have. Our struggles can be fertile ground for astonishing growth. But, it takes time and it can't be rushed.

Life is not necessarily easy but it can be a tremendous experience.

The Miracle Life Saver

Dr Janet Hall

It was the trip of a lifetime – trekking in the Himalayas. I was both amazed and delighted when my fourteen-year-old son Robin brought home the leaflet from school inviting interested boys to take up this fabulous travel opportunity. Robin was usually a cautious person who did not seek out adventures. A seasoned traveller myself, I saw this as a terrific chance for him to widen his view of the world and agreed that he could go.

I was even more amazed and delighted when his father committed to going on the trip as well! (Robert and I had travelled through India almost twenty years before on an overland bus trip from Katmandu to London. I especially remembered his lack of enthusiasm for the crowds and local food in India.)

Since our marriage breakdown eight years earlier, Robin and his dad had not had a lot of opportunities to do 'boy's stuff' together, so this tour promised a wealth of bonding experiences . . .

Father and son set off with the school tour while mother and daughter, Pamela, had a holiday in Bali together. When we met again at home, I was not surprised by my boy's typical taciturn response to my inquiry about his trip – 'It was fine, Mum. Oh, but Dad almost died.'

Suffering from an overdose of shopping therapy and jetlag at the time, I thought he was making a joke and let it pass – you know the sort of boy's joke: 'The food and conditions were so bad that Dad kept saying he was going to die!'

I didn't find out the true story until the night of Pamela's birthday, six months later. Though separated, Robert and I always did our best to put up a united front when the children had a birthday and so had taken them out to a teenager-approved restaurant. Robert and Robin were having their usual dry banter when the conversation turned to their trip to India.

To my surprise, Robert recounted the most amazing tale of his near-death experience.

The tour group was given the chance to do a white-water trip down the Ganges.

Everything seemed straightforward in the briefing and Robert particularly noted the instruction to hold onto your paddle if you should fall out. The adventure started off well, with time to note the magnificent scenery of the mountains surrounding this ancient river. It was awesome to think that they were way out in the middle of nowhere, where few people had ever been.

Suddenly they entered white water and in a freak spin, Robert fell out backwards into the water.

He went under and was tumbled violently and savagely in the water's huge splash. As he struggled to keep his head above water, he saw the boats disappear around a bend. He kept being dragged under and his mouth was full of brown Ganges water. He fought desperately to keep breathing and tried to swim for the bank. Then his heart almost stopped – there was no bank! The river had cut through an immense gorge and was flanked by huge cliffs of sheer rock.

Robin looked out in terror as his boat swept around a bend and he lost sight of his father. The boat in front had already beached and the instructor was scrambling along the rocks in hope that he could get back to where Robert had fallen out. Robin threw himself out of his boat too early and almost got swept away by the raging waters too! He bashed his leg on a submerged rock and thought he had crushed his kneecap but kept forging for the shore. Clutching his leg and limping in pain, Robin anxiously followed the instructor and was aghast when he saw that there was no sign of his father in the foaming river.

Meanwhile, time and time again, Robert was hurtled into the rock and then tossed back into the raging water. Dragged under by the waves he felt himself losing his fight. His clothes and especially his sandshoes were weighing him down even further. Valiantly he held onto the paddle as instructed, yet that also seemed to be dragging him down. Each time he tried to swim towards the edge he could get no foothold in the sheer cliffs. He was starting to black out and felt his chest fill with water. He thought to himself, 'So this is how you are going to end it all – drowned in the Indian wilderness.'

As he went under for what he thought was the last time, he thought he could hear something through the blur of white water noise. He somehow heard Robin's voice screaming, 'Swim, Dad, swim for your life!'

Inspired by the love he caught in that cry, somehow, Robert fought back against the suck of the downward pull of the water. He let go of the paddle and thrashed both arms and legs towards the direction of the bank. A miracle happened then – there was a break in the cliffs and his feet touched down in shallow waters. He floundered to the safety of the dirty bank and lay in pain, battling for each breath and going in and out of consciousness.

There he was found and helped to safety where Robin was waiting for him with big hugs and big tears.

Normally the life of a party, Robert said he didn't have much heart for the joviality of the evening get-together that night. He sat apart and brooded about his lucky escape. He felt that he had almost let go of his spirit and will to live. It had taken the love of his son to reconnect him with the essence of life.

Appreciation

JENNY SMYTH

Growing up in the country was a happy experience. Our farm, still run by my brother, is in the Yarra Valley and I am thankful for those formative years, dealing with rural things. The homestead was always full of produce from the land – the vegetables and fruit, which we enjoyed as they came into season. The garden was my world and outside the hedge, I treasured the wildlife and wild-flowers.

The polio epidemic helped excuse me from attending school until I was ten and then my life changed considerably.

My father, Geoffrey Haggard, had been a prisoner of war in Turkey for three and a half years during World War I. He had been First Lieutenant of the submarine, the Australian AE2. This had been damaged in the Dardanelles, but the crew had survived, being captured as they escaped the sinking vessel. Those years in captivity, deprived of normal comforts, with poor food, extra punishments such as solitary confinement if they misbehaved and with nothing to read, do, see or hear, was an experience that had wrought quite an impact on a young, fun-loving man.

After a while my father was invited to share some of his experiences, sometimes talking to schoolchildren on the wireless about the war and his experiences in it. He also marched on Anzac Day and was compiling a book. He was very keen that young people should know and appreciate this wonderful country, and our freedom. As World War II approached, he became anxious about our defences and protecting Australia.

He was a vital, passionate, worldly kind of man, charming, with sea-blue eyes that could imagine far beyond our horizon. To my mother's dismay, my father re-enlisted with the British fleet and was expecting to go to Singapore.

This may have been on his mind as he walked along the railway line that ran through our property at Woori Yallock. He was found, killed by a stone thrown up by a passing train, with a mark on the side of his head; just a blow to the temple, no other damage.

Everything seemed different after that, and the home I knew changed. We three children, I being the youngest, were expected, and wanted, to cope and contribute to the upkeep of the farm, while my loyal, wonderful mother – a shy, quiet person – endeavoured to run the farm and bring us up with the help of her family. She managed the farm with some local help, and I enjoyed being a stock rider and collecting stores in the old buggy.

I was delighted to start school. I found English grammar and maths a bit of a mystery to unravel, but I was top at biology and could gut a rabbit better than anybody!

Brother Geoffrey joined the navy straight after school and attended the signing of peace with Japan. After that he was pulled out of the navy to run the farm, albeit rather unwillingly.

Our mother had learnt many things during those war years with no able-bodied men on hand. She could start the pump for river water for the stock and home, and work the engine that made the electricity for the house. She kept everything going. She also worked for the Red Cross and the Comforts Fund, packing parcels for the armed services overseas, some in prison camps as my father had been.

She realised that had my father gone back into the navy, as he was expecting to do the day he died, he may well have been captured in Singapore and suffered more deprivation there. How terrible that would have been. She quietly witnessed husbands and sons returning home, settling back, thankful for the peace they had helped secure.

My mother had struggled to keep the farm running to hand on to the next generation, and when we were all grown up she married again to another naval man who had returned from the two world wars.

Those early years imbued much within me, and returning to the homestead wakes and refreshes my soul every time. I am thankful our old home is still in the family, it's a wonderful example of perseverance and continuous hard work through four generations of amazing people.

Parents

MAUREEN WEINER

When I was a child, I looked to my parents for guidance.
They were my heroes. They knew everything.
They held my hands and they lifted me up.
They taught me to see and I learnt to listen.
They picked me up and they gave me hope.
I drove them mad – and they loved me.

Now that I am older, I look at my parents,
And I see the child in them.
Now they look to me for guidance
and a helping hand.
Now I must be their eyes and their ears.
They are the ones needing support and hope.
They too can drive me crazy,
but above all, they need my love.

Music Judy

JUDY MCARTHUR

During the seventies, I was a young mum when an anthology of women's essays edited by Gwen Wessen was published. Its title, *Brian's wife – Jenny's mum*, summed up for me the anonymity that overcame many women at the time.

Being fortunate in having a husband who encouraged me to return to the preschool education field, I happily embraced my three roles. Fifteen years later, when we were in our mid-fifties, Graham was diagnosed with early onset dementia. His dismissal as managing director followed. He became seriously depressed, his self-esteem plummeted – to him his all-important role in life was over.

To relate the profound effect my husband's disease had on our whole family could be another story, but the loss of a friend, communicator and lover was overwhelming for me. I foolishly gave up my job as a kindergarten teacher in the misguided thought this would help Graham. But now there were two of us wallowing in self-pity, and me toying with self-destruction.

Wise counselling enabled me to see that, if I was to be an effective carer, I must have a challenging outlet to sustain myself. Returning to sessional kindergarten would take me away from Graham for too long a period each day.

The gift from a friend of his (late) wife's keyboard, inspired me to consider the idea of becoming a visiting pre-school music educator, filling a perceived gap in programs. I made posters, accumulated a basket full of percussion instruments and interesting props, and 'Music Judy' was born.

The venture was taken up first by playgroups, and later by childcare centres and kindergartens. I keep the fees very low, pick and choose the days or hours I want to work, and have now developed a regular clientele. When things get tough at home and I feel valueless, it is my music group that keeps me going. To pull up outside a centre and hear small voices shout, 'She's here. Music Judy's here,' makes me feel so special.

When, or if, Graham needs someone at home with him constantly, I will scale down my clients, but I will also pay for someone to come into our home so that I can still focus on my interest.

I urge all carers, whenever possible, to try to keep your own special identity. It will certainly help you to keep your perspective and sanity.

Visiting Rites

KATHRYN DAVIS

She sat twisting the strap of her bag, pulling it through her fingers and tying complex knots along its length. She kicked at the bag as it swung between her feet but apart from this she was still. Not just her eyes but her whole body was focused on the man lying in the bed in front of her. He was all she saw; everything else was white. Even the noise was white; buzzing and humming and beeps that didn't register with her unless they took too long to come. She heard his breathing. Heard it in her own lungs and throat as she began to inhale in time with him. Breathe. Breathe. Breathe.

One hand crept away from its work fretting at the bag strap and floated towards him, balked, hovered, then returned gently to her lap. Breathe. Breathe. Breathe.

In one sudden movement her hand flew toward him again and settled around his wrist, curved like an inverted cradle. Her thumb stroked across the back of his hand, leaping over the IV line at each pass. Her other hand continued its work on the strap of the bag. If she couldn't speak, couldn't scream, perhaps she could torture the bag into screaming for her. She cried, but didn't seem to realise it.

As I sat in the chair beside his bed after the last surgery I remembered all the times before; the first operation when reality had already started to slip away, but he still knew who I was and still reminded me of himself; the time he had a stroke in the recovery room and no one noticed; the time he died on the table and I cried because they brought him back to all this pain and confusion. That time there was enough of him left that he told us he would rather die than be cut again. But it happened again, and again.

I remember a time, not in the hospital, when he looked me right in the eye and said what a shame it was that I had died. He said the same thing later to someone else and I had to explain that he meant Carey. That he had confused our names or our lives, something. I was so ashamed.

So many times, Daddy, since this illness first took hold, I've been embarrassed by you and for you.

And so, the last time, I sat beside his bed with nothing left between us. He didn't know me and there was no vestige of him that I recognised. His face was blank when he looked at me and everything I said confused him. Then, just when I thought he would stay a stranger forevermore, he rolled away from me and I found him again. His hospital gown gaped open down the back and his broad and freckled back was turned to me. I reached out and touched skin as soft as a baby's, and I was ten again, five, eight, six, a child in summer when summer stretched forever. The local pool where I would cling to his back in the deep end, my arms barely reaching around his neck as he took me down through the cold green water to sit in silence on the bottom of the pool. He and I the only people in the world until I ran out of breath. (How did you always know when, Daddy?) Then he would pull us back to the light and the noise and we would laugh. I felt so loved, so safe. After, he would buy us each a Spearmint Choc Wedge to eat as we walked back to the car. Hot sun burning my shoulders, the pavement burning the soles of my feet, green ice cream running down my arm, walking in his shade or holding his hand. (Every summer I burned and peeled; never tanned. I got that from you, Daddy.)

He doesn't remember. This time, for the first time, I felt glad there wasn't enough of him left to remember, because I loved him again. I would hate if he knew enough to know what he had become. (I miss you, Daddy, and am glad you're not here.)

The most important thing I ever learned from my father wasn't something he told me, or showed to me. It wasn't something he deliberately or knowingly taught me, it may even have been something he was unaware of himself. What I learned I learned by sitting at his bedside during the last days of his life. I learned that there is no accurate measurement of love. It is not something that can be weighed or calculated. You cannot point to it like a page on a book and say, 'this is the day I loved you most', or 'this was when I stopped loving you, when you did this thing'. It may have a beginning, but that beginning can be known only sometimes. Real love has no end and no limitation. Instead, where once there was love there will always be love, even where it has been lost to other emotions; love will still be there no matter how hard it is to see or to bear. It might break your heart but it will never leave you alone.

Love is our Healing

GREGORY LANDSMAN

It has been more than thirteen years since my grandmother died in my arms, yet not a day goes by that I do not think of her with deep gratitude and a love that still warms me from the inside out. Over the years I have experienced love in different ways, but the love my grandmother gave me showed me that love is our healing and our only hope for a joyful life. My grandmother healed so many of my hidden wounds through love in action. She taught me that a gift of love does not have to come in a box, it can be in a smile, a touch, a kind deed or a silent blessing.

As I write this I recall my immense sadness on my return from Tokyo at finding my Ouma ('grandmother' in Afrikaans) very ill. Each day she looked frailer than the last and for a while I refused to accept that she would not make a healthy recovery. Doctors suspected she had lung cancer, but she would not allow any tests, as she did not want to have her body cut open. No matter how much I begged her to get help, she refused. She believed that she had lived a full life and didn't want to spend the remaining years in and out of hospital care.

Every day I spent with her I cherished. Yet there were so many questions that burdened my heart and mind. I wrestled with trying to understand how someone who had been so strong and dynamic was now so weak and fragile.

One morning I went to visit her and found her still in bed. This was unusual because by this time she was usually being bathed by the visiting nurse, but the nurse had just phoned to say she could not make it this morning. As I sat next to Ouma on the bed I looked into her eyes and my mind drifted back to my earliest memories of her. I recalled moments of truthful loving, how her plump, tender arms used to form the most comfortable cradle for me to lie in. She would rock me from side to side, and had this wondrous way of laying kisses on my forehead in between verses of the songs she sang to me.

Ouma looked after me as a child and every afternoon at five o'clock she would ritually bath me with the precision skill of a racing driver. The face cloth would weave in and around my ears and over my entire body, ensuring nothing was missed. She would gently wash the soles of my feet, giving them a quick tickle. When I hopped out of the bath she wrapped me snugly in a towel and we would laugh like best friends.

Sadly the joy I experienced at home with her did not extend into my school life. From the age of six I was beaten by other children for looking different and by one particular teacher for any number of reasons that she would come up with on a daily basis. I had trouble reading without stuttering and every morning my grandmother would wake me up at six o'clock and I would snuggle next to her in her bed so she could help me practise my reading. Every morning she assured me that I was a clever boy who just had a very bad teacher.

One particular day I was beaten repeatedly by my teacher. Firstly she hit my knuckles with the side of a ruler for not replying quickly enough to arithmetic times tables, and then I was given thirty cuts (lashings on the palms of my hands with a cane) for stuttering in front of the class as I read. The pain was so intense that each cut took my breath away. I tried to fight back the tears but couldn't and they ran down my face.

I felt humiliated and hurt and ran all the way home to seek the safety and comfort of my grandmother's arms. My eyes ached as much as my hands, which were red, raw and swollen. Without saying a word, Ouma gently looked at my hands the way a person looks at an injured bird. She reassuringly ran her fingers through my hair and marched me back to school at such a racy pace that I struggled to keep up. Ouma was like a hurricane about to do serious damage.

She flung the door open and stormed into the classroom, taking the teacher by surprise. Her small, powerful hand lurched upwards and grabbed the teacher's throat, pushing her against the blackboard. The teacher, wide-eyed with fright, struggled to get away but Ouma's firm grip and big belly held her prisoner. In an authoritarian tone Ouma said, 'If you touch my grandson again I will personally break your neck.' Then Ouma walked towards the wall unit that housed all of the teacher's prize canes. Ouma snapped them all effortlessly in half over her knee, much like you snap matchsticks with two fingers. The children sat in silence, looking on with horrified fascination, as though an action movie was being played out in their own classroom. 'This is the last time you touch him!' Ouma shouted at a high pitch.

We walked home together, her arm affectionately resting on my shoulder. While Ouma talked about the stupid teacher, I cried a little and then we laughed. My grandmother had this incredible knack of being able to untangle my anger and sadness just by making me laugh at her comical expressions. Through the laughter I always felt healed.

As I sat on the bed with her reflecting on these incidents, it was difficult to believe how much she had changed. Her big, love-filled body now resembled an overblown balloon that had been deflated. She was a shadow of her former self. Her dark skin hung loosely off her bones and her crown of black hair was now thin and white. The only thing that hadn't changed was the warmth of her eyes and the love that they reflected.

As we sat on the bed I said to Ouma, 'Let me bath you.' She smiled and said that was okay, the nurse would be here tomorrow. I insisted and reluctantly she accepted. When we got to the bathroom I undressed her as she had undressed me as a child. Her frail limbs did not allow her to sit in the bath, so I put her in the shower, but she was too weak to stand and nearly fell over, so I jumped into the shower fully clothed to break her fall and hold her up. I was drenched, but she was safe.

I took her out, wrapped her in a big towel and picked her up like a tired child. She put her head on my shoulder and said, 'In all my life I would never have thought I would live to see the day you had to bath me.' For the first time my grandmother cried in my arms and I was able to support her in the way she had supported me. We both wept. We had travelled a long journey together and overcome many obstacles, not only as grandmother and grandson, but as true friends who shared a mutual respect and acceptance of each other.

While we did not exchange many words on this day, our hearts seemed to have a language all their own, chatting like never before, about gratitude, friendship, life and love. Her eyes and her gentle touch revealed many emotions that wrapped themselves tightly around my heart. It was at this moment I learnt that when a person's heart is filled with love, no words are needed to convey it.

As she died her face had a veil of love over it. She gave me a wide smile that let my heart know how much she loved me and in a sweet, gentle voice, murmured, 'You are a good boy who will always be blessed.' Then she took a deep, long breath that lasted for an eternity. She seemed to savour it, much like the last drop of good wine. I saw the strength of her love in her eyes one last time, and as she closed them, soothing tears filled with life flowed ever so gently down her cheeks.

I took comfort from her painless death and felt a sense of gratitude for the blessing of having been loved by her. What I feared most about her death was that my life would be empty. But I learnt that love did not end when Ouma died, it kept on growing and growing. My grandmother left an imprint of the love she shared with me deep in my mind and heart. This inspired me to feel continually the presence of her spirit, and through this her love lives on forever. Love continues to grow when we remember a person's goodness and through these memories, we keep love alive. This is the power of love.

Self-Acceptance

A Successful Year

TOTTIE GOLDSMITH

It looked as though 1998 was going to be a very successful year. I had just finished a season of *Grease*, the musical spectacular, following straight on from a radio breakfast stint with TTFM (we finished up winning our ratings for the year, I am proud to say). I had become pretty much a household name in 1997 with a controversial television series called 'Sex Life', and I was being paid to speak at functions, open venues and at times just be somewhere.

Life was fun, active, interesting and profitable. I had been the main provider for my child for five years, and I was now able to afford a nanny to help me with the responsibility of 5 a.m. starts and commuting to Sydney every week. I felt as though I was doing a pretty good job of life. I felt independent, strong and like I was on a roll that nothing could break.

Well 1998 started out as planned. I had job offers, high earnings, great friends and a healthy child. I had started to feel the pinch of working so hard and juggling a young child, but didn't know how to get off the treadmill. In the entertainment industry we are brainwashed that we have to take the work while we can. I had taken only one holiday in five years.

I knew I was tired but I didn't have the time or the patience to collapse. After making the very big decision to leave *Grease*, I joined the cast of the *New Rocky Horror Show*, which included a pay cut, a complete move to Sydney and a new kindergarten for Layla, but it also gave me the opportunity to expand on my skills.

I was still earning a good salary, performing in eight shows a week and discovering a range in my voice I didn't know I had, thanks to the persistence and belief of the musical director.

It was about June of that year that, unbeknownst to me, my life was about to take a dramatic turn. The media were full of warnings about water pollution. We were told to boil all our water, which I promptly did, but somehow one of those bugs got through my filter system and into my gut. I didn't feel well and with my complaints of stomachache and bowel problems, my doctor suggested I go off wheat. He didn't relate my discomfort to water, and neither did I.

The weeks went on, I ate no wheat, the shows continued and I began to get weaker and weaker. Six weeks later I was diagnosed with giardia. I was treated with a heavy dose of antibiotics, which took away my stomach problem but left me so weak that I was unable to carry my own body weight around.

The diagnosis was too late and I could no longer walk down the stairs that took the cast backstage. After taking three weeks off and barely being able to stand up or lift my head off the pillow, I had to raise the white flag. It was the hardest thing I have ever done. I had to admit defeat, something that didn't come easily to me.

As the days, weeks and months went on, I got sicker and weaker.

At one point I didn't answer the phone for months, because apart from being too weak to talk (if you knew me, you would know how bad that was!!) I was also ashamed of the state I was in. I was always so happy being able to help people and being the shoulder and strength for everyone; I didn't know how to deal with my new state of being.

I didn't know what was wrong with me. No one seemed to know. One doctor suggested I was depressed, so I tried anti-depressants. No result. Chinese herbs, acupuncture, hypnosis for stress – you name it, I tried it. After three or four frightening and physically intolerable months, my aunt suggested that I go and see a doctor who specialised in chronic fatigue syndrome at Sydney's North Shore Hospital.

The blood and urine tests came up positive with many viral infections and showed that I had also had glandular fever, but it was the giardia from the Sydney water that broke the camel's back. At least I felt some sort of validation as to why I had been so unwell. The question now was, 'How do I get well, and how did I allow myself to get so sick in the first place?'

The next eighteen months were filled with complete and absolute frustration, extreme loneliness, intense physical discomfort, overwhelming fatigue and a real sense of panic about the future. I had no idea how long the 'syndrome' would take to leave my body, and most of all I felt guilty about the state I was in. I was feeling like a failure as a mother; I could barely get Layla to school, as the nausea and weakness made it terribly hard to drive, and standing up for more than about ten minutes at a time was difficult.

So now my work began. I knew I had to look back over my life and somehow work out why, when my life appeared to be going so well, did I get an illness that would isolate me so completely from the world, and practically bring my flourishing career to a standstill.

I began to ask for help for the first time in my life. I contacted CFS help lines and responded to letters that were so kindly sent to me by other sufferers. But my greatest help, I discovered, was my relationship to God. I became more spiritually connected than I had ever been before and I knew I had not been isolated, but that I had isolated myself. It was time to discover who the adult Tottie was, what my values were, how to be alone, who I was in relationship to others and why I was so vulnerable.

I had been involved in an industry of insecurity and jealousy (especially the theatre) and I didn't have strong armour. I was wide open to taking on other people's pain and too needy of others' approval. During my convalescence I learnt not to be so hard on myself. I learnt how to walk away from people who were disruptive and aggressive. I learnt how to close my door, take the phone off the hook and be alone. I learnt how to pray for strength when I was in pain or afraid and, most of all, to believe in the power of the mind. I learnt that being vulnerable doesn't mean being weak; instead, I see it as an asset to being more in touch with the world around me and closer to my true feelings.

My life is very different now. I know who I am and what I really want out of life.

Most of all, I thank God and the God in me for the people who stood by me and wanted nothing more than my health and happiness.

You Never Know

RON CLARKE

In 1955, when I was eighteen, I had set some world bests at a junior level in both the mile and the 3 miles. Less than twelve months later, Herb Elliott came along and made mincemeat of these. History abounds with outstanding juniors who never quite made it to the top in senior competition. It looked very much as if I were destined to be another one.

Not that I had tried too hard. I was always more interested in playing Australian Rules football, getting established in a career, and settling down to the joys of raising a family, than I was in athletics, and the 1956 Olympics showed me just how good the international runners were.

Funny that, but watching the likes of Kuts, Delany and Brasher inspired young Herb (who was almost exactly twelve months younger than I) to say, 'I can do that.' At the next Olympics in Rome in 1960, he set new figures in winning gold in the 1500 metres. I looked at the same men doing the same things and said, 'I can never do that,' and got on with my life.

Not that I had any regrets. I was going with Helen, now my wife of forty-two years, I had passed my accountancy final examination and qualified as a chartered secretary as well. I trebled my chartered accountants salary with my first senior appointment as an accountant; married Helen; started the family; played football with Essendon Reserves and then with Hastings on the Mornington Peninsula; and dabbled with inter-club athletics during the summer.

In August 1962 the IOC selected Mexico City to stage the 1968 Olympics. I would have said I had no hope of ever competing in an Olympics. Fate intervened. I broke my ring finger so badly playing football it became permanently bent and I could no longer play. So I took up athletics again, training for the first time during the winter cross-country season. I improved so much that I scraped into the Australian team in Perth for the Commonwealth Games, where I fluked a silver in the 3 miles. Then one evening at Olympic Park after another twelve months of solid training after work each day, I managed to break my first two world records. That's when I began to think about both Tokyo in 1964 and Mexico City in 1968. Internationally I was a babe in the woods. I had competed in just the one race, the 3 miles in Perth, so I did not really think too much about Mexico City. My mission was to do well in 1964.

Unfortunately things did not go as I had planned and I came away from Tokyo disappointed with my two main runs there in the 5000 and 10 000 metres. Now Mexico City loomed large, as I certainly did not intend running all that much longer. I found that I could fit the running in after work okay but with my two elder children approaching their teens I wanted to spend more time with them.

At over 2500 metres above sea level, Mexico City posed a serious problem for distance runners. Professor Becker, the United Kingdom's leading physiologist, even predicted someone might die competing at that altitude due to the low levels of oxygen. In 1967, I went to Mexico City with my doctor, Izzy Zimmerman, who was a sports medico as well as a GP, and we struck up a friendship with the French medical team. (France sent four specialists to Mexico for the four years before the Games to experiment and monitor the reactions to altitude in all the Olympic sports.) I knew then, from their research and my personal experience, that Mexico City was going to be impossible.

The RSPCA protested about the equestrian events being held at such a height, so the Olympic authorities agreed to transfer these to the coast but nothing could stop them holding the track and field at the main stadium. After all, they said, it only affected a few events (from the 1500 metres and over) and was fair to all. The problem was, it was not fair to all. Any distance runner born or bred at high altitude had naturally developed more haemoglobin in their blood systems to combat the lower oxygen content in the air, and their genetic advantage in absorbing oxygen into the blood tissue was also clearly superior.

So we all went to Mexico City knowing a miracle would have to occur for us to stand a chance against the Kenyans, Ethiopians and Mexicans. Realistically we knew that there were two races being held for each of the distance events – one for the athletes from the high altitude countries and another for the rest of us.

Despite all the evidence, deep down I still thought maybe there was a chance. The 10 000 metres should have been mine. I had the experience of a previous Olympics; I was now an experienced international competitor, and during the months before the Games I had proven to be a lap or so better than any other 10 000 metre runner in the world. So I hung on. In fact, the first twenty-three and a half laps (of the twenty-five) were the easiest I had ever done in a 10 000 metre race, and there were just four of us left – three mountain men and me. I forgot the first rule of survival at altitude and had a go when the pace was applied with one and a half laps to go. Suddenly it was like running down a long tube and all I could think about was reaching the finishing line.

I woke up with an oxygen mask on my face and Brian Corrigan, the Australian doctor, swearing under his breath. My tongue was so thick I could not speak, so I gave him the thumbs up and gradually came back to life. After setting seventeen world records in the three years immediately prior to Mexico City, after my collapse there I would never run close to one again. In fact, four years later, doctors discovered the mitral valve in my heart had been damaged and would need replacing.

Was it all worthwhile? Undoubtedly! If it had not been for the broken finger, I would never have rediscovered my talent in athletics. If I hadn't met and married the girl I did, I may not have received the help and encouragement that is so necessary to juggle a career and family with international competing.

Life is full of 'ifs'. It seems to me that it really is a matter of appreciating and making the most of whatever comes your way.

Fashion Failure?

JULIA KAY

'I am fat and ugly, and I'm going home now.'

'That's fine with me.'

'I hate you, Mum.'

'Same.'

This is a typical interchange between my daughter and me during a shopping expedition to buy her some usually much-needed new clothes. That's if we get to the shops at all.

Cathy is nearly seventeen years old, intelligent, strong minded, sensitive and stunningly good looking. She is extremely photogenic and modelled for women's magazines when she was younger. Her beautiful body is reminiscent of paintings by great artists from Reubens to Picasso – striking facial features, feminine curves and a tiny waist.

But for Cathy her looks and particularly her body shape are now the cause of recurrent dark, depressed moods, self-doubt, shame and embarrassment. Faced with racks of clothes designed not for bodies with hips and thighs, but for straight-up-and-down willowy frames, Cathy sees herself as a fashion failure. Her gloom can last for days, particularly if we come away from the shops empty-handed, or worse still, with clothes that she thinks make her look even fatter or uglier than she already is.

No amount of talking, explaining or supportive comments from me can make her understand the fact that it's not her but the clothes that are the problem. Cathy has had fashion advice from some high-profile clothing experts like Simone, a gorgeous older friend and ex-model, who has a similar body type and has learnt how to choose clothes which complement rather than highlight curvier body parts. Simone's inspirational tips, however, haven't helped boost Cathy's image of her body, which, she is convinced, is unacceptable by today's scarecrow standards.

This attitude to her body is a far cry from that of the boldly confident young child who danced and performed both on stage and off for anyone who would watch. Now it is an internalised, socially critical gaze that harshly judges Cathy's body for her.

So, what will be the outcome for Cathy of this negative teenage body image? Will she regain the confidence and composure of her childhood days? Or will she succumb to crash diets, obsessive exercising or eating disorders such as anorexia or bulimia? These paths are only too familiar to me, having endured as a girl and young woman the brutal criteria for success in the ballet world, where prepubescent, emaciated builds were prized.

Cathy will probably not be a ballet dancer or a model. But she may be a brilliant mathematician or physicist. Her abundant intelligence, wisdom and growing maturity will, I am confident, assist her in forging an excitingly productive path for herself, with fashion becoming an enjoyable accessory to her life rather than a controller of it.

In the interim, I will resign myself to weathering many more shocking shopping trips with her.

Perspective

Ian Haigh

As a scared little boy of seven, I hated the darkness of the ward in a rambling old Victorian country hospital where I stayed for five months in 1952. But that was nothing to my parents who knew their son was paralysed with polio, at a time when hope for a good recovery was at a very low ebb indeed. Poliomyelitis scared everyone – and badly.

For months on end there was an intermittent parade of stern doctors and kindly nurses, always heavily masked, who fed and toiletted me as quickly as they could, then scuttled for safety outside. My ill-framed questions were deftly deflected by everyone I asked – no one half a century ago was about to try and explain to a little boy what had happened . . . much less what might lie ahead.

Dad bought me a tiny toy policeman on a motorbike; it was all I could play with and, oddly, I have it on my bedside table to this day.

On one of the interminable mornings, a nurse with smiling eyes above her mask announced a 'great treat' – a real bath. Vividly I can recall that vast old iron trough of steaming water being tested for temperature with a gnarled, matronly elbow. Then my rather pathetic naked frame was lowered into water that was just a few degrees below boiling point. The already nervous nurses had no idea why I erupted into banshee wails, until they saw the rapidly changing colour of my skin and realised I had no way of even trying to get out. The nerves lacing that weathered old testing elbow had been well protected by years of serious toil, making bunion-like skin. There was minor scalding – and I've had very few baths since then . . .

But my recovery from polio was excellent. It took a long time, and there is virtually no physical legacy, but I began to notice the effect my perceived 'condition' had on people I met. I'd always been treated well but like a baby . . . even as a seven-year-old those who spoke to me seemed to drop my age by five years, and talked oddly.

How many mentally unimpaired people who *look* different say they are treated oddly as adults? The disability, because that's what it was, of having people treat me differently became an enormous problem for me – not something debilitating, of course – but it made me angry and it affected my perspective on life. I began to think I *was* carrying a very real social incompetence.

One man changed it all. I was working with the developers of the Dinner Plain ski village as it took shape in the lee of Mt Hotham in Victoria's high country. Houses were being built and had to be sold – the whole place was for sale.

One of the first buyers was a man named Paul, who bought one of the more expensive houses that had been a display home for the village. It was felt that we could generate a little publicity centred on him. He was a vigorous, vibrant bloke and happy to help. Paul owned a shipping container business in Port Melbourne and an appointment was made for us to meet.

Opening the door to his office I was mildly surprised that he didn't rise to shake hands – but Paul hadn't risen to his feet for twenty-four years, not since a horrendous car accident had robbed him of that ability.

My composure was absurdly shot to pieces and it must have shown. Then Paul said, 'What's the matter with you, man? Come on, we'll go in my car.'

And we did. Within an hour all of my discomfort had gone – and I subsequently came to know him well in the snow country. Paul 'skied' in a sledge contraption; he drove an all-terrain motorbike into remote and beautiful areas of the high plains; he entertained splendidly; his house was magnificent, his friends were legion; his business thrived – nothing fazed Paul.

For me deep shame was the catalyst that rid me of this absurd 'disablement' paranoia – shame is splendid as a vehicle for self-analysis.

Paul will never know the debt owed to him – and it was all so simple.

He never allowed himself to see himself as different from 'normal', and apart from anything else, it was both presumptuous and simply selfish for me to do otherwise.

A Weight off My Mind

GLORIA KROPE

One Saturday afternoon in August 1999 I was leafing through my photo albums of 1978, the year I was crowned Miss Australia. I had to send some press cuttings and photos with a story I was submitting to the publishers of a book on the history of the Miss Australia Quest.

I hadn't looked at these albums in over a decade and as I turned the pages I was overcome by a profound sadness and longing. The slender and vivacious twenty-two-year-old smiling in countless publicity shots had become a fat and despondent woman of forty-four, unrecognisable as the glamorous beauty of 1978. How *could* I have let that happen?

Of course, I was well aware of why I had slipped off the rails. I experienced a major lifestyle change in early 1989 when I returned to Melbourne after working on Hayman Island as the resort's public relations manager. My career changed direction again when I was appointed executive director of The 500 Club, the Liberal Party's most successful and influential supporter club. Working with many of Australia's leading business identities and politicians was challenging and stimulating but the downside of this exciting new career was a deskbound, sedentary lifestyle light years away from the active days I enjoyed on Hayman Island. The long hours and tight deadlines eventually took their toll and I started to suffer from chronic stress. My hectic work schedule regularly forced me to skip meals and I'd end up grabbing takeaway or junk food on the run. I had little or no time to exercise and in less than two years I blew up from size ten to size fourteen.

I started dieting and soon became a victim of the yo-yo diet syndrome, with hunger and deprivation triggering bouts of bingeing. This became a pattern that would more or less repeat itself over the next few years, although I did have brief periods when my eating was relatively normal and disciplined. My weight fluctuated dramatically as I tried every new fad diet, searching bookstores and magazine stands for the next quick-fix miracle cure. Nothing worked, of course, and by the mid-1990s I weighed in at around 80 kilograms.

The years of battling with my weight took its toll on my personal life. I became reclusive, avoiding friends and social occasions. My self-confidence vanished and my self-esteem plummeted to an all time low. In desperation I tried therapy, for by now depression had become a permanent companion, albeit well hidden from my friends and colleagues. My first and last thought each day was, 'How am I going to lose this excess flab?' I spent a fortune on useless exercise equipment (thanks to my insomnia I was a sitting duck for all those early morning infomercials).

By the late 1990s I weighed over 90 kilograms and despaired of ever looking good and feeling healthy again. I wore layers of black clothing to hide my figure and when I glanced in the mirror I saw a stranger with triple chins and a bemused, forlorn expression.

That winter's day in 1999 was a turning point because it forced me to confront how deeply unhappy I was. The quality of my life was abysmal for someone who had been so vital and energetic. It was time to get my physical, emotional and spiritual health back on track. I had lost the better part of a decade to obesity and depression through my self-defeating behaviour. It was time to take stock.

I decided to hire a personal trainer, something I hadn't tried before. I started a weight training regime and cardio program. The weight training helped to alleviate the stress, but I still battled daily with my food intake. I overate if I was hungry and most of the time I was confused about what to eat because of information overload. Every book and magazine article I had read trumpeted a different scientific approach to successful weight loss.

I flirted with the 'high protein – no carb' diet for a few weeks and dropped 8 kilos but there was a side effect – I 'hit the wall' each afternoon and ran out of steam. What else could I expect on 20 grams of carbohydrates a day? I knew that this was just another quick-fix solution that was destined to fail.

Then I received a timely phone call from an old acquaintance, Beverley Pinder. She and I knew each other from my Miss A days when she represented Australia in the Miss Universe pageant that same year. Beverley owned a successful public relations company and one of her clients was Jenny Craig. She recommended I try the program as she had great faith in the product. I decided to give it a go. I made a resolution to stick to it no matter what. What I didn't count on was how easy it was going to be.

In early December 1999 I went to the Jenny Craig centre in

Prahran and weighed in at a whopping 89.75 kilos. I met Kerryn, a terrific girl who was to be my consultant and advisor throughout the duration of my weight loss. I took home a week's supply of food, some educational literature and a ton of determination.

Incredibly, I lost 1.75 kilograms that first week. Without starving. Amazing. I continued to lose around 1 kilogram each week over the next few weeks. I couldn't believe it. I noticed how much more energy I had; I could walk up a flight of stairs without collapsing. Instead of falling into an exhausted heap each evening I went cycling or roller-blading or walked my dogs. I had energy to burn. One day I'll never forget I was power walking when suddenly I broke into a run . . . and kept on running and running and running. I felt like Forrest Gump.

Instead of starving myself (which was so deeply ingrained in my consciousness as the panacea for weight loss), I was eating three meals and three snacks every day. My metabolism fired up again and I felt healthy for the first time in years. My skin glowed and my eyes sparkled. The stress that I had lived with for years no longer got the better of me. I stopped turning to food for comfort when I felt overworked or anxious. I exercised instead and because I had so much energy it was a pleasure not a chore.

No matter how busy I got I *never* allowed myself to skip a meal. The Jenny Craig menus were tasty and convenient. It was like having a personal chef and I no longer had to think about what, when and how much to eat. The program was effortlessly integrated into my busy schedule and I found myself looking forward to each new day rather than dreading the inevitable battle with food.

I started to feel happy, vibrant and energetic again. Hunger, starvation, deprivation, guilt, misery and depression were no longer a part of my life. I sold or gave away my old clothes and went on a shopping spree buying size ten. The day I put on a pair of jeans again was a day for celebration. I had lost 35 kilos in under a year and felt reborn.

Interestingly, the body sculpting with weights and the slow, steady weight loss has changed my body shape. I am now more of an hourglass than a pear shape and because I don't restrict any food groups I don't suffer cravings, especially for fatty or sweet foods. I indulge myself occasionally with treats, but in moderation. I still enjoy an alcoholic drink from time to time, especially a glass of French champagne, but these days I am less inclined to party hard because I value my new found health.

I have learned to appreciate that eating a balanced and nutritious diet is integral to a healthy mind, body and spirit, and I continue to enjoy an exercise regimen that is simple and fun to maintain. Today I am bursting with self-confidence, have renewed self-esteem and have found a measure of happiness and contentment that a few years ago seemed unattainable.

When Enough is Enough

ATHOL GUY

During seven years of Seekers reunion concerts from 1993 to 2000, one of the lasting impressions for all of us after every show – and there were some 250 plus in total – was the number of young children sitting with families and singing every word of nearly every song. It gave us great pleasure to comment in interviews about this fact and the obvious appeal of the music to all generations. Very satisfying indeed.

We imagined that these youngsters had instinctively found something in the melodies or the lyrics, or perhaps they had been endlessly sung to sleep or pacified on long car journeys via the rhythm of the road and taped recordings.

Whatever it was, we've always been made to feel a part of the Australian 'family' and their evolving lives, with our music a key ingredient in ceremonies, celebrations and poignant farewells.

Whilst this is mostly all very warm and fuzzy, here is one moment that suggests that from time to time a little less could mean a lot more in terms of continuing appreciation and loyalty for us and the music!

During our first five concerts at the Sydney Opera House on the last tour, the following conversation was overheard at interval in the ladies wash room.

First child – approximately eight years old: 'Did you enjoy those songs? I knew all "Morning Town Ride". We learned it at school.'

Second child – approximately twelve years old: 'Yes. I knew all of them because I was given the Seekers complete five CD set.'

First child: 'Is it over now? They didn't sing "Georgie Girl".'

Second child: 'Don't be silly. That's only the first half – we have to go back inside.'

First child (after a silent pause for thought): ' Oh God. Does that mean we have to listen to Mum singing for another hour?'

Sorry, Mum, it sounded pretty good from where I was!

Night Terrors

EVELYN M. FIELD

It is very hard being a middle-aged psychologist. People tend to think that I always cope with life's ups and downs. It must be the blonde tips in my hair. 'You always look so calm,' people say. That's when I whisper to myself, 'Yes, like a swan, serene on top and paddling for grim life underneath.'

Miriam, my daughter, died many years ago. On the whole I have managed reasonably successfully to cover up the big black hole that is inside me. Of course, I use lots of techniques such as make-up, clothes, a confident manner and a strong voice. I also rely heavily on family and friends and the occasional piece of chocolate. People don't see what's inside, they just see my smooth facade.

But sometimes at night there is no facade. There is just sheer terror. The terror I feel when I wake up and recall her passing. It was far worse for many years after she died. Then I would wake up at night petrified. I did not know what to do with myself. Eventually I would go to the dining room and get a small glass of Baileys. That always worked. I would go back to sleep immediately. Once, a teacher overhead me say that I had run out of Baileys and was using a small glass of port, because Baileys was too expensive. The following day Adrienne Glanville brought a bottle of Baileys to work for me. I will never forget her kindness.

The years have passed by. I manage to sleep pretty well at night. The secret is to be exhausted and drop into bed, although my doctor would say it is due to hormone replacement therapy. However, whenever I hear that another parent, with whom I feel some connection, has lost a child, I know that I am in for a bad night. That's when I put the miniature bottle of Baileys, which I picked up on an aeroplane, by my bedside table, just in case. I cope by knowing that it is there.

Earlier this year Rebecca, my other daughter, moved into a house with a garden. She wanted her dog, Millie, to live with her. That meant that Tessie, the old terrier, was now all alone. I talked to my vet and ended up with a little white fluffy papillon. This means butterfly in French. So I call her Bufy. She is really a small dog with a big heart. She is intelligent, caring and extroverted. One day she will sit with clients, as Tessie does now. Perhaps it may help you to know that I use butterflies a lot, on my letterheads and business cards, and as part of my model. They are my link with Miriam, because she loved them. They are also used as symbols for Compassionate Friends, a group for parents who have lost a child.

Some time ago my mother decided to write her memoirs. This is a pretty good feat for an eighty-year-old, except that she ended the memoirs by talking about her recent great-grandson and Miriam. The problem was that I should have looked at the manuscript during the day, sitting in my little glasshouse, surrounded by my colourful indoor plants, sipping a cup of hot chocolate. Instead, I had to read it quickly and return it to her the following day. So, after a long day of work, I hopped into bed and read the manuscript. It was hard enough reading about her life before the war, and discovering that my grandmother did actually die in a concentration camp. By midnight I had got to the part where she mentioned Miriam.

Eventually the pain will pass and life begins again

I tried to sleep but the familiar terror struck again. This time was different. Sitting on top of the doona cover was a warm little white fluffy puppy dog snuggling up to me. I put my hand on her soft, furry body and she gave my hand a lick. Then amazingly, the middle-aged psychologist felt she could cope with the terror.

Many people have to face very dark moments in their lives. I learnt that you can find ways to face the pain, deal with it and find new meaning in your life. Eventually the pain will pass and life begins again.

Anonymous Meeting

BRIAN BELL

I'm talking to no one, but people can hear me
Telling the truth of the way it has been.
Feeling the depth of acceptance so near me
Comforts my soul till my world is serene.

Words come to life where the stillness is caring,
Hearing my version of fantasies past.
Everyone present is peacefully sharing,
Healing a hurt that would otherwise last.

How does it function, so simple a notion?
How can this talk help a body to heal?
How can a spirit that's drowned in life's ocean
Rise to the surface by making things real?

How can the guilt and that shame that forever
Held my reality just disappear?
Maybe it's my being willing to sever
Connections, by having another soul hear.

I'm talking to no one but everyone's straining
To grasp all the meaning I need to convey.
Now that it's out, little pain is remaining,
And I'm coming closer to living today.

The Mountain

PHILLIPA CHALLIS

The majesty of the Cliffs of Moher on the west coast of Ireland, the sheer power of the ocean as it crashes relentlessly on the black granite rocks, is truly awesome.

I was travelling around the south of Ireland on a seven-day bus tour and was enjoying every place visited. The fact that I was using crutches because of an injured leg did not hold me back in any way. I tackled every new path and staircase with enthusiasm – I had to see it all.

The memory of my visit to the cliffs on a beautiful summer's day is etched on my mind forever. There were pure white puffs of cloud in the clear blue skies and an invigorating wind blowing, which caused people to lean into the wind as they walked. I remember being full of resolve and determination as I started to climb a very steep hill that had extremely shallow, deep stairs. Not to be daunted by the steepness, I looked just in front of me and carefully took one step at a time.

Halfway up the hill it started to rain. I called on the good Lord for the challenge he was giving me as the 'liquid sunshine', as the Irish call it, started to fall, making the well-trodden steps slippery. It made me question his judgement.

'I've not complained about the difficulty of getting on and off the bus and the fact that I might miss out on seeing everything,' I thought to myself. I was thinking how good I had been, being my usual bright and cheery self as I struggled with the obstacles put before me because of the crutches. Running the full gamut of self-pity, I said out loud, 'I let the rest of my companions from the bus go ahead so as not to hinder them.'

As the skies got darker and my breathing heavier, I said, 'I'm not complaining about the steepness of the climb, so why this challenge Lord?' And so the tirade went on for no one in particular to hear, as I gingerly looked upwards to where I was headed.

Just then a good-looking young man came over the top of the rise. Like me, he too was walking cautiously in the liquid sunshine. He too was on elbow crutches – except he had only one leg. As we drew level and exchanged a smile, I counted my blessings and was especially appreciative of the fact that my crutches were temporary. I only needed them until the broken bone in my ankle healed.

When I finally reached the top, I stood and took in the wonderful view and thanked God for the lesson I had received.

Starting Over

Professor Carl Wood

I've had a successful life when one measures success by accomplishments at work, but until recently deep down I thought that I had failed in the most important thing in life: a happy, close relationship with a woman.

I've had two failed marriages, and I feel that this was mostly due to my own problems. I've also had several female friends with whom I have been briefly involved. These kinds of short-term liaisons suited both parties at the time, but they lacked an honest exchange of feelings and the deep mutual understanding that forms the foundation of a happy long-term friendship.

Finally I met my emotional resurrection. She was a tall, slim woman, much younger than I, with three children, two divorces, a war voice and direct expression of thoughts and feelings.

After some months of cautious advances we finally went away for a weekend together. We had a marvellous time but when we discussed our relationship, we decided that our families and the difference in our ages made the whole thing impractical. When we returned we didn't see each other for two days. It was unbearable, and we began to see each other again.

For the first time I was completely honest with a woman. I could now express my feelings; I could laugh, cry, be happy or sad and talk about anything – religion, life and death, sexual behaviour, spiritual feelings, our own peculiarities, loves and hates and anything we could think of.

We are both happy and whilst we will not have long together because of my age, we are keen to experience the beauty of our love and we are not afraid to cry about the future loss of each other.

We both think we will always be together in some way.

Life on the Land

SOPHIE WAJSMAN

'Don't worry, it's all character building.' Harold, my father-in-law, was to say that repeatedly over the years.

I'd grown up in inner-city Melbourne but I fell in love and here I was living with Steve in the Mallee. My friends were amazed that I could survive, living seventy miles from Mildura. I loved a chat and was famous for being able to strike up a conversation with total strangers. Now, apart from Steve, there would be days, sometimes a week or two, before I saw anyone else.

I had grown up with rather romantic notions about life on the land, but one incident brought home the reality of it. Our son, Jake, was only about one month old and, to begin with, I was already exhausted from constant wakeful nights. It was a stinking hot day, we had no air-conditioning, and I was feeling pretty cranky.

Steve was over at a neighbour's property about ten miles away. Suddenly the phone rang. It was Steve and he was talking quickly.

'We've just been hit by a dust storm and it's heading your way. I want you to shut all the windows and doors, and stay inside. You'd better be quick or everything will be covered in dust. You've got about two minutes before it gets there.'

I put Jake down on the bed and ran around closing everything. By the time I'd finished, Jake was crying and when I looked out of the window all I could see was a solid wall of red dust. Everything else had just disappeared. I couldn't even see the front fence that was only ten yards from the verandah. Small branches and clumps of earth were being hurled around. Every now and again I'd hear things crashing against the house with such force that I was scared a window would break.

With everything shut, it wasn't long before the house felt like an oven, and the hotter and noisier it got, the more I felt trapped until eventually, I just burst into tears. I don't know who was howling the loudest, Jake or me. We must have been a pitiful sight, me in my sarong and thongs, Jake wearing next to nothing, shiny with sweat, the pair of us blubbering out of sheer frustration.

I picked him up and held him up to the window. 'Look at this,' I shouted. 'This is quality of life. I hope you're enjoying it.' At that moment I felt so awful, just totally miserable. I wasn't coping as a new mother, the constant heat was driving me mad and I couldn't help wondering what would happen to us as a family if I suddenly discovered that I really couldn't live in the bush.

Gradually, as the dust storm subsided, so did my anger and frustration. I was supposed to be comforting my baby and instead I was adding to his distress. Eventually we both calmed down and by the time the dust storm had passed, and the house was open again, Steve came home. For him it was just another day.

Most people on the land are used to having to deal with the odd dust storm or flash flood. They don't see their lives as anything romantic or particularly special. They just do what they have to do to survive. I was to learn that lesson over and over again during my time in the bush.

Until you try, you don't know what you are capable of

There were many times that I found myself wondering whether I had made the right decision to live in the country, such as during the dust storm. And I'm sure that, even though Steve never once said so, there must have been moments when he questioned whether he had made the right choice of partner for his lifestyle.

My time on Wampo taught me that I was stronger than I thought I was. I was never going to be totally competent in the bush, but I was always willing to try and I found out that country people will forgive a lot as long as they know you're prepared to have a go. I learned that until you try, you don't know what you are capable of.

The Piano

ANTONIETTA VENTURA

When I was around ten years old, I had been aggravating and apparently delighting my family most nights with my 'drawer piano'. Any drawer that was a portable size would do. In retrospect a possible explanation could be that it had been a particularly silent and frustrating year.

My English was too limited to make friends in my new convent school. Classes seemed to be behind the standard I had been accustomed to, but I had been placed in a class below my age. The greatest horror of all was that we had to write in pencil whilst I had long mastered pen and ink and script. There was some sensitivity to 'newcomers', a word I learnt to recognise.

Without ever leaving her home or being able to speak the language, my mother, Anna, soon discovered that piano lessons were available at the school. One day my elder brother walked me through the mysterious but exquisite inner world of the convent to the music cottage. A long relationship began with Sister Leila. Piano classes brought back pleasure and challenge to my days.

Some time later, my brother came across a piano that needed a home. After what seemed to me to be a very long delay, arrangements were finally made for its collection.

In those days our family was quite extended, including some borders – the sons of friends that my parents were asked to keep an eye on. So there were two borders, two brothers, one visiting fiancée and an occasional visiting semitrailer driver. Eventually everyone managed to confer and they decided that collecting the piano would make a good Sunday deed, and so pacify a tenacious and enthusiastic little girl.

My mother and I stood outside in unspeakable excitement and waited. Soon the semitrailer stopped in front of the house. We anxiously watched the lads unloading the piano. They were in a jovial mood, unaware of what was going to happen next.

For some mysterious, unexplained reason someone, not the driver it seemed, decided to move the long truck. His bravado, together with inadmissible ignorance, caused the whole truck to jolt to such a degree that, with helpless desolate reality, the piano crashed spectacularly to the ground in front of our eyes. It created an unforgettable and unique thunder of sound together with a visual spectacle of individual ivoried keys flying in mid-air to create a fireworks display of notes and dust. So vividly too I can remember the insensitive laughter of the 'lads' busily hiding embarrassment and regret.

For many weeks later, Anna's beautiful, soulful gaze followed me everywhere, accompanying my own lonely acceptance of this loss. Of course, there had been loss already. The loss of country, language, dear loved ones never to meet again, identity, heritage had insidiously taken hold in our hearts, but this visual, palpable loss is more memorable and easily accessible. Of course, there were many other losses to come.

In the face of interrogation from Sister Leila, shyness, embarrassment and unwillingness to expose the situation made me answer a ready 'yes', the piano was home and in place for hours of practice. I agreed, I was a lucky girl. This unusual situation went on for many years. Sister Leila was absolutely certain some days I had definitely practised for many hours, particularly when I passed all my piano exams. I look back and see the pattern of the mutations of each day as I visualised the notes and their sounds. Tone was achieved by pressing on my thigh at any quiet moment.

Eventually I bought a piano, but not before I had left school. Then life took its hold and doubt set in about whether I really had the talent to proceed with a musical career of any significance. However, privately, my love of music has sustained me so many times in a multitude of different ways.

Grief

A Life Worth Living

MARGARET SHEEHAN

My first-born son was so special in many ways. Martin was born a very healthy 6lb 14oz in a little bush nursing hospital at Charlton in Victoria. He looked like a mirror image of his father, with a cute turned-up nose, black hair and a smile that lit up his entire face.

He seemed to be a normal healthy infant who thrived on all the attention his doting parents and extended family bestowed on him. It was not until he was about four months old when he started eating solids that things began to change and his health deteriorated. There were frequent bouts of diarrhoea, some vomiting and ear and chest infections.

I was assured by my doctor that these were normal childhood infections, but he referred Martin to a specialist to monitor his asthma. I was most surprised when on a second visit to the paediatrician in Melbourne my son was admitted to hospital with severe asthma. This was to be the first of many visits to hospital.

There were times when Martin was very lethargic at home and would fall asleep in his highchair after eating breakfast and having just woken from a good night's sleep. It was after one of these episodes that I took my precious baby to Melbourne and pleaded with doctors to find the cause of his illness. By this stage I was expecting our second child and felt unable to cope with a new baby and a sick child.

We ended up staying in the city for weekly blood tests to determine whether there was any change in his white cell count. After all this time we were looking forward to going home to our little house on the farm. Finally it was the morning of his last blood test. I went to wake Martin to get ready for our visit to the doctor, but to my absolute horror I was unable to rouse him. I wrapped him in a blanket and raced him to the nearest hospital, speeding through petrol stations to avoid traffic lights.

When we entered casualty I was berated by the nurse for wrapping him up as she believed that he had convulsed because he was too hot. When I explained that I was unable to even raise a temperature in him she calmed down a little. The doctor was quickly called and he immediately administered some dextrose and I was delighted to see my son return to consciousness and give me one of his beautiful smiles.

I wanted to take him home there and then, but the medical staff now believed that there was something untoward about his health and the time had come to investigate the situation thoroughly. For one month he stayed in hospital and underwent various tests to try to reach a diagnosis of his condition.

I arrived at the hospital early one morning to the sound of him crying as they tried to put an intravenous line into his arm so that they could take continual blood tests during the day. The splint and apparatus became too difficult for this eighteen-month-old boy to manage for any more than a few hours. The results of the blood tests proved that he had cyclical neutropenia (low neutrophil count) and a low white blood cell count (leukopenia). Tests on his faeces and small bowel indicated a fat malabsorbtion problem. In many ways this was a relief, but we were yet to reach a diagnosis. Cystic fibrosis, which had been suspected, was ruled out – so now the dilemma.

It was New Year's Day 1979 when the paediatrician summoned my husband and me to the hospital with the all-important results. The diagnosis was Schwachman Diamond Syndrome, a very rare condition suffered by only a few children in Australia at the time. When I asked the doctor for the prognosis, he said the words I never thought I'd hear: 'I can see no reason why he would not grow up to be a strong and healthy man.'

My son's diet remained the same but he was to take pancreatic enzymes before every meal to help the digestion of his food. He immediately started to show signs of thriving with normal digestion, more energy and an increase in weight. It was such a thrill to be able to take my little boy home and get him ready to welcome his new brother.

As Martin grew older he never complained about his frequent asthma attacks which still persisted, or having to take the awful powdered enzymes before every meal. His gentle nature endeared him to everybody, but especially to his younger brothers and sister. They looked up to him with admiration and love as he grew to be a tall, well-developed teenager.

He went to agricultural college after passing Year 12 and then as part of his course he went to work as a jackeroo on a large sheep station named Collinsville in South Australia for two years. The joy of Christmas after he had been away a year was complete when he returned unannounced on Christmas Eve to the family home. He had grown into a healthy, strong man and we were all so proud of his achievements.

This was the last Christmas we would share, as he was taken from us in April of the next year – 1998 – in a single car accident, as he drove to town to play his beloved football with the local team.

The doctor's prediction did indeed come true. He did grow into a strong and beautiful man, only to have his now healthy life cut short by a tragic accident at the age of twenty. His life is still an inspiration to all of us but we will always wonder why we had to lose him after he had won so many previous battles of life.

Time to Grieve

SALLY BROWNE

EARLY 1998 | I finally close my fashion business.

I have had a ball, I have had enough, and I have enough.

Fashion is no longer an exciting challenge.

What's in, what's not; who's in, who is hot . . . who cares! I'm bored!

The time is right and ripe for me to pursue other business interests and new adventures.

MID-1998 | I see a sign and it haunts me. 'Don't let fear get in the way of your dreams!' I had always wanted to get up as high as I could in the Mount Everest region, but I am afraid of heights. Despite that, I embark on a dedicated training program and fall in love with bushwalking, climbing and cardioworkouts.

LATE 1999 | I am ready for my first major adventure and set off with a wonderful group of people for Nepal. I had expected a physical challenge, and it was excruciatingly demanding at times. I had not expected it to become an emotional challenge and a turning point in my life.

High up in the 'big hills' it is cold and dark by 6 p.m. No clubs or pubs, no entertainment. At night we tell stories . . . personal stories, funny or meaningful stories and mountain stories. One story in particular struck a chord deep within me.

Three guys were making an assault on K2. They came to a crevasse and put their ladder over it. As the first climber made his way across, the ladder slipped and he vanished into the deep, dark hole. His two mates hurriedly loosened and lowered a rescue rope, felt a weak tug on it and then a stronger tug, and very slowly they began to raise the human weight. Gently lifting him onto the snow and laying him down they stared at this breathing human and then stared at each other. They could not recognise him. It was a completely different person.

The guy they had rescued had been on a climb much earlier that day. He'd slipped into the crevasse, hit a ledge, lost consciousness and later regained consciousness – hence clung to the rescue rope like grim death when he felt it. They also got their guy out too. Incredible, wonderful, remarkable.

As we trekked and climbed higher the next day I thought a lot about this story. On reflection the K2 story was somewhat like my life: a huge adventure, involving mateship and risk, resulting in some incredible surprises and some wonderful outcomes. I had also experienced times that felt like I was skating on thin ice and I had fallen into a few deep, dark 'personal ravines'.

Around 9 p.m., alone in a tiny tent on icy snow (it was minus nine degrees), I was exhausted but too cold to sleep and my mind drifted back to my deepest darkest ravine.

EARLY 1978 | I had two small sons aged five and three and I was three months pregnant with my third child. The fashion business was booming; the marriage was not.

I was trying to play the impossible role of fashion designer, businesswoman, den mother, wife and domestic goddess.

My husband (and finance manager) was flirting heavily with one of our staff. As I got dumpier and plumper, they seemed to get flirtier and, I suspect, dirtier. All too much for me, I confronted my man, confirmed the dalliances and sadly realised it was time to flee from home with the children, my bruised dignity, a suitcase, a sock of spare change and an airline card (my husband had never given me a credit card). It was 2 a.m. I arrived at the airport with a tired child tucked under each arm, determined to get as far away as possible from my broken dreams in Melbourne.

EARLY 1978 | PERTH, 8 A.M | I called my fashion agent, bless him. 'Hey Buddy, you know how you've been nagging me to come to Perth. Well, I am here.' Poor guy. Two months before my arrival he had a peaceful home, a beautiful wife and a great dog. Six weeks before I arrived he and his wife discovered they were going to have a long-awaited baby; two days before I arrived their dog had puppies. Shock, horror. Now his home housed two pregnant women, two small children, one dog, six pups and a fashion agent wondering what the hell had happened to his life. They lovingly welcomed us into their home to stay until I sorted myself out. I became their cook and housekeeper.

No one in Melbourne knew where we were. I felt cheated, alone, frightened. The days were dreadful, filled with despair and the dilemma of how I could continue to provide emotional, financial and physical support for my beautiful boys and the expected baby.

I pondered, cried, thought, cried, looked for jobs and cried again. I was desperate. I decided I would try to have a 'spiritual awakening', hoping it would light my path to the future.

I prayed and made an 'appointment' with God. Ten a.m in the park, tomorrow. (We working girls make appointments for everything!)

The children and I were at the park early. No signs from God at ten, still no sign of God at 11 a.m; at midday we gave up and trundled home. I poured a bath, jumped in. Oh hell, my body was covered in spots; a red rash had crept over my whole body. Then I remembered one of my staff had had German measles before I left for Perth. Rubella. And I had been living in a home with another pregnant friend. Thanks a lot, God. This spiritual awakening is working a treat.

Frantic, I changed the sheets, cleared the fridge, packed the kids up, called my fashion agent and his darling wife at their office to give them the dangerous news and moved to a hotel. Waited three days for spots and fever to vanish, called home, caught flight, saw gynaecologist, tried to repair marriage, comforted confused children, and went back to work. Phew! The other woman had left.

Word of my dilemma carrying a rubella-affected unborn baby got out and my many well-meaning friends took it upon themselves to offer help and advice. 'Get rid of it.' 'This baby could be so affected it could ruin your life. You can't go ahead.' And the other end of the scale, 'This is your lesson, you must not interfere,' to 'God has given you this baby.'

STILL 1978 | After three weeks of tests, with the baby alive and kicking in my tummy, twenty-five weeks old by now, my gynaecologist made the decision to terminate. I did not and could not have made this decision and was relieved it was out of my hands. No one told me what was going to happen. Probably out of kindness.

When you terminate a pregnancy at this stage, the doctor injects something into your womb. You lie alone all night with your baby kicking, slower and slower, while it begins to die, eventually, maybe twenty-four hours of hell later, your body realises it doesn't want this baby and you begin to self-abort and go into a normal birthing pattern.

Because it is all so awful the medical staff leave you pretty much alone, no doctor for delivery, no team cheering you on. Alone and lonely you go through the labour and your baby enters the world. Warm, wet, an almost dead baby; maybe she was dead. I wept and wept; they whisked her away, no name, no sympathy, no explanation, and no funeral. Gone.

I am in the maternity section of the hospital in the middle of happy new mothers; sweet babies and the bustle of nurses. My body begins to produce milk for my dead baby. Day two they bind my breasts, never mentioning my baby. Day five they sent me home.

I bounced back into my life: mended the marriage, got on with nurturing my boys, designed a few more frocks, and got gloriously busy to cover my pain. Total denial.

1998 | For twenty years I carried the grief. I could not confront the cruelty of the process of this birth and death, the total lack of sympathy, empathy or burial ceremony or ritual. This precious part of me, this life treated so flippantly. It's over, get over it.

1999 | Back in Nepal, towards the end of our trek, our leader Jamie Duff decided we would have a group ceremony. During our time together we had shared our triumphs and tragedies. At 6 a.m.

the next day we set off up a craggy rocky mountain. We sat separately, reflecting on past pain, lost loved ones, broken hearts and hopes. We made personal offerings in memory, with paper, pencils, little treasures and sparse high-altitude bushflowers.

We set up a human chain gang to gather rocks, then we began to build a structure. One by one, we buried our tributes and our 'pain' in the base. We covered our treasures with small stones, then built our huge monument higher and higher. The centre was hollow and we filled it with incense and fragrant branches. We lit a bonfire, then we prayed, cried, talked, hugged, shared secrets, read meaningful passages and alleviated past, internalised pain. After quiet peaceful contemplation, we set off down the hill.

The ceremony was an extraordinary and cathartic experience for me. I felt so light as I bounded down the hill, at peace at last and completely free from years of guilt and pain from never bidding farewell to my baby. She was finally given her precious burial ceremony. High up in the Himalayas there is a monument that holds a little book of prayers, songs and poems, bound in string and beads, wrapped in a prayer flag with love, a tribute to her unlived life.

One of our great indigenous leaders had once said to me, 'How people live and how people die is not our business. Loving them is our business.' This statement lives on within me.

Finally, twenty years after my daughter's birth and death, I was ready and able to whisper, 'My darling, how you lived and how you died was not my business. Loving you was my business, and I loved you deeply as you lay in my arms dying and I love you today as a free spirit. Bless you, baby gal.'

My Husband

SUE CARR

It was a very exciting time in my life and for my small family; there was an addition to our ranks to make four, and a new extended family of five others. Alistair and I celebrated our engagement party with family and friends. Three days later my father died of a heart attack in his dispensary. Wonderful for him, as he did not suffer, but a huge shock and loss for me and my mother, one from which she never fully recovered.

I remember following the funeral cortege on a day of 40 degrees in February and wondering how and why the people in the streets which we passed were still going about their daily business. It seemed that they were unaware of what had happened to our family. I was twenty-one years of age; my father was forty-nine.

In the following months I attempted to assist my mother in picking up the pieces of her life, to feel excited about my forthcoming wedding in December and to come to terms with the huge loss of my father whom I respected and adored. In time, the gap was of course filled by my future husband, Alistair, who was constant in his support; he helped me through this incredible 'learning about life' curve.

Then it happened again. One evening nine years later, Alistair – Tax, as he was known – and I were having dinner with close friends in Eltham. Late in the evening he felt a tightness in his chest and we rather naively thought it was the rich food and wine. As we drove home I had to stop the car many times on the journey to Camberwell as he felt intense, sharp pains in his chest. I was calm as I helped Tax to bed but I was sure that I needed to act quickly. I remembered as a young girl how little action was taken when my father experienced a tightness in his chest. He was a pharmacist and always knew best. I realised that I may be about to lose Tax.

I immediately telephoned our neighbour and good friend, who was also our doctor, and by 3 a.m. we had Tax in a specialist ambulance on the way to St Vincent's Hospital. I went home and tried to sleep, but at 6 a.m. when I rang the hospital I was advised to come in immediately. I rushed to Fitzroy. The shock was overwhelming. Still in casualty, Tax was attached to wires monitoring the effects of a serious heart attack and to tubes assisting his breathing. It reminded me of the time I arrived at my father's pharmacy in 1967 to find a hospital stretcher entirely covered being gently carried to a waiting ambulance.

Somehow we got through it. We were determined he would not die, and although he had two further attacks Tax left St Vincent's a few weeks later, ready for a new life that would be different from the one we had shared before.

It was extraordinary how we adapted to the fight to maintain his health and to find ways to reduce the effects of ongoing heart disease (which we discovered some seven years later was caused by impending renal failure). We could not rely on cardiac or renal physicians to maintain his healthy condition; we had to take action and balance our lives of a hectic family and work schedule with a careful diet and quiet times. We were determined to live life to the fullest. Our baby son, Nick, made it all the more important.

In the end, fourteen years after the first heart attack and many months spent in coronary care from further severe attacks, we lost Tax to renal failure.

The fight had been worth it though. We were told Tax had enjoyed many years more than was forecast. We had learned to be well informed; to leave no stone unturned, to understand and to heed every warning sign by learning to monitor the heart condition regularly at home; and, importantly, to never give in.

I also learned to be independent, particularly having observed how my mother's lack of independence destroyed any chance of her opening a new chapter after her life with my father. This provided me with the vision to move forward continually and to not live in the past or for the future. I have not taken for granted the people closest to me, because without them life is meaningless. This is particularly relevant as the entire extended Carr family of five have now passed away.

St Cecilia's Day

Dr Colette Rayment

Today, 22 November 2000, I am in Amsterdam. I have intentionally not made any arrangement to meet friends or colleagues and my agenda is entirely my own. In fact it is even unknown to myself.

It is St Cecilia's day, the patron of music, musicians and composition, made famous in old and recent times by poets celebrating in verse the music so familiar to their ears. For me the day has even more significance; it is the twenty-sixth birthday of my son, who died when he was thirteen.

At six his passion was for Van Gogh, for whom our painterly next-door neighbour had inculcated a love in the childish mind. He had a poem published at ten. As far as music was concerned, however, it was for him, a labour of love – not for the cello or the music, itself, but for me. Like his brothers, he had made a contract with me to continue music lessons until he finished school. A realist and an ironist at thirteen, one of the last things he said to me as he was dying was:

'And I was supposed to play in the concert today. Not that I really wanted to.'

He added sardonically, 'I was doing it for you.'

This, I knew, was true. The lure of the football team and the magnetism of the girls in his class were never threatened by any devotion to the cello. But play it he did, and quite well, according to his acute sense of loyalty and honour.

So here I am in Amsterdam contemplating how to spend the day in this city away from my family and clearly, for all my determination to be strong and wise as angels, in need of solace.

At moments like this (and anyone who has 'lost' a child will tell you) there is a great need to think and act holistically. You need to care for body, mind and spirit – to nurture the need for reassurance, wellbeing and even a hoped for moment of union with such a child on such a day.

My first choice is to receive the holy bread – a spiritual breakfast if you like – to begin the day. (Later in the day I will eat well and also take care to nourish the mind.) Happily I have been told where to find a short morning Eucharist in the famed Kalverstraat, a popular shopping thoroughfare running off Dam Square and housing everything from contemporary art to McDonald's and including at least two flourishing chapels. The place I sought was called the Begijnhof, a seventeenth-century home for semi-religious women. This is how my day began.

'Solace on St Cecilia's Day' tells the rest of the story of my Dutch St Cecilia's day, 2000.

Grief

In search of solace on St Cecilia's day
I set out for the Begijnhof
as backing vans bleep out
their monotonous drone –
the first two notes of 'Für Elise' –
done to death in childish toys
now a faulty needle
in a tram-track groove
of mud and sand around
the renovating Dam.

A man passes by wheeling
a double base ahead of himself
through the grit and roar of cranes.
Overhead the Kerk carillion
has clearly had enough:
amused baroque embellishments,
'I could have danced all night',
say it all. 'Greensleeves' lures
passers by to coffee (not ice cream)
and in the Nieuwe Kerk Kafe
the thinnest longest fish-netted legs
pace in patent platforms
way below a red smile flashing
to the peals of 'Yankee Doodle'
expatriated to the Old World.

Over omelet met brood en boter
I reject the Concertgebouw offerings
of Werkman, Schien and others
and take a taxi to the Rijks instead.

No no not that either: follow under
the Roman arches and hail Van Gogh
in an Exhibition of Light:
Javanese and Sumatran light houses
and Fresnel's fabulous lens, Gauguin's chair
under gas and arc lamp and then
the music of the spheres: *Starry Night*
on the Rhône River: I see
your six-year's-old self shouting
up the stairs of the Jeu de Paumes
'Van Gogh, Van Gogh!' you yell, yellow
chair wheat sunflowers cornfields
dazzling above your golden head.

Back in the permanent collection
where one should have begun
I come face to face with Scheffer's
Christus Consolator surrounded by
a chained slave, a Greek freedom fighter
and – a mother embracing
the body of her child . . .

Back, back through the arched Rijks;
but now the air is full of music,
strings and songs of the busking Altai-Hangai.
This is a new delight to find
Asia here in Europe: I stop to look
but mainly to listen
and suddenly I am as free as
the Mongolian steppes and
timeless as the Gobi.

Robert Shannon

DAVID WESTON

On the corner of my office desk is a framed photo of my son and me taken at a function. Tucked in the left-hand bottom corner of the frame is a clipping from a brochure of a mate. A photo of a suntanned handsome man with the smile of a true winner grins into the camera while seated in a wonderful vintage car. He is what a female friend calls a DDB – drop-dead beautiful man.

The picture haunts me every day. I sometimes think that I will take it out of the corner of the frame, but I can't. No, I won't because I don't want a day to pass without thinking about the impact this person had on me. The tragedy is that the photo and the memories are all that I have left because this most dynamic of human beings died suddenly earlier this year.

I have experienced the deaths of parents, the untimely death of one of my son's best friends when she had all of the potential in the world. She was only sixteen. But never before have I felt such grief as when the person in the photograph died. I literally cried for weeks. He was no saint. In fact, at times I described him as the uncle from hell. He was wicked, egoistical, loud and obnoxious, and yet at other times as tender as a young child, full of the joy of life. His name was Robert Shannon.

The year before he died, Robert asked me to attend a strategic planning day for the company he had founded some twenty years before. I was an outsider to his business, the Shannon's Corporation, the business of insuring and selling through auction classic and collectable cars. Gathered for the workshop were his key managers, his suppliers (the insurance underwriters Shannon's used), his marketing consultants and the directors he had appointed as a board to guide him and of course the facilitator.

All of those present knew the business well. They talked about their projections for growth, their customer base, the gross margins and how they delivered customer service. My role was to be the devil's advocate, to ask the questions that only an outsider could: 'What would happen if Robert died or sold out?' How prophetic, but I had no idea.

What I did see however was that the staff did not appreciate the uniqueness of the business that they worked for. The words formed in my head like one of those inspirational flashes in cartoons when the light bulb illuminates. The words just blurted out, 'This business is unique. It exists for two reasons – to indulge Robert's passion for being around classic cars and so that he can raise money for the causes in which he is involved.'

Eventually, Robert confided in me that he was negotiating to sell. His problem was how to reinvent himself from Robert 'Shannon's Corporation' Shannon to something else. But before he did sell he was determined to have one or two corporate flings – especially to be a sponsor at the Australian Grand Prix.

On the Monday before the Grand Prix, I got the phone call. Robert had been found dead at home. But what! What cause? How would his staff cope (he was the classic, out the front leader)? He had the Grand Prix auction on in two weeks' time.

I cried deep gut-wrenching tears unlike any tears or sorrow I had ever felt before. The rest of the week was a blur. His staff rallied and the show went on. At his funeral Father Bob said prayers and tried to help us understand but I know he found it as hard as us.

'Robert was only forty-eight but he packed ninety-six years of living into those forty-eight years.' As the service went on in the Church of St Peter and St Paul in South Melbourne, the whine of the Grand Prix cars in their first practice session at Albert Park could be heard. He would have loved that. My son, the one in the photograph frame, came to the funeral with me but left soon after to visit the grave of his friend who died at sixteen.

We rallied on the Grand Prix day. As we arrived at Albert Park we heard that the Shannon's International Sport Car Race had to be abandoned because of a pile-up on the first lap – how would Robert have reacted?

Only a week before he died we had been at the Lord Mayor's Charity Day at Flemington Race Course, another Shannon's Charity contribution dressed up as a corporate sponsorship. We bumped into Father Bob. 'Say a prayer for me, Father,' said Robert as we parted. I hope to hell he did.

The face smiling out of the photo in the corner of the picture frame is not someone I once knew, but who has died. It is Robert alive, confident, winning and making lots of noise, fun noise, and exuberance in a human form. I guess he's reinventing himself in the other world. I hope they are into passion up there.

A Parent's Story

SUE WILKINSON

I remember it vividly. I was standing in the school quadrangle listening vaguely to the droning voice of the school principal. My mind was elsewhere. I was trying to figure out my future. A difficult thing to do for anyone, but by the end of assembly I had come up with a foundation for the rest of my life. I wanted a career, a husband, perhaps some children, a house, a couple of dogs and a creative hobby. It was perhaps not that exciting, but I was happy enough with my first draft. When the principal signed off from the morning spiel and sent us forth into the classrooms I went off armed with my foolproof plan.

I completed high school, studied and embarked on a career of teaching intellectually disabled children. The career, the house and one dalmatian by the name of Daisy were accounted for. I met Anthony at a party and fell for him immediately. Soon we were an inseparable couple. We both wanted children but felt we needed to wait a while. We put our efforts into our careers and hobbies. In my spare time I learnt how to paint. I was the happiest I had ever been; the only thing missing was a baby.

Two weeks after a romantic trip I made an appointment with my doctor. The lines on a simple urine test confirmed my suspicions. I was pregnant. The schedule was set. I was due 18 November. It seemed so very far away. I drove straight in to see Anthony at work. He was ecstatic with the news of impending fatherhood. We told our families immediately. We were bursting to share our good news. They were all so happy for us.

I didn't drink or smoke. I avoided our cat and watched my diet. I read everything about pregnancy and childbirth in sight. Having a baby consumed our every moment together. We talked constantly about plans, the nursery and the birth. Together we looked at hospitals, and decided upon a birthing centre at a local public hospital. We wanted a minimal intervention birth.

Anthony pampered my every need. We enjoyed our time together, the three of us. I went along to my regular doctor and midwife visits. Everything was normal, or so I thought. At eighteen weeks we heard the heartbeat. We were so happy. On a small monitor we saw our baby moving inside me. We were reassured that everything was normal. We watched the ultrasound over and over again at home. On our second ultrasound we found out I was carrying a boy.

In the twenty-ninth week we attended our first antenatal class. We met other expecting parents. We compared bellies, expected dates and pregnancy stories. It was such an exciting and informative evening. It was difficult to sleep that night, and I thought it was a mixture of excitement and worry. I complained to Anthony of a rough night. I had a shower and got dressed. My belly seemed even bigger than normal and the baby seemed high, almost under my ribs. There was a trickle of fluid down my legs. It was then the roller coaster scooped us up.

I contacted the Family Birthing Centre and after a short question and answer time the midwife instructed me to come into emergency. We navigated our way through peak-hour traffic. We did our best to remain calm, but the fluid was trickling out each time I moved slightly. We eventually made it to the hospital and I was helped into a cubicle. Within minutes I felt a strong surge of fluid escaping. A doctor was quick to examine me. She told us that there were a variety of possibilities now that my waters had broken: labour may begin; an infection could develop, signalling the need to get the baby out of my womb; or the baby could remain safely in the womb for the next eleven weeks. It was obvious now that every hour the baby remained in my womb would be considered a bonus hour. It was a very confusing time. There were so many new faces, medications, procedures and technical terms. Our minimal intervention birth plan was thrown to the wind. I was given an injection of steroids to aid the development of the baby's immature lungs and antibiotics to fight infection, and was placed on a drip. The next twenty-four hours were difficult. I was moved to a ward where it was possible to stay for the duration of my pregnancy, however long it may be, and put on a drip of ventolin to help ease the pains I was having. The ventolin did ease the pain, but added to my feelings of disorientation. Anthony and my parents were very reassuring but we were all so shocked. Prematurity was not known in my family and the pregnancy had been progressing normally.

When the ventolin course was complete the pains returned. We timed them. A nurse helped me through each pain. The decision was made to move me back to the delivery suite. A surgeon spoke to me briefly and told me that the baby needed to be delivered, as an infection had developed. I was moved to theatre for a caesarean. I was in a lot of pain and extremely frightened. Anthony sat beside me; we looked deeply into each other's eyes. I could see his fear, but he smiled through his anxiousness. The surgeon began the procedure, and within minutes I looked up to see a little purple baby.

Our baby. Our son. He weighed 1600 grams and was 40 centimetres long. My heart was filled with such love. He was beautiful. I reached out to touch him, but without any coordination my touch missed. I had been prepared for the situation of not being able to hold him, but it was difficult. Our moment of joy turned quickly to fear. We waited to hear his cry. He never did. In the corner of the room a team of people surrounded him. The voices I could hear were distorted, and I was unable to see what was happening. I could hear a strange hissing of air, and knew that they were trying to get him to breathe. I wanted someone to tell me what was happening.

Anthony and I were so confused and frightened. We waited. The sound stopped, the voices continued. I felt a chill run through me. After several long minutes we saw our son, alive, in a humidicrib on his way to the hospital neonatal nursery. Anthony was asked for his name. Henry James was given an identity.

I was moved to a recovery area where Anthony joined me. Then the paediatrician came and stood by my bed. He had the 'I'm so sorry' eyes, the look that says 'Prepare yourself, I have something horrible to tell you.' He told us that Henry was very sick. 'Sick,' I thought. 'He's alive!' But sick? How sick?

Whilst in recovery Henry had been given an X-ray. It showed he had a congenital abnormality; specifically, a left diaphragmatic hernia. There was a hole in his diaphragm and his intestines had moved through the diaphragm and into his chest. His immature lungs were barely functioning, and his left lung had not fully developed because of its lack of space to grow. He was struggling even with a ventilator. We were told the next forty-eight hours were going to be the most difficult and there was a real possibility that he would not survive. He was now too sick for the neonatal nursery and needed to be taken to Intensive Care at a nearby hospital.

I went to see him before he was taken away. Outside in the hallway my parents and Anthony were crying. I thought I was too late, but Henry was alive and preparations were being made for his transfer. My time with Henry remains blurry. The transport team gave us two polaroids before leaving. I was now going to be separated from my baby, not by rooms, but by kilometres. Surely this wasn't really happening. Surely I would wake up in the morning, in my own bed, pregnant. Anthony held my hand until I fell asleep. He stayed the night by my bed.

I woke early. I saw the hospital room. This was no dream, this was real. Anthony was still by my side. My parents walked into the room as I was waking. The smiles on their faces told us Henry was alive. They had sat by him all night. They told us about the care Henry was receiving and gave us two polaroids the nurses had taken. He looked so tiny and vulnerable lying there, connected to the machines. It was difficult to be so far away from my baby. The day passed slowly and we counted each and every hour. By the end of the long day we were starting to feel a little more confident about Henry's survival. At 1 a.m. I called Intensive Care. A friendly voice spoke. She was the nurse looking after Henry. She asked me how I was feeling and showed genuine concern for my predicament. She told me that Henry was no longer stable. She suggested that if possible I should come in to see him. The shake in her voice seemed to indicate that perhaps Henry was in real trouble. I phoned

Anthony, who had gone home to get some rest, and told him to come quickly. Every minute waiting for Anthony seemed like an hour. I watched the clock tick slowly. I desperately wanted to be with Henry, hoping he didn't die before we arrived. When we reached the hospital the nurse told me that since our conversation Henry had regained stability. I tried desperately to understand everything she said, but I was still on painkillers and was in such a state of shock. I understood that Henry was stable, he was on life support, still within the dangerous forty-eight-hour period, and I was unable to do anything to help him. I felt such a surge of powerlessness. I was physically and emotionally exhausted and felt so sick being out of bed, but we stayed with Henry for a few hours. A single touch reassured me. I wanted dearly to hold him, protect him, help him, but it wasn't possible. We cried, and started to question 'Why? Why us? Why Henry?'

The next morning was brighter. We had been informed of accommodation at Henry's hospital. Anthony made arrangements for my transfer. I hated being separated from my baby, and at midday, only thirty-six hours after Henry's birth, I was discharged. No longer on painkillers, I could see Intensive Care clearly. There were other children, on similar beds. Computer screens had lines and numbers, machines beeped and ventilators wooshed around me. It was terrifying. Reality hit and it hit hard.

I felt so helpless and stupid. I had no idea of the complications of prematurity and had never even heard of a diaphragmatic hernia. The doctors were not confident of Henry's ability to make it through, as he was faced with two substantial problems. There was the realistic possibility that Henry's treatment could give him brain damage, blindness, deafness or more. Our love for Henry was unconditional. We wanted him to survive regardless. The doctors tried to keep our feet on the ground, but we clung desperately to hope. It was all we had.

I was producing breast milk and had been so looking forward to putting my baby on my breast, but I was taught how to express using an electric breast pump and every three to four hours I would go into a room to express. I adapted to writing Henry's name on each bottle, sterilising procedures and storing my milk. We started to document Henry's life. We took photos and began writing in a diary a nurse had made.

Time took on a new perspective, and eventually the critical forty-eight hours passed. Henry was doing well. He had a long road ahead, but we developed a margin of confidence. Each hour continued to crawl by, and each day lasted an eternity. Anthony and I had our maternal and paternal instincts but not the normal parenting environment, so we did what we could. We wiped Henry's eyes, held his hand and talked to him constantly. We read him stories and pulled the tail of a musical toy to distract from the relentless beeping machines and the thumping of the high-frequency ventilator. We placed little soft toys in his bed. It was heartbreaking, but we kept going.

On 10 September Henry was stable enough for surgery. The surgeon had large hands and a gentle face. He told us of the procedure and relayed a feeling of confidence. He informed us of the risks, and they worried us, but we continued to cling to hope. My parents, Anthony and I waited in the Intensive Care waiting room. We attempted to remain calm. The colour drained from our faces as we walked paces within the tiny room. We held each other. We cried and we waited. In our minds, if Henry could make it through this operation, he would have a greater chance of survival, a greater chance of coming home.

Three hours crawled by before Henry's trolley was wheeled past the waiting room door. He had survived the operation and was being returned to his area within Intensive Care. After several more excruciating minutes the surgeon walked down the hallway towards us. I checked his eyes for the 'Sorry' look. It wasn't there. He smiled. He told us that the surgery was successful. Henry's intestines were now out of his chest and where they were supposed to be. His lungs now had enough space to form. We celebrated his strength, and for the first time the roller coaster seemed to slow a little. We were able to catch our breath.

We adapted to living at the hospital; our old normal life seemed so far away. For five more days we watched the outside world scurry through their normal lives from large windows. We wondered when we would be able to take Henry into the outside world, away from the machines, away from the hospital. We talked about all the things we could do with him, places we would go and things we would do together as a family. Each day signalled a little improvement and we felt confident enough to allow Henry some visitors. We began to make arrangements for the upcoming weekend for Anthony's parents to meet their grandson. We were enthusiastic for them to see our beautiful little boy. My parents visited daily. They kept buying Henry toys and things and would sit with him each evening. They wrote in his diary and took photographs at every opportunity. The love and dedication they showed saddened me. I felt such overwhelming guilt. I felt responsible for putting everyone, including Henry, through this. I began to question my diet, my lifestyle. I wanted a reason for Henry's condition. There wasn't one to be found.

On 16 September our worst fears were realised. Henry showed signs of an infection. The word sepsis still rumbles through my brain over and over again. Henry's usual pinkish skin had changed to a murky grey. The surgeon said he would attempt surgery if Henry became stable once more. That surgery never eventuated. Henry's heart stopped beating. The doctors gave us five-minute updates, until eventually he was stable. We refused to sit in the waiting room any longer, and told the doctors we wanted to be with our son. They were supportive of our needs, and warned us of Henry's stability and his now bruised and bloody appearance. We cried when we saw our little boy. His chest was now very bruised and there was blood in his ventilator tubes. Doctors explained that Henry had been given heart massage and more medication. It was horrific seeing him like this. We stroked Henry's body gently. We told him of our love for him. Within minutes a beep sounded that I will never forget. I looked to the monitor that I had studied for thirteen days and watched his heart rate jump around erratically. Doctors and nurses sprang into action. It was frantic, and once again they began heart massage. Watching those thumbs pressing up and down on my baby was terribly distressing. I felt so helpless, so pained. Someone in the room sat us down and gave us tissues to wipe our eyes. The thumbs kept moving up and down, up and down. Henry was not responding. Finally he was separated from the tubes that had maintained his life. Henry died in the arms of his daddy at 11.40 a.m. that morning.

Anthony passed Henry to me, his little body now limp. I held him tightly. This was my first hold. I felt the crash of my heart as it fell from my chest and onto the floor. I was oblivious to the world around me. We went to a nearby room where we could be alone. Henry's eyes were closed and he had a gentleness on his face. For the first time in thirteen days all was quiet except for the words we spoke and tears we shed. There were no doctors or nurses, no noisy machines. A little while passed and a nurse asked if we would like to give Henry a bath. We did. We dried him gently and continued to talk to him as we wrapped his body in a bunny rug. In our minds we had failed as parents. We had watched him die. We felt helpless and useless. We hated ourselves for not being able to protect him. We took hours to say our goodbyes, it felt like minutes. Leaving Henry in the room was incredibly painful. We left our hearts and love of life in that room.

Mum, Dad and Anthony's brother held us and helped us gather our things. Then we went home. It was a long and painful drive. I was numb. Only hours ago we had been sitting by Henry's bed confident of his progress. The thought of leaving Henry in a cold room alone distressed us. We wanted to organise the funeral quickly. As with so many other things over the last thirteen days, we had no idea of what to do. We never thought that we would have to organise our son's funeral. I called a local funeral director and made an appointment for the next day.

The next day the funeral director brought around a small urn decorated in teddy bears. She was very gentle with us, and helped us through the possibilities. Anthony and I had discussed everything, and decided upon an unattended cremation and a memorial service. We chose an outfit for Henry to wear and gave the funeral director a musical toy and a gold angel to be cremated with him. That night Anthony and I prepared a service that celebrated Henry's life and showed how much we loved him. It was our job as parents to do the best we could. We asked Anthony's brother and a dear friend to read for us at the service. They were invited over and together we read their scripts. My parents wrote a beautiful letter to Henry and offered to read it at his service. We were so thrilled that they wanted to share such a personal letter.

On the morning of the service it rained, but the sun somehow managed to shine between the clouds. Family and friends filled the chapel. We were astounded by the number of people who attended. I could hear continuous sobbing from every direction. Although difficult, the service was beautiful. We were rich in support. The roller coaster was still roaring, emotional highs and lows welling up such confusion.

Anthony and I had made plans to scatter Henry's ashes at Warrnambool. We had wrapped the urn in a bunny rug and I held it tightly in my arms. The urn moulded to my body. It was the longest time I ever held Henry. We arrived at Warrnambool and located a favourite place of ours. It was a mountain overlooking a lake and the ocean. We walked to the top and laid down flowers. We wept as we scattered Henry's ashes and said our goodbyes. We sat there oblivious of time, only noticing the day was ending by the sun sinking behind the mountain. Eventually we had the courage to say a final goodbye and started the walk down. I was awash with feelings of abandonment. Anthony pointed to some ducklings bobbing for food in a river. He said the most reassuring thing: 'Look, this is a place of love and life. It is a place of families and birth. This is the place for Henry.'

I face real fear every day. Fear that I will forget, fear that I am unable to live a happy life and fear of losing my sanity. My whole world has collapsed around me.

Our family and friends had so much trouble dealing with our grief. We were new people, sad people. Most admitted that they didn't know what to say or do. Some people had so much trouble they avoided us. We were so appreciative of those who continued to say Henry's name and wanted us to talk about him.

There were great acts of kindness and compassion. People would go out of their way, showing initiative, not waiting for the reply to 'If there is anything I can do.' Some friends rang almost daily; one cooked us dinner; another wrote a poem; Anthony's sister created a needlepoint; my brothers planted trees in Henry's memory; some friends sent cards and flowers on Henry's due date; a family friend prepared all of the food for after the service and our florist donated all of the memorial service flowers. We were also given rose bushes to plant in our garden. We were pleased that people were acting on their hearts.

Having a son born prematurely in a traumatic birth, hearing a life-threatening diagnosis and watching Henry undergo treatment and losing him has changed me, my perceptions, my relationships and so much more. I have come to the following conclusions.

I am still a mother even though my son is not in my arms. Maternal instincts don't just go away. Most people don't know how to cope with grief. They don't know what to say or do.

Friends become strangers and strangers become friends.
Some days I cry a lot, some days a little, but I still feel the same on the inside.
Some days I am better at juggling my emotions.
Grief makes me say what I think in half the time.
Anthony continues to grieve with me. He needs me as much as I need him.
I respect that he grieves differently to me.
I am vulnerable.
I hate the roller coaster.
I shouldn't feel guilty when I smile.
I shouldn't push myself too hard.
Sympathy cards soon get replaced by bills.
Everyone you tell has a story to tell.

Not everyone is a good listener.
It's not fair, it's not right and we didn't deserve this.
I wanted to be normal again but didn't know what normal was.
Being sad isn't selfish.
I had to pick up the pieces of my life and learn who I had become.

Still numb with disappointment, Anthony and I made the decision to have more children. We felt such guilt when we admitted that we wanted another baby. We talked to each other about how we felt. We didn't listen to people who said 'Wait.' We didn't listen to people who said 'Do it straight away.' We listened to our hearts and each other, and started trying to conceive when we were ready.

We somehow thought that having another baby would be like replacing Henry. It wasn't. We thought that by having another baby, we would be closer to forgetting Henry. We couldn't. We wondered if others would think another baby would be an answer to our grief. It didn't matter what anyone else thought. We decided not to tell others of our plans to have bubba two. We felt our lives had somehow ventured into public property and we wanted to have some space, some privacy, some time to ourselves.

After a pregnancy that seemed to last longer than nine months I gave birth to a healthy baby girl on 26 December 1999. That first week was very emotional. I waited for someone to come and take her away. I looked into her cot in amazement that she could breathe without the help of life support. My heart was filled with so much love and at the same time so much pain.

The roller coaster rides continue to rush us through so many ups and downs, so many highs and lows and so many twists and turns. Here we stand, dizzy, disorientated, without our son but with a happy, inquisitive little girl. We made it through hours that we thought would never pass, and through days and weeks when we thought it impossible, but we did it. People have often said that they doubt their own capabilities to make it through such a tragedy, but I always make the comment that this was not my choice. It has taken a lot of hard work and sheer determination to keep moving forward and not to allow myself to immerse myself in the bitterness that comes with grief.

It's two years on now and I wonder where the time has gone. I wonder how things might have been. What would Henry look like. Would his eyes be brown like mine? I have too many unanswered questions and only one photo album filled with the memories of a special child who inspired me to be more, to think more and to do more.

Unlike the dream-filled school girl, I can't imagine where we will be years from now or how we will be feeling, but whatever we do I know we will be missing our son, thinking. 'Henry would have . . . Henry should have . . . Henry could have . . .'

Forgiveness

I am Lucky

ANNIE ROBERTS

At the age of twenty-one, the world was my oyster, or so I was led to believe. I was in my final year of a primary education course. I was free and happy.

Suddenly, my world was shattered. My once respected and hard-working father was arrested and jailed for his involvement in a six-million-dollar heroin deal. Six federal police searched my home and interrogated my mum, while my sisters and I sat in the lounge room contemplating our future.

There were to be a few changes in our lives, including more financial responsibility for the family and weekly visits down to Parklea or Long Bay jail.

I was looking forward to beginning a new year as a twenty-one-year-old. However, the year did not begin as I had hoped. My grandfather passed away on 1 January after being ill for some time. Two weeks later, my mum had a life-threatening asthma attack. My sixteen-year-old sister and I had a doctor and four ambulance men striving to keep Mum alive. It was a relief in a way to see Mum settled and safe in the Intensive Care ward, breathing easily. I reluctantly kissed Mum goodbye and told her I loved her, which is not something I usually say, but I'm glad I did.

I was going away to a Rotary Camp for a week for a gathering of young people who had been captains and prefects in school. I suppose I was happy for the distraction, yet felt uncomfortable being away from home.

I rang Mum on Tuesday when she was discharged from hospital, and she sounded tired. The next piece of information took me by surprise; Dad had suffered a massive heart attack and was in Blacktown Hospital under prison guard. Mum went on to explain that she was going on the train the next day to visit him. I was worried about Mum going down so soon after being in hospital herself.

The next day I kept myself busy organising an activity. When I went to the office to ring home, my friend Ruth was at the door. The look in her eye told me there was something wrong. 'Is it my dad?' I asked. 'No,' Ruth said. 'It's your mum. She died!'

She had had a severe asthma attack on the way home and had collapsed at Blacktown railway station. I lamely repeated the message, my mum's dead, my mum's dead. I don't know if I was trying to convince myself of a truth I could not begin to comprehend.

So there I stood the following day, in a hospital that had my dad upstairs attached to a heart monitor – and handcuffs, and my mum downstairs in the morgue.

That was thirteen years ago.

I have had to learn to live with the pain and loss. I have learned to live with the fact that my mum did not see me get married or get the chance to meet my husband or future children. But I cannot change what happened.

I have always tried to find positives in a difficult situation. Fate can really knock you off your feet. I never thought in my wildest dreams that I could ever describe myself as lucky. But now I do.

I am lucky because I am completely and utterly in love with my partner of thirteen years. I have a job I love. We live in a beautiful, peaceful part of the world. I am grateful for the life I have now, after going through the usual depression, guilt and blame phase.

I have learned to talk with my mum in a spiritual way, just in my head. I am open to the signs in life that tell me she approves or supports the decisions I make. As for my dad, he served nine years and died in August 2000.

At the absolute worst time in my whole life I never thought I could feel lucky, but I can honestly say I do feel lucky and appreciative of the life I have. It is a common thought that there are always people worse off than you. You have little control of your destiny except to find positives.

Reflecting on a major event in your life, years later, is scary because you are entering a world that caused you great pain and sadness. However, if you then look at how your life turned out and the direction fate took you, it can be quite bizarre. You ask yourself did I suffer such grief to fully appreciate an amazing level of happiness?

My life took a particular path and I met my husband, best friend and life companion, all in one man. Yes, I am lucky.

The Burden of Forgiveness

CAMERON SCHWAB

When you are a kid, you don't have much cause or reason to give your surname. Those who need to know it do, and a child's life is such that they are rarely required to divulge this piece of information. You are simply Cameron, your mates are Davids, Craigs, Gregs, and generally there is more than one of each. Your whole identity is locked up in this single piece of information.

Mr Stratton, our Under-10 football coach at Essex Heights, used to write our given names up on the blackboard when selecting the teams. There was no need for surnames, even though there were names that appeared on the board more than once.

We had two Camerons in the team, but the coach did not have to explain which of us was playing where. The other Cameron was one of our better players, and was generally named in the centre, whereas I was more likely to find my name consigned to the back pocket.

I would sometimes pretend to myself that it was me who was named in the centre, or the pivot as Mr Stratton used to call it. This was a carefree time, when ability was irrelevant when it came to ambition. Imagination meant everything.

The other Cameron was certainly one of the coach's favourites. By mid-year the other Cameron became Cam. I stayed Cameron for the rest of year.

I cannot recall exactly what time of life I stopped becoming Cameron, and became Schwab, or Schwabby to my mates. I think it was in my late primary school years when I crossed the ire of one of the older male teachers, who asked sternly, 'Schwab, who do you think you are?'

Most of my mates went through the same transformation, and those innocent first names were lost as young children metamorphosed. The lucky ones simply adopted derivations of their surnames. There were a few Maccas, Smithies and Hutchies, a couple of Mitches and a Nicko. The less fortuitous were given names that resembled their unfortunate body compositions, features or functions. Among my group of mates we had a Puddin', a Snozza and a hapless Captain Stinky. I guess I was lucky to be Schwabby.

By the time we got to the Under-13s these nicknames were all on the blackboard, and even the coach became known by some extraction of his surname.

However, some things never change. I had made the back pocket my own. Ability was beginning to overhaul ambition.

It was around this time that I realised that my surname carried with it a special significance. I was picking up a prescription for Mum down at the local chemist, when the pharmacist looked at the name on the script and looked down at me and asked, 'You any relation to the umpire?'

I knew enough at this stage to know that my Uncle Frank had umpired a VFL Grand Final, and I answered the question accordingly. He then asked, 'You any relation to the bloke at Richmond?' I could answer this question with greater certainty, because the bloke at Richmond was Alan Schwab, my father and Secretary (as they were then called) of the famous Richmond Football Club. Once again I answered the question politely, puffing my chest with a sense of pride.

The pharmacist grunted and returned five minutes later with whatever it was I had come to collect. He handed over the package and some advice.

'Tell your old man to sack Tom Hafey, he's past it. Put Francis Bourke back on the wing where he should have been left in the first place, and tell Neil Balme to get a haircut, he's a disgrace.'

That evening I passed on the chemist's pearls of wisdom to Dad, and waited for the response. I thought he would get angry with the chemist; after all Dad doesn't tell him how to pack his shelves. But he just looked at me and smiled and said, 'He's right about one thing, Balmey does need a haircut.'

From that point onwards, my own identity and that of my father were linked. Whilst Dad was not a politician, or even a famous athlete, he had a burgeoning profile in a game that captures the passions of an inordinate number of Victorians.

And the game had captured my passion. I loved it, and continued to love it well past that day of reckoning when I realised that I would never make it out of the back pocket. I was never going to be good enough to play at the highest level, but in no way did that dilute my obsession for the game that was to become my life and my career.

I could live out this obsession every day. Dad would come home, most often late in the evening, and I could hear first hand whether or not Royce Hart's knee had recovered sufficiently to take on the Blues that weekend.

I was just so proud to be Alan Schwab's son. I carried the surname around like a badge of honour, flashing it whenever the opportunity arose, and often it did. He was my hero.

My hero died seven years ago, suddenly, aged fifty-two, in a hotel room in Kings Cross. He would not have liked the way he died – it was so unnecessary. But he did, and we carry on. We also carry on but with a burden: the sadness that never leaves you. The fact that you still need a father. The fact that you still need a hero.

The burden of grief, not just your own but of others. I shared the loss of a father with my sister and brother, and we did what we could to support each other. But I also shared Alan Schwab as a hero with hundreds of others.

I found myself being invited to functions and get-togethers that Dad would have attended but I was not entitled to attend in my own right. For a couple of years I became a proxy Alan Schwab. They could still have their Schwabby.

We learn from death as we do from life

None of this left a lot of time for me to grieve in my own right; I was too busy grieving on behalf of everyone else. This was one-way grieving, and in many ways I was just too sad and angry to grieve anyway.

Now, I am not sure what I miss most, the father or the hero. Perhaps they have always been so inextricably linked that I do not know the difference. Most of the time, having your own real-life hero was more important. If nothing else it made me a very charitable child in terms of my expectations of Dad as a father. As I grew older I became far less charitable, and I judged Dad harshly.

We learn from death as we do from life. That is perhaps my greatest lesson. Heroes and fathers are indeed human, and they have human failings. They make mistakes. I have now learnt to forgive.

I am a man now, and I am also a father. A life replaced. My son's name is Lachlan, but I am sure he will be Schwabby one day, and he will have to work that out for himself. I hope he wears the moniker with pride, as I did. More than anything, I hope he also learns how to forgive.

A Different Start

CAROL ROJO

I have a very vivid memory of being huddled in a circle on the footpath with the neighbourhood kids. I was about eight at the time and we were sharing secrets. My friend said, 'My dad has gone. He lives in another house.' I said, 'My dad isn't my real dad.'

I didn't have a good reason for this, just a feeling. I always felt different.

One day my mother told me, 'Your dad isn't your real father. Your father is Italian, that's why you are so dark.' I remember feeling confused by the other kids' taunts: 'You're dirty . . . your skin is brown, we're not playing with you!'

Shortly after this my mother had her first breakdown. She went away. I felt guilty that this was happening because of me. I had feelings of isolation and abandonment. Why was she leaving me?

This was all too much for an eight-year-old. I would fantasise about my biological father rescuing me; all I wanted was to feel loved and secure. My mother would never tell me his name and through my adolescence we never talked of him, as to me the pressure seemed too much for her to bear. Although I thought of him often during the years, having my own family seemed to fill the gap; however, I still had this void.

Finally I decided my mother owed me the chance to work through this myself. At the age of forty-three I could wait no longer and I asked her for his name. I couldn't believe it when she told me. It was all so simple; I found his name in the telephone directory, listed under a business. Adrenalin pumped through my veins as I picked up the receiver to dial.

His secretary answered. She said he was out and could she take a message. I left my name and phone number. During the next few hours I felt high with anticipation and fear as I waited for his return call. The phone rang. I found myself trembling with excitement as I listened to his voice miles away. We talked and I asked if we could meet. He replied, 'With all my heart.'

I wept for joy over the lost years, I was walking on cloud nine. We arranged to meet at a certain place and time. I couldn't wait and finally the day came. While waiting with anticipation many things crossed my mind. Was he really going to turn up?

My heart was pounding as this handsome man approached me. It was hard; my mind stopped working. All I could do was stare at him. Over lunch I asked many questions so at last the puzzle finally took shape. That afternoon came and went too quickly, and every day I think how lucky I was that I had the courage and encouragement from my husband and family to pursue this life-long desire to meet my biological father. The bonus was I also really liked him.

Better to Have Loved and Lost

JULIE AUNGER

I met Kim, the love of my life, when I was fifteen at a coffee shop in Rundle Street with my sister Suzanne. He was so good looking, a champion swimmer and his reputation was hellish.

Three months later he rang and asked me out. It was a holiday weekend and everyone was away and he said I was his last hope. Flattering! I fell in love with him that day and have never stopped loving him.

We were passionately in love for the first few years of our courtship. Often he'd have to stop the car and kiss me passionately, making me tingle all over with desire for this beautiful young man. He said he'd love me forever and one day we would marry.

Kim and I were engaged when we were twenty years old and we married in October two years later. Shortly afterwards we had our two wonderful children, Nicole and Craig.

But there was a flaw in our happiness; Kim attracted women like 'bees to a honey pot'. Beautiful girls and friends fell in love with him and flirted and he, being a man with a large ego, had many affairs. A couple of times he fell in love and left me, but he always came back vowing his lifetime love.

Kim was an excellent father and loved being with Nic and Craig. He taught them not to fear life, to be their own people, and to have a go at everything. They had so many wonderful adventures with their dad and he taught them to waterski and snowski; ride horses, motor bikes and push bikes; and drive cars. He taught them to enjoy sport and be strong.

Following many tumultuous years, both personally and financially, Kim and I became relatively settled in our relationship and continued to share our mutual love of our children. Eventually, we were fortunate enough to build 'Garfield', our dream home, together. 'Garfield' is my paradise, my life's dream. It is such a special place.

One Saturday night my daughter, my son and his girlfriend, Sally, had just finished dinner when the doorbell rang. My mother, Joy, was standing at the doorway with her hair standing on end. My heart sank. I knew there was bad news. I could read the sadness on her face and her body language was one of great despair.

'What's happened? Is Dad all right?'

She told me that Kim had been killed that afternoon in his helicopter with another friend Lesley Sangster. I screamed and my body went into shock. The grief overwhelmed me. The man I had loved and who had been my life for thirty years was dead. My strength, my protector was dead. The father of my children was dead.

Somehow you survive tragedy and life goes on.

I wanted to keep the business that Kim and I had started together for my son to take over after he finished university, so after the funeral I went to the office every day to learn all about the business. The general manager (who became CEO) of the business and I had always been wary of one another and now he and his wife, who had been Kim's secretary, were very resentful of me as they considered that the business belonged to them.

Over the next few years the company never reached budget and eventually outside auditors were appointed. Unfortunately, they also proved to be incompetent and never really informed the shareholders of any concerns.

In March 1998 I was called in by the bank to put up my beautiful home 'Garfield' as collateral for the company as there was a huge cash flow problem. I was devastated because my home was my security for my old age, and I had owned it mortgage-free.

Unfortunately, despite my son's efficient crisis management and his ability to reestablish the business, the company ran out of time. The damage of ten years' bad management and thieving had taken its toll and the company went into liquidation.

I was horrified to find myself in this situation, particularly when I had trusted supposed professionals and, on some occasions, friends. As a widow, I felt vulnerable and at the mercy of ruthless businessmen who were only there for their own gain.

The last few years have been bad for me. I attempted suicide and felt that I couldn't go on. But recently a dear friend has shared her Buddhism with me and I have found the teachings of the Dalai Lama to be logical. They show the truth about reality. Every day I meditate and I try to awaken my ignorant mind.

I am learning about attachment and how to let that go, that everything changes and that death is part of living. I am now happy and enjoy watching where my mind and thoughts can take me.

Letter to a Son

BRIAN BELL

Dear Brian,

I am your mother, and I have just come through childbirth for the third time. You are the result.

The doctor held you up in his hands, smacked you on the bottom and said to me, 'It's a boy and he's got a bad foot.' You won't know how much having no toes on your right foot will affect every part of your life, because I will blame myself for it and carry the blame so deeply that you will not even know it's there.

Across the road some children have been playing and one just called out 'Brian', such a nice name!

The doctor will tell your father that he is not to smack you, so all the anger he is carrying from his own father will come out as emotional abuse. When you are four, he will not only smack you, but pull you across the floor by the ears, or the hair, punch you in the shoulders until you feel the pain there all day long, and verbally abuse and threaten you.

I, being only a mother, will sadly have to stand by and let all of this happen.

Don't expect any Christmas or birthday presents from us, for we are not at all rich. And anyway, as Jehovah's Witnesses we are not allowed to believe in those pagan rituals. If you need clothing around these festive times, however, we may buy it and call it a gift. This may confuse you.

At school you will do extremely well, but you will be badly treated by the teachers and students. There will be one teacher who understands you and in his class you will score 953 marks out of 1000, the highest in the class by a wide margin. This, of course, will not be good enough for your father. Being left-handed will be another heavy cross for you to bear because it will mean your writing will be criticised. (If only they knew!)

Because I was brought up in the Depression, you will listen well when I tell you that you have to save money. At seven years of age, you will overhear me tell a visitor that you 'are a good little saver' and you will think that this is the first time anyone has ever said anything nice about you. Of course it is not, but as we can't say nice things to anyone's face, you are not to know that. And hearing it will make you save even more, becoming a slave to possessions and money. This will help to make you think that you are successful.

Most of your cousins are girls and have been brought up to think that they are better than boys. You will not feel good in their presence, until one day, when you are nearly forty-seven years old, you will meet a cousin who has travelled the same road as you and come to the same truths that you will come to. She will tell you of her memories of how cruel your father was to you, and her validation will be good for you.

You will marry at twenty-four to a woman who was molested by her mother's father, but she will not tell you that. You will have a son and then a daughter. When your daughter is sixteen, your marriage will be swiftly falling around you, but your daughter will see the change in you and you will share a closeness that she has never had with her mother.

She will reveal to you that a cousin molested her at the local swimming pool when she was younger. In the following two weeks you will learn about your wife's similar history and also my own, with my brother raping me when I was very young.

By some strange linking of coincidences and with your heightened awareness, you will be contemplating all the things that have happened in your life and you will lead yourself back to a belief in God, denied for twenty years. This God will be different; accepting rather than wrathful, part of everything rather than separate from everything.

A few months later you will go to a party held by people from a co-dependency group. There, you will be talking to someone about loneliness and that man will do you the greatest favour. He will tell you not to eat, drink or otherwise medicate your loneliness; rather, to go home and sit in it. That night you will write your first serious poem.

Four years later you will win the Henry Lawson Award that I always coveted, and this will be but the beginning. Some weeks after you accept the prize a woman will come up to you at a dance and say, 'A couple of years ago you gave me some of your poems and when I finally got around to reading them I realised that I was not alone. This changed my whole life.'

This sort of feedback will keep you on your path and it will happen regularly, and to you it will mean more than any statue or award.

Further along the way you will write a poem called 'Colours' and when you send it to me I will jealously tell you that it is inaccurate. But whenever you recite it, people will feel the love in the poem in their own way.

That's about all I can tell you for now, but beyond my not being able to understand you in those later times, I pray that you will find your own place in this world.

With as much love as I know,

Your Mum

Turning Point

DEBORAH GRAY

My mother took her own life. I found her. In the following weeks I wondered how I could ever erase such a shocking memory. I dreaded going to bed and, worse, waking in those tortured early hours.

News travels fast; extraordinary kindness arrived from the most unexpected places. A friend wrote a note suggesting that when one door closes, a window opens, the first sign of faint optimism.

One morning, my mother came to me in a dream, her face so vivid, no trace of pain, the most radiant euphoric smile. She looked at me with such love, then turned and walked through a door.

Since that dream, I have been filled with an amazing inner peace, a positive belief. I treasure my good health and believe each day is precious, but the greatest gift I have been given is I no longer worry about things that are simply not important. I am happy within.

I feel so lucky. Thank you for this gift that had eluded you, Mum. Somehow I believe you had something to do with it.

Wisdom

Madeleine's Country

JOHN LEARY

Back in the mid-seventies I was serving at the Aboriginal mission at Daly River when Geelong artist Gerry Dingeman was visiting the North with his two teenage children. Just by coincidence there was an Aboriginal family visiting at the same time, and they wanted to go back to Port Keats. I thought it was a good chance to show Gerry a bit more of the Territory, so I got out the four-wheel drive and everybody hopped on board.

There would have been about twenty of us jammed in that jeep. The Aboriginal family was made up of about five or six adults and a host of children, including eight-year-old Madeleine. Madeleine was the typical Murinbata kid, skinny, alert, lively, with a 'dream-time' depth in her eyes. She was there with her mother and grand-mother, her aunts and cousins – in their culture: Family.

Straight away everyone got on well. Being an artistic type, Gerry was a person of great sensitivity, with great interest in people, and in many ways rather a poetic person.

Of course, by the time everybody was rounded up we left later than I expected. What I wanted to do was to detour off the Keats track about 20 kilometres to Kurapink, which is a sizeable creek at the foot of some rocky slopes. Somewhere up in those rocks was Popungala, a remarkable cave with its ceiling completely covered in Aboriginal paintings. I knew this would make quite an impression on Gerry. Little did I suspect the impression it was to make on all of us . . .

As I said, we left too late to make Popungala before nightfall. So we decided to camp on the banks of Kurapink, which we reached at about 5 p.m. The women used branches to sweep the ground clean as they usually do, so that no snakes or scorpions would creep up on us. I had shot a kangaroo earlier and it wasn't long before we were sitting down to a four-star meal.

That night Gerry got onto all sorts of questions about Aboriginal customs and legends. The old lady particularly told many dream-time stories that even had the Aboriginal kids enthralled. Gerry reciprocated by telling Dutch stories – the boy with his finger in the dyke, and so on. Then they started dancing, and Gerry and his kids did some Dutch dances, and this went on till the early hours.

After boiling the billy next day we took off into rather dense scrub. We reached the foot of the Macadam ranges, left the jeep at the bottom and climbed into a shallow valley. The kids were running everywhere, climbing over rocks, having the time of their lives.

We had climbed into the range for what must have been about twenty minutes and were getting towards the top, when suddenly Madeleine just stopped. She began calling out in a high trilly voice at the top of her lungs.

She called out who she was: 'I am Madeleine; I am the daughter of Djakul . . .'

Then I realised what it was all about. It should have occurred to me: Djakul was one of the owners of this place. This was his country, and since country is always passed down patrilineally, this was Madeleine's country too. But not the country of any of those others there, even her mother, though they were all from the same extended family.

Everyone stood still. (Gerry said afterwards he came out in goose pimples all over. I didn't tell him I did too!) This little voice, clear as a bell, vibrant with intensity, calling out her name, her father's name, and all the ancestors she knew. This place was, after all, their country too, and their spirits were here all round us.

She walked on ahead. I didn't realise we were so close to the cave. She walked around to the right and there it was – quite a big cave, with a high ceiling, and all of it painted in the most breathtaking shapes and colours: sun's rays, fish, turtles. There seems to have been some kind of chemical reaction over the years, centuries really, and you can't rub off the ochres. They've become sort of glazed.

Madeleine wouldn't go into the cave. She walked out onto a ledge just around from it, overlooking the Moil plain with the sea in the distance, and she just stood there with her little chest out and arms back. She must have stood there for about five minutes in that very proud, commanding attitude, and we stood there watching. Then suddenly she relaxed and came back and joined the group, as though nothing had happened.

We took photos of that beautiful place, but as far as Gerry was concerned, of all the sights that day, Madeleine standing looking over her country was the one that took hold over all the others. His painting was one of those creations he just had to do.

My Journey

DIANE DEEMING

My first home was memorable: one room in a condemned tenement building in Glasgow for my parents, my baby brother who slept in the bottom drawer of the dresser, and me. We were poor – but so was everyone else.

We had no hot water or electricity; we were always cold and often hungry. When our school shoes wore into gaping holes, Mum would stand us on a piece of cardboard, draw around the shape of the shoe and make insoles.

We ate the basics. The humble tattie could be tortured into so many appetising dishes, and we always had chips. Bread and jam was a wonderful filler and a pot of soup could be watered down to last a week.

With the arrival of my second brother, we moved from the slums to the luxury of a council flat on a housing estate. Both my parents worked, so being the eldest I had to shop, clean and prepare the evening meal. I also had to take one brother to and from school, and the other to a relative to be minded before I could go to school. This involved two buses and sometimes a three-kilometre walk, regardless of the weather.

I left school when I was fifteen years old. There was never any question of furthering my education, I had to get a job and contribute to the household budget. I had a wonderful diversity of jobs and would try anything. I was skilled at nothing, but always managed to bypass the long dole queues in a depressed Glasgow economy.

My family left for Australia on an assisted passage in 1965. I planned to join them the following year. I was nineteen and in love (for a while). Six months later I was involved in a car accident. I had numerous leg and arm fractures and was in traction for three months. I only just escaped being an amputee.

As soon as it was medically allowable I paid my ten pounds and departed for Australia, arriving in Melbourne on 4 January 1966. The moment I limped onto the tarmac at Essendon Airport I knew I was home. What a country – all that lamb – and so cheap!

I joined Ansett Airlines in 1969. For my interview I wore a yellow wool dress four inches below my buttocks, two hairpieces and two sets of eyelashes. I dabbled with the truth somewhat by saying that I had excelled at school with numerous A levels, but unfortunately I had no proof or reports as all records were destroyed when the school burned to the ground!

I got the job and stayed with Ansett for twenty-eight years. During this period I married a handsome, charming English soccer player. Unfortunately, his looks and charms were irresistible and I divorced him in 1976. I worked predominantly in the sales and marketing area for Ansett and talked myself into a newly created promotions manager position, which I developed by trial and error and loads of 'front'. I was the 'Profile Person' for Ansett.

When I was forty-three, to my utter disbelief, I found myself pregnant.

I confided this to only a few close friends. I was only twenty-three weeks into the pregnancy, when during an early morning sales meeting I had pains and spotting. 'Nuisance,' I thought, so I left my office for an hour to visit the doctor. My cervix had almost completely dilated and my daughter was on her way into the world seventeen weeks early. I was rushed to hospital.

My baby was given a three per cent chance of survival. I was confined to bed for eleven weeks – my one-hour absence from the office extended to six months. In the halls of industry it was rumoured I had been taken to hospital with . . . a nervous breakdown? . . . Cancer? . . . Asthma? . . . A baby? 'God, she's too old!'

On 19 January 1988 my life changed forever – 'Hello Maryanne!' My return to the work force would have been even more difficult had I not been so enamoured of my little girl. She was perfect, a real battler. I worked predominantly with men, and I think to this day that they were embarrassed and didn't know what to say. Although one woman did give me a lovely patronising pat and said, 'Well, dear, you still *look* the same!'

It wasn't easy, but then what is? I was on my own with a family to support. I coped, I juggled and I balanced. Maryanne had every possible minute of my time and Ansett had the rest.

I elevated myself above the gossip and innuendo and went full steam ahead as before, only now I wasn't as available for after-hour functions or the 'up front' stuff. It was thought I would fall apart with the pressure, this middle-aged woman who had gotten herself pregnant, and a single mother to boot!

But I pushed myself harder and the more I was excluded, the more I challenged. I wasn't the favourite daughter, but that was just too bad, I needed the job.

When Maryanne was two years old I was offered another position with our office in Adelaide. I packed the car with clothes, toys and the baby, and we arrived in South Australia in January 1991, knowing no one. It was difficult trying to break into this community. Being a sole parent, I was not readily embraced. I advertised in the local paper for someone to pick Maryanne up from care, which would allow me to break into the Adelaide networking functions. To our great fortune, we found Mrs Low, a wonderful woman who became a grandmother figure for Maryanne for many years.

I left my career at Ansett in 1998. Not to pursue other interests, or for health reasons, or to tour Australia in a four-wheel drive. I left Ansett because it was time for me to go, but I will always be grateful for the little, fat, bald executive who had a passion for yellow wool dresses, hairpieces and false eyelashes.

I look back with great fondness and gratitude at the events that form the learning curve that is my life. I continue to grow, taking on new challenges and grasping opportunities along the way. I may never have had a college education, but my school of hard knocks ensured I was well equipped with an abundance of common sense. Everyday I am thankful for my daughter, my health and the wisdom to make decisions that enhance my life. We get only one shot at this life. *Make sure it's your best shot.*

A Life Set with Challenges

GAI WATERHOUSE

My life as a horse trainer has been a very fulfilling one: thirty-seven group one winners; a New South Wales trainer's premiership; five Doncaster Handicaps; five Metropolitan Handicaps; a VRC Derby winner; two Magic Millions winners and over 150 black type races. That I would train nearly 1000 winners since I took out my licence in 1992 was once only a dream, but I can safely say my dreams have turned into reality.

Despite my success, I have endured along the way many challenging situations, which have taught me a lot about people and myself.

I was brought up in Sydney, the only child of Tom (known as Tommy) and Valerie Smith. In that lies a story in itself, but I have always felt privileged to have had them as parents. My father in particular was, prior to his death in September 1998, a mentor and inspiration in every facet of my life. He was a determined man who, in his lifetime as a horse trainer, won every major thoroughbred race on the Australian calendar several times and won the Sydney trainer's premiership a record thirty-four times – thirty-three of those in a row. Being such an ambitious person, he may have been seen by many as demanding; however, I can unashamedly say I was the apple of his eye and he would do anything he could for me. (That was good and bad growing up as a strongminded young girl, as I probably got my way a little more than I should have.)

I never realised I wanted to be a horse trainer until I was in my thirties. I had always toyed with the idea of being involved in racing and I often helped out at the stables during the holidays. However, when I finished my final year at the Convent of the Sacred Heart in Sydney, I went to the University of New South Wales to take my Bachelor of Arts majoring in theatre as my ambition was to pursue a life in the theatre. This was much to my parents' dismay as my father thought acting was not real work. On one occasion he came to see me in a play in London, he could not understand why I was involved in such an industry, yet he was still proud of me even though he didn't like what I was doing.

When I returned from London I worked in the media and continued acting, securing roles in Australian soap operas.

In my late twenties I married my husband, Rob Waterhouse, who was from a famous Sydney bookmaking family, and we subsequently had two children, Tom and Kate who are now nineteen and seventeen.

Prior to taking out my own licence in 1992, I was Dad's foreperson at his stable Tulloch Lodge, assisting with the training of a large string of horses.

In the 1996–1997 season, four years after I was granted my licence, I had trained ten group one winners, which many thought remarkable as I had been training for such a short period of time and had only a small number of horses in work. In many ways I could not believe how easy it was and couldn't understand why everyone didn't become a horse trainer. However, it did not take long for things to change. Around 1998/1999 my stable hit a lean patch. I couldn't work out why the winners had decreased. Even Rob was asking me why I was not training the number of winners that I had previously. Many people were critical of my lack of two-year-old winners. It was time for reflection and re-evaluation.

It was the same time that Dad died. He was my mentor and advisor, and suddenly he had gone. It was a difficult time for me. Rob took the family overseas to have time together to reflect. It was at this point in my life I came to the decision to follow the advise of my father.

I started to think about all the things he had told me that I had not paid attention to when he was alive. It was an invaluable time, as it was the turning point in my training career.

My life has thrown up many challenges, and will continue to do so. It took a tragic situation such as my father's death to make me value his advice. His philosophy was to train horses as athletes and to get them really fit before starting them in a race.

This season 2000–2001, which ends in July, will be my best ever, so far having trained 146 city winners and 204 in NSW alone, and goes close to emulating Dad's remarkable season of 1975 when he trained 156 city winners.

It's Never Too Late

DOUG MALOUF

Dreams and hopes are funny things. As adults we're told they're important, yet as children we were smacked about the ears and told to 'stop dreaming and get on with it'. Some adults never outgrew that syndrome. They're still getting the metaphorical smack around the ears and told to stop crying for the moon. And that's a catastrophe.

My story may not have the emotional impact of many others in this book, but I sincerely hope it can help someone realise that it's never too late to chase and catch your dreams; it's never too late to learn something new and it's never too late to change. My story is about how I stopped losing and started learning.

I have to admit I had a bit of a mental block about learning during my school days. I had it all figured out. You started school at five and during the next ten years you learnt the basics like reading and writing. You did as little maths as possible – well, I did anyway

– and avoided as much history and science as you could manage. To add some spice, you constructed a few unidentifiable objects from wood and metal, did just enough homework to keep the folks and teachers off your case and failed final exams in style.

Was I worried that I didn't get straight As in every subject? Of course not. I'd fulfilled the minimum government requirement and I had a job to go to. Life was about to really start. School had simply been somewhere to go to keep me out of Mum and Dad's hair until I grew up. And at fifteen I was grown up. I pretty well knew everything about life. At least life in country Canowindra . . . Safe and predictable.

I began work with Dad in our country store. He was a good storekeeper and by the time I was twenty, I too, was a good storekeeper. Dad insisted on values and service, and I'd embraced these, and at that ripe old age considered my education was complete. That was until Mum and Dad did the unthinkable: they sold up and we moved to the city.

Suddenly life was very different. The safety and predictability of the country was no longer there as a backstop. I got a job and was still selling, but my confidence was taking a beating. The skills I was so proud of weren't the skills I needed in the city.

I moved around trying to fit in and going nowhere fast. I was standing still. And you know what they say about standing still: *everybody eventually passes you, so in effect you've gone backwards*. It was a very bleak time for me.

Then two things happened. The first was when I turned to real estate. Now remember this was in the sixties, and industry training programs such as we have now were virtually unheard of. And I must also be honest and say I can't tell you that this decision to have a go at real estate was a deliberate career move. It was more like a drowning man clutching at a toothpick to stay afloat. I really still had no idea where I was going or why.

The second hit me after four weeks of dealing with the public. When the customer knows more than you do – you're in trouble. The problem was – well, I didn't know what I didn't know. It's a state called unconscious incompetence. You're lousy through ignorance. That was me. Now I was not only unhappy, but afraid and way out of my depth. And flat, dead broke. Something had to give . . . *Me!*

It's been my experience that no matter how much adults say they want to change, it rarely happens because they want it to. Adults change because something happens to make them change, usually a crisis. That's what happened to me; I was in crisis. And there was only one answer: education. I had to educate myself. I had to change.

There's one good thing about hitting rock bottom – and that is if you hit hard enough you might just bounce. It's that or lie there and wither away. I bounced and the propellant that kept me moving upwards was a mixture of fear and desperation. You can laugh about the proverbial light bulb and how long it took me to find the switch, but by now I knew that to survive I had to be as good as I could be at this job – and that it had to be more than a job.

I enrolled in a correspondence course on real estate. For four years I diligently wrote assignments and posted them away and then anxiously awaited the responses. And you know what? I realised I was enjoying learning. I could see where it connected with my life and my needs. I was moving forward; I wasn't losing any more – I was winning.

Now that I knew where I was going I couldn't wait to get there. So, next came a Real Estate Valuation Certificate course – and from there I just couldn't seem to stop myself – I had to have more. I read every book directed at self-learning that I could get my hands on. And then I discovered audio tapes. What a motivational joy! I found myself starting every day listening to the great achievers of life, absorbing all their wise advice. And it was paying dividends. I was becoming more effective in my work and more confident in my life. And believe me – any teacher I'd had through those ten gruelling (for them!) years of school would never have recognised me. I was hard pushed to recognise myself as the same person, and that's probably because I wasn't really. So many of my attitudes and habits had changed and all because I'd finally had the sense to realise that the more knowledge I acquired, the more successful I became, and not just in a financial sense – in a complete sense.

I suppose that's why at forty years old I found myself signing up for university. And for this episode of my formal learning I was going to be a real student, not just a backside on a seat taking up air space.

Just as long as you keep sight of your dream

But I also learned that the actual 'learning' wasn't enough. I had to apply it. That application saw me develop my own real estate chain, develop my own speaking business, my own books, manuals and tapes and my own training systems that have taken me all over the world.

So, what is my message? That I'm a legend in my own bath water? I hope not. My message is: change rarely happens because we'd like it to, but usually when it's forced upon us. But even then we've got choices and I believe we're never too old and it's never too late. For me personally, education is no longer a burden I have to carry – it's carrying me.

And the great news is that it doesn't have to be all formal. Just getting out to observe and mix with the high movers in your industry to see what works and what doesn't will be worth a dozen university degrees. The point is, it doesn't matter. Just as long as you keep sight of your dream, gather every bit of knowledge possible to help you to get there – and learn to duck. The ear-whackers will still be there, you just need to step out of their reach.

Bush Fathers and Sons

A.R. Morrison

In the summer of 1967, at 'Oolambeyan' station near Hay, I saw a ghost. Not a misty apparition, but clearly a man leaning against the mantelpiece with one foot hooked across the other, smoking a cigarette, his free hand tucked into the side pocket of a Donegal tweed sports coat. It was my father, who had been dead for ten years.

He was a true bushman, a sheep station manager for over thirty years, variously at Richmond and Blackall in Queensland, and Broken Hill and Warren in New South Wales. For all those years this quiet and reserved man carried in his wallet a frayed letter on buff military paper.

> No. 615, Sergeant J. A. Morrison, C Company, 23rd Battalion, A.I.F.
>
> This NCO acted as platoon sergeant during operation near Beaurevoir, east of Peronne, on the night of 3 October 1918.

> He displayed extraordinary coolness and courage under heavy machine gun and artillery fire. By his example, he was of invaluable assistance to his platoon commander in getting the men through the enemy barrage and on to their objective. On reaching the objective, he made a valuable forward reconnaissance in daylight.
>
> His tireless energy and excellent conduct were of the highest standard and acted as a great incentive to his men.
>
> His Majesty the King has graciously approved the award of the Military Medal.
>
> (Signed) J. C. Robertson, Brigadier General, commanding Second Division.

We hardly knew one another. Like many bush children I had gone to boarding school at ten, then spent five years jackerooing in the back country. We lived lives apart, and contact was desultory. Our relationship was one of mutual respect, even pride, but formal and restrained; deeper feelings were never articulated nor emotion shown in those times.

In 1956 I was managing a sheep stud operation south of Narrandera, and Dad had come out of bored retirement for a six-month spell as relieving manager of 'Oolambeyan', itself a merino stud about two hours drive away. The conventions of the time were such that no stud man would ever step on to a competitor's property. So we spoke on the phone, but nothing more.

Then a mutual friend arranged a meeting when we were both in Narrandera buying station stores. It was just an hour or so of drinks at the New Criterion Hotel, where we chatted happily about the trivia of station life – the country, the season, stock and wool markets. But it was the first and only time we ever spoke on a man-to-man basis, and it was great fun.

The next time I saw Dad was a few months later at Concord Repatriation hospital, where he lay dying as a result of his World War I injuries. He could hardly speak, but struggled to rasp out, 'You're young. Don't waste time.' Just that, and no more.

Five years later I found out more about the man I briefly knew. Barty O'Donovan was a tough little station handyman and bush carpenter who divided his time between 'Oolambeyan' and another Hay district station. We met by accident in the village of Carrathool, and he told me of Dad's arrival at 'Oolambeyan' in 1956. Barty was last in line for orders, and when Dad detailed him off to repair gates, Barty quipped, 'Understood, sarge.' Being an old-style station manager and something of a martinet, Dad was quick to put him in his place, and heated words were exchanged. Then the penny dropped – Barty had been 'C' Company runner, and the two had not seen one another since 1917. I asked what transpired. 'He did the right thing, son. He stood me aside, we hopped into the ute and spent the rest of the day in the Carrathool pub.'

I visited Barty once a year for the next few years, and each time we went through the same routine. He offered me a rum, and as we contemplated the first sip he would look up at the ceiling at an angle of forty-five degrees and say in a sombre voice, 'Your Dad's crossed over the great divide.' I would nod, and he would go on, 'Never forget the last time but one I saw him. It was hopping the bags at Villers Bret, and he said, "Can you make it, Bart?" and I said, "All the way, sarge . . ."' The story would vary each time as to location – ranging from leave in Cairo to a café in France. Then Barty died.

So when I visited 'Oolambeyan' in 1967 for the first time since Dad was there it was an emotional event. The manager and I were sitting in the homestead breezeway yarning quietly and having a few beers. I looked up and saw Dad, looked up again and he was gone. It was an illusion induced by a combination of tiredness, emotion and beer.

I was young at the time, busy, in a hurry and going places. The message was there for me to pick up but like many young people driven by ambition, I only partly heard it. Relationships and people are there and then they are gone. You only get one opportunity. Make the time, make the best of it and keep talking. I hope my sons, for better or worse, know me for what I am, and we have the opportunity to know one another as men. I know for sure that we have to work at it.

Willing to Change

MARGARET PORRITT

Life keeps moving and you constantly need to change and adapt along with it.

I was married at nineteen, had three sons by the age of twenty-six and was divorced at thirty-two. I was left to support myself and rapidly discovered the many trials of single parenthood.

To support my boys and maintain some sense of sanity, I took the bull by the horns and became an employer rather than an employee. I saw it as the only way to re-gain independence after a twelve-year marriage and a bitter divorce.

I purchased a small fashion boutique in the west end of Melbourne and within three months opened a second store. For ten years I retained just these two stores and built a strong reputation in inner-city Melbourne. I was a true success in my own city and I didn't even know it.

As my sons reached their teens and became more independent

I opened another six stores. The secret of my success was always to listen to my customer and add value to their lives.

When the recession hit in 1989 I was in the wrong position at the wrong time with the wrong product. I had experienced amazing success for twenty years where everything I touched turned to gold – this was about to change.

During the recession my gut instinct told me that it was not the economic downturn that had altered my business results, it was me. I had stopped listening to my customers and I no longer focused on adding value but on making money. Sometimes success can be like a drug. The more you have, the more you want.

There's an old saying – 'For things to change, first you must change'. Nothing could have been more pertinent at this time in my life. I knew for my business to survive I first needed to rebuild my team. We had lost a number of staff due to difficult financial times so I had to work with a small team of twenty-five.

We proceeded to engage in New Age Training and, from a personal perspective, I shifted 180 degrees in the way I ran the business. It went from a totally autocratic business where no one made a decision but me, to one where I learnt to say, 'I don't know, what do you think?', and to empower my team to have ownership and responsibility around the business.

While learning to let go I realised that there was still a role for a strong leader. However, genuine leadership is not about disallowing choice, creativity and decision-making but encouraging all these traits that bring job satisfaction and pride.

In the years between 1990 to 1995 I sold my house and mortgaged all my assets. To me, my house was a dead object but my business was a living, breathing entity that needed all the investment I could give. My only focus was on what I needed to do for my business to survive.

Between 1992 and 1995 I opened twenty shops and closed twenty-one. Through this process I managed to consolidate in six prime locations. By 1995 I had the right team and the right position but still the business was haemorrhaging.

The same year I launched Feathers by Margaret Porritt, a label developed from listening to my customers and adding value to their lives. We ensured clothing was supplied in a wide size range and would suit any woman, from full-time mother to full-time worker. The magic was back. And the winning formula was our team, our product, our focus and our location. However, we were still missing one ingredient – marketing.

We ventured into a marketing campaign in 1996, with myself on billboards, posters and in our shop windows stating, 'I couldn't find them, so now I design them.' I might add, this was not a pleasant experience for someone like me who does not even like having her photo taken. When you are fifty-five and size fourteen it is very hard to see pictures of yourself all over town.

The positive response to this campaign showed that I had finally given my customers exactly what they wanted and needed – honesty and a designer who endeavoured to truly understand their needs.

It is life's way of giving you a tap on the shoulder

The business has continued to go from strength to strength with stores in Sydney and a diffusion label, appealing to a younger market, that was launched with unbelievable success.

The reason Feathers stopped growing was because I had stopped listening and, while the world was in revolution, I refused to adapt to change and did not read or see the signs.

As soon as you begin soaring on the high of life's success, things can just as easily come crashing down. From experience, I have learnt that this happens when your focus shifts in the wrong direction and you are unwilling to change. It is life's way of giving you a tap on the shoulder. Accept your mistakes, swallow your ego and move on. And remember, adapt to change at all times.

The Lesson

David Bardas

When my father died suddenly, I left my law studies at the University of Melbourne to join the family business of Sportscraft and Sportsgirl. I was twenty-three, untrained and with no experience in business or the fashion-retailing industry. Looking back now, I describe myself as 'not knowing what I didn't know', which was probably an advantage.

Our advertising agent at the time was a man named Cy Cater, who handled other small retail and fashion accounts. One day I was in his small cubbyhole of an office sitting in on a job interview. The job applicant said he 'had done Commerce'. Cy asked, 'Yes, but did you finish it?' The applicant replied, 'No,' to which Cy said, 'Well, don't talk about it.'

From that brief exchange I got the message that if you didn't have the persistence, discipline or courage to finish something, then you didn't have the right to talk about it as a qualification. So I slunk away and reopened my books and reapplied myself to the unfinished law degree. I finished it part-time even though I never had any intention of working as a lawyer.

Mick Hull, another of my mentors, further reinforced this message of how important it is to complete a task once you have started it. Mick had been a squadron leader in the air force, and was, in the early 1960s, joint managing director of the company. Mick gave me a small book called *A Message to Garcia* soon after I started work with him. It was about a forward scout going behind enemy lines to deliver a lifesaving massage to a comrade, and being told, 'don't come back unless you deliver the message.' Mick's message to me was that in war you lose lives, not just profits, if you don't complete an assignment. The principle is the same.

Years later, I read John Bertrand's inspirational book *Born to Win* after his crew won the America's Cup from the Americans for the first time in over one hundred years. Before the last deciding race the score was three–all and John was already a national hero. As John pushed off for the final race after years of training and practice, his wife, Rasa, said to him, 'You haven't won anything yet.'

For me, these words simply reinforced Cy's message of some forty years earlier – that you haven't achieved anything unless you successfully finish what you start.

Open Your Eyes

DANIEL JOHNSON

I studied civil engineering back in the 1970s at the University of Vermont in America. I was one of many others who had no idea what to study. I was good at maths and science so I took the advice of my parents and went into engineering for no other reason than, as my mother said, 'You'll be able to get a good job when you graduate.' The fact that I wasn't interested in engineering never entered the selection equation.

So I spent four long years struggling through a degree that I neither enjoyed nor found of any interest at all. That didn't stop me from studying hard, very hard, because the subjects did not come easily to me. So I learned plenty and became quite proficient in civil engineering calculations.

I was a sophomore (second-year student) and Bill was a first-year graduate student in the business school. We became good friends. This was very unusual. He was several years older than I and the only graduate student I knew. We both had a passion for skiing and met one day on the slopes of a small ski resort, Mad River Glen, not too far from the University. We spent many days over the next two years skiing together and riding the chairlift back up.

We got to know each other well. Bill told me about a most unusual question on one of his first exams in graduate school. It was an industrial psychology course. All the questions were essay format and very complicated, except the final question. The professor asked, 'We have all been in this department late in the afternoons and seen the woman who cleans the department. What is her name?' Of course, Bill thought this was a sign of the professor's unusual sense of humour and wrote, 'I don't have a clue.'

When the tests were returned, Bill along with every other student in the classroom lost credits for not knowing the woman's name. An upset student challenged the professor, saying, 'How could you possibly reduce our scores on such an unnecessary question?' 'On the contrary, it was the most important of all the questions. The theory we learn in this course will be of no value unless you get to know and care about everyone you work with,' was his response.

Needless to say everyone in the class learned the woman's name. That professor made an impact.

I never even met the professor and he made a lasting impact on me. That was one of the most important lessons I learned in all four years at university. Here I am in the year 2001. I work at a company with 150 employees and I am the only person who knows every single employee on a first-name basis. I also know many of the carpenters and painters who have been remodelling our offices recently. Showing I care about others has taken me further and farther in life than any textbook theory ever could.

I am now a specialist in what most organisations call 'human resources'. I prefer to say 'people'. I realise now that of the many reasons I am in the 'people business', one is because I have applied that one lesson every day since I learned it on that chairlift at Mad River Glen, Vermont.

One little story, one big impact.

Wisdom on a Tram Ticket

GEOFF MUIRDEN

About forty years ago, when I was a teenager, Melbourne trams used to have little philosophical gems, only about one line, printed on their tram tickets. They don't do that now, and haven't done it for many years, but maybe someone in the tram section back then was a philosopher and wanted to enlighten the masses, making his little contribution to our welfare. We should be grateful to this unsung hero for making our lives just that little more enlightened.

One tram ticket had this brief motto: 'What you think upon, grows'. As I've grown older, maybe in some ways I've also grown wiser, and it's now possible for me to see how much is packed into this little snippet that slipped into the unconscious mind. Maybe no philosophy department will call for its students to write an essay on that saying, but it's packed with meaning.

It means we attract to ourselves the kind of thoughts, feelings and experiences that suit the way we align our thoughts. A stamp collector, for example, will come across stamps all over the place while the unobservant, not alerted to this hobby, would never notice.

Those of a semi-mystical bent have coined the adage: 'As within, so without', meaning that what we really believe in our inner being becomes actualised in the outer world.

There's the old saw about the pessimist looking at half a glass of his favourite liquid and saying, 'It's half empty,' and the optimist looking at it and saying, 'It's half full.' The irony is that both are right, depending on their own frame of reference.

You may have had the experience of being in a school where fellow students mocked any slowness to understand a lesson or a question. You may have felt mocked when saying something in public that the teacher or fellow students thought was stupid. They didn't have to say it out loud, it was just a feeling.

What you think upon grows

Maybe you think I'm rambling from the points but I'm not. When I look back, sometimes in anger, sometimes in sadness, at my anti-learning experiences in school, I remember the tram ticket adage: 'What you think upon, grows'. As a hapless student I was being encouraged to think upon how inept and stupid I was. This created a conflict between the desire to know – since it's natural to want to learn – and the unreadiness to risk being ridiculed.

What you think upon then becomes a conflict and creates anxiety that can be resolved by either going for it with the grim determination to get through it – crash through or crash – or by making the best of learning and resolving to be gentle with yourself even if others aren't.

When older people face new challenges and try to avoid them, maybe they have a distant memory of their schooldays when they tried to learn something new and failed or were mocked for trying. That's when they can retrain their thinking and let the love of learning grow instead of the fear of failure. They need not regard failure as death blows. Thomas Edison tried over a thousand times to make a light bulb before he succeeded, and every time he failed, he said he had learned another way that wouldn't work. He's the same man who said: 'Genius is 10 per cent inspiration and 90 per cent perspiration.' He may not have travelled on a Melbourne tram or seen the tram ticket but he knew that 'What you think upon, grows'. Instead of listening to a little voice in his head that jeered and sneered at failure, he chalked it up as one more failure on the road to success. So can we.

And the last word: what I thought upon grew into an article for this book. What you think upon may create a new and better life for yourselves and others. Go for it.

Childhood Dreams

MAUREEN WEINER

When I was a child, I had my dreams –
Magic castles in the air.
I could be whatever I wanted to be –
No matter what my looks or capabilities,
Nothing was impossible.
I could fly through the skies, conquer the world.
I was the beautiful princess.
There was always a prince charming to fight the dragons,
There were always fairies and magical beings at the bottom
    of the garden,
Always that pot of gold.

And then I grew up.
I learnt that if you wanted a castle, you first had
To build the foundations and lay the bricks.

I learnt that the only reality was what you saw in the mirror
each day,
What could be numbered and counted,
Named and valued.
I learnt that the only treasures worth having were those in
the bank.
I learnt that fairies only live in story books,
That there are no demons –
And there are no knights in shining armour.
I learnt about life.

And, now that I am growing old,
A strange thing has happened.
I have once again found my dreams.
I realise now that my dreams are my realities,
That my true reflection lies, not in my mirror,
But in the way I lead my life.
I know that the best place to build castles
is in the air.
And I know that the things of value
Are not those that can be measured or quantified –
They are qualities like love and compassion.
I know that demons do exist –
They have names like hate and greed.
I know that the magical beings still live in my garden –
You call them Nature.
I have once again found kindred spirits –
My shining knight.
I have learnt to fly.

Inspiration

Say 'Yes'

EDDIE MCGUIRE

When you are a kid growing up, most of the time people tell you what you can't do. Don't touch that. Don't say that. Don't do that. Not many people ever tell you what you *can* do. It takes courage to say 'yes'. It takes very little thought to say 'no'.

When you say the word 'yes' you are taking on the responsibility of making something happen. 'Can you open the door?' 'No.' Then you sit down and continue what you are doing. 'Can you open the door?' 'YES.' Then you have to go to the trouble of getting up and dealing with whoever is there. But who knows what might be waiting.

I had a saying when I was a young reporter that you never get a story sitting at home. You have to get involved, make things happen. I have always thrown myself into projects with passion but also with optimism. Problems are challenges. Successes are springboards to bigger things.

I was lucky when I was a boy. I grew up in Broadmeadows and

my parents constantly gave me positive reinforcement and took an interest in all areas of my development from sport to music to education – everything that I did. As a family we were all intimately interested in what each other was doing and we actively supported, barracked for and protected each other. Despite all this, like everyone else, peer group pressure takes its toll.

When people outside your family circle are telling you that you can't achieve, that you shouldn't do extra training, that you were mad for doing your homework, that you had to know someone to get anywhere in life, it wears on you. When you start to achieve but receive criticism instead of praise you question yourself as to what it's all about.

Luckily for me I attended a pie night at the St Dominic's Under-11 football club when I was nine years of age. The guest speaker was a man I didn't know much about until it was explained to me that Alan Killigrew was a former North Melbourne and St. Kilda football coach, that he had been wounded in the war, that despite being small in stature he was a rugged rover when he played, and that he was best known for his rousing addresses. Naturally, to a boy aged nine, any man who had played football was a god. That he'd also coached took him, in my eyes, to an even higher plane.

When this bent old man stood up to speak I didn't see a bloke past his prime with a curved spine, nor that his head was cocked at a strange angle I saw two eyes that burned with enthusiasm and life. I saw a man who had seen plenty in his time but still had a love of life. His body may have been world weary but his soul was young.

He launched into a rousing speech, and his salient point is as profound to me today as it was back in 1974. Killigrew said, 'What ever you do in life, try and be the best at it. It doesn't matter that you don't ultimately achieve your goal but that your goal is to be the best and that you do everything in your power to achieve it. It doesn't matter whether it is studying, playing sport, being with your family or sailing paper boats down the gutter after a downpour, always try to be the best you can be.'

At a time when I felt that so many people from mates, peers, teachers and the media were telling me, 'No, you can't do that,' here was a man who was telling me it was my duty to try hard. It was my duty to try to win, and there was no shame in defeat if beaten while giving of your all.

Later I came across a speech by the US president Teddy Roosevelt. It was known as the 'man in the arena' speech. It was not too different from what Killigrew was trying to say.

> 'It's not the critic who counts: not the man who points out how the strong man stumbles, or where the doer of deeds could have done them better. The credit belongs to the man who is actually in the arena, whose face is marred by dust and sweat and blood; who strives valiantly; who errs, and comes short again and again, because there is no effort without error and shortcoming; but who does actually strive to do the deeds; who knows great enthusiasms, the great devotions; who spends himself in a worthy cause; who at the best knows in the end the triumph of high achievement, and who at the worst, if he fails, at least fails while daring greatly, so that his place shall never be with those cold and timid souls who know neither victory nor defeat.'
>
> *Theodore Roosevelt*
> Citizenship in a Republic;
> Speech delivered at the Sorbonne, Paris, 23 April 1910.

To me that says it all.

Olympic Flame

GINA RENNIE

I am trying to encourage my children to live life and not just to watch it; to be spontaneous and adventurous and to grasp life by the hand.

During the 2000 Olympic Games held in Sydney, I became more and more inspired as I watched athletes from many countries stretching themselves to their limits. I was overwhelmed at their courage and perseverance, and was pining to let my family feel and touch the Olympic spirit.

We saw and embraced the opening ceremony on a large screen with twenty other people and I could see the children's eyes light up at the wonder and splendour of it all. There was our wonderful Olivia Newton John singing, our faster than fish dolphins swimming, our artistic and athletic champions putting on the best show on earth. I was so proud that our large island, with its relatively small population, could produce so many exceptional athletes. When Cathy Freeman won the 400 metre race, it was the final impetus for me to join in a world for once united in a joyous cocoon of movement and mass.

We were very stretched financially but I decided that somehow we would get there. Late one night I told my four children to pack their bags, as we were going on an adventure. At midnight we left to travel the 870 kilometres from Melbourne to Sydney, arriving the next morning with the children full of excitement after sleeping peacefully for the whole trip. I knew that we couldn't stay long so I decided that we would pack as much activity into our day as we could. I wanted my children to see the Olympic flame that had come to represent hope, endeavour and a united world.

Sydney had gone all out to make its transport exceptional and its new double-decker trains were luxurious. As we travelled from Sydney to Homebush, sitting next to athletes, spectators and volunteers, it felt as though we were going on a joyride; people of all nationalities were discussing the dips and highs of the events they had been to or participated in. When we arrived, the children nervously protested, 'Surely we can't go in there, we don't have tickets.' 'Don't worry,' I told them, 'we'll ask if we can go and have a look around Homebush.' In true Olympic spirit we were told that of course we could explore.

We sat and watched the Olympic flame and I talked to the children about what it meant. I told them that I hoped its flame would always keep their hearts warm and that its spirit of achievement would always inspire them to achieve their best. I told them I hoped they would have the confidence to believe in themselves and in some small way help the world to be a better place so that one day the world would be united in peace. We heard the roar of the crowd inside and I felt that we didn't even have to be inside at the events. The life spirit of the 100 000 people inside cheering was all around us. We were there!

That night we travelled as far out of Sydney as we could to find budget accommodation, hoping to pack in a full day of activities the next day. I had managed to get reasonably priced tickets to one event, Greco Roman wrestling, which was to be held at beautiful Darling Harbour. We woke early the next morning, leaving our car at a station some way out of Sydney.

The wrestling was raunchy and fun and we all felt very international having the events announced in French first. Next to us sat a Canadian family with four children. The parents were working as teachers for a year in Australia. Around us were Americans, Chinese and many other nationalities, waving their flags and cheering. After a simple lunch spent peering out to Darling Harbour, we got fully into tourist mode and inspected the huge tourist boats perched on the bay, took the monorail around the city and saw athletes we recognised. That's when we saw a very tall Chinese athlete who was the longest person I have ever seen. Everywhere excitement, enthusiasm and a feast of international fervour struck us.

Later that night we drove back to Melbourne, napping on the way as we got tired. To our family, the long drive there and back was worth it. We will always remember that we were a part of the Olympic Games and our lives will always shine a little brighter for it. We know that if you want something hard enough, just maybe your dreams will come true.

Celebrate Living

NADA GLAVIC

Don't accept your existence, rather celebrate your living
On a journey to finding yourself,
On a journey coming home to yourself;
Our relative self is our body, mind and soul.
I used to exist, now I have a life to live.
As your body needs food so does the soul,
Feed it and you will be fulfilled;
Life is for living, now get on with it.

Open your eyes, heart and mind

Open your eyes, heart and mind and you will see,
feel and learn
Life itself is beautiful, it's people who ruin it.
I've met a lot of people and now I've met me;
Don't wait for opportunities; create them yourself.
If you never sow the seed, you will never pick the fruit.
Do not worry needlessly about the things
you cannot change,
Rather put effort into things you can.

You Make Your Luck

JOHN KNOWLES

I was a country boy, born in Murchison, Victoria. When I was nine years old, my father brought the family to the city as there were more opportunities in the 'big smoke' for his three sons. By the time I was ten, I knew exactly what I wanted to be – a carpenter, cabinet-maker, builder. I'm sure my earliest recollections of climbing over floor joists instead of playing with coloured blocks like most three-year-olds helped shape my future. I was driven by a fierce desire to achieve, not necessarily financially, but to overcome the challenges of my limited education.

When I was seventeen my father gave me a thirty-five-feet frontage block of land in Rosebud, a favourite Melbourne beachside holiday destination. It took a long time to save enough money to build my first small spec house, a weatherboard holiday home. My brother Graham and I worked all hours of the day and night to finish it. Eventually we sold the house for the princely sum of

£2260, and continued to build and spec our own homes on the Peninsula. In total over the years we must have constructed and sold about twenty houses.

During this time the building business was booming all over Victoria. I realised that to continue doing well I had to locate areas that would be suitable for new homes, so I chose North Balwyn and later Ivanhoe. This was quite risky but both these areas worked in our favour.

My next venture, and my first marital home, was built on twenty acres of land we purchased in Mentone. We subdivided and developed it over the following four years. Following this I purchased land in Brighton where I built the home that still houses my family to this day.

In 1974 we had a dream to create a special place where older people could retire and live a great community lifestyle, rather than become isolated in their own homes. Our first retirement village was built for the Frankston Baptist Church; we built seventy units, which sold so quickly that we had to build another sixty. This was the first privately owned retirement village in Victoria and only the second in Australia. To date we have completed close to 3000 units around Victoria for older Australians.

It's not all been easy. There have been many frightening times when we thought we would lose everything, but we believe in what we do. Perhaps my success is an example of the 'Little Aussie Battler' high work ethics: integrity, inspiration and lots of perspiration!

My greatest satisfaction is in knowing I have done what I pledged to do as a schoolboy from a humble working-class background with limited education.

I've enjoyed all the good things that go with the success, but I've enjoyed and appreciated far more the things that money can't buy, such as the priceless friends who stick with you through the good times and the bad.

The Game of Patience – Thai Style

JAYE WALTON

At the beginning of 1960 the fickle finger of fate traced a flight plan from London to Adelaide. At that time Australian travellers were still sailing with the British, Italian and Greek shipping companies much more than flying.

If the flying choice was made, it was necessary to have at least one stop-over in the Orient. I was travelling alone as a young married woman, but I was not at all in fear of the unknown. In fact when I was young my father was employed by the British India Company and we had spent many years exploring Eastern cultures.

When the airline manager suggested that I stop over in Bangkok, the spirit of travel and adventure that I had inherited from my parents took control of my planning. Today my choice would still be the same, and truly as Omar Khayyam says, 'A single step can lead to a journey of a thousand miles.' In my case that first step and my first visit to Bangkok has dominated my life and led to a journey of a million miles.

On an April day in 1960 the weather in Bangkok was extremely hot, as I now know it always is. It was very dry and the sun was burning bright. Tourism was only beginning at that time in Thailand, and in my ignorance I accepted a hotel reservation for a centrally located hotel. Today I would insist on a riverside hotel, as the mighty Chao Phrya River acts as a lung in the often polluted atmosphere of this huge, throbbing city.

I joined three other tourists for a sightseeing tour, which culminated in a visit to the Grand Palace, including the temple of the emerald buddha. It was a public holiday on this day, and the king of Thailand, King Bhumpipol Adulyadej, was due to change the raiments on the emerald buddha. I found myself surrounded by a sea of people, all sitting quietly on the ground, mainly in the shade of the pavilions. No one was pushing or shoving or talking in raucous tones. These people were waiting quietly for their adored king to perform a traditional ceremony.

I had discovered Thai patience. It dominates and controls every aspect of Thai life. Everything does not have to be done *now*. Everybody does not walk at top pace all the time and people do not shove and push to be first. Thai patience seems to enter one's thinking by an osmotic process; suddenly we are aware of it and if we are sensible, we try to emulate it.

Nowhere is patience more obvious and indeed essential than in the creation of indigenous Thai handicrafts. In 1976, after continually travelling throughout the kingdom with her husband while he was introducing alternative crops to opium and planning much needed irrigation systems, Queen Sirikit began talking with the women living in the provinces and discovered the handicrafts that were part of the everyday lives of these people.

In the north of Thailand the hilltribe people were adept in

cross-stitch designs. In the north-east the women wove the most complicated geometric designs into pieces of silk for everyday wear, and in the south, a particular swamp grass was used to make basket-wear for daily use.

Her Majesty had the foresight to realise that without strong encouragement, these indigenous handicrafts could slide into oblivion. Furthermore, the queen was aware of some of the difficulties experienced in these far-flung rural areas, caused by draughts or floods and the resultant crop failures. All the talents of these poor farmers' wives had to be garnered and used to increase the family income.

Her Majesty founded the SUPPORT Foundation: the letters represent supplementary occupations and related techniques. The Foundation began in the north of Thailand where Her Majesty selected fifty people to be trained in the preservation and production of the Northern Handicrafts, working under a canopy in the gardens of Bhuping Palace, on Doi Suthep mountain, a little above Chiang Mai.

Today throughout the Kingdom, 50 000 members of the SUPPORT Foundation, under Her Majesty the Queen, are working in the production of exquisite products, while, at the same time, increasing the family income and improving their quality of life. These people would otherwise be poor and insecure.

Her Majesty travels throughout the year, spending two months or more in each location. Adjacent to each of the palaces, training centres have been established and during the periods of Her Majesty's visits, teachers from outlying villages have the opportunity to extend their own talents, in 'Train the Trainer' schemes. This enables them to return to their villages and further train the villagers, ultimately giving them opportunities for increased incomes.

While residing in each area, Her Majesty makes almost daily visits to outlying villages by sturdy four-wheel drive, bump-defying vehicles, or where necessary, by helicopter. Seated on a cushion, on a mat on the ground, at a low table, Her Majesty talks with villagers, paying them cash-in-hand for their handicrafts, as well as paying them for being members of the Foundation. There is no middle-man in this finely tuned operation.

If it were not for Her Majesty's foresight, these exquisite indigenous handicrafts would have disappeared and farming families would be much poorer. The delicate character of Thai handicrafts depends on patience; patience to weave extraordinary Mudmee silk; to create the finest needleworks of art; patience to make Liplow fern-vine handbags and baskets, or to weave krajute reed mats and patience to create superb delicate pottery.

Whenever a visitor travels to Thailand, efforts should be made to find the local outlet for SUPPORT handicrafts. Once a year at the beginning of December, for people unable to visit the Provinces, a huge SUPPORT Foundation sale is held at Amporn Gardens. It is here that the purchaser needs patience as the crowd is overwhelming, but patience pays off and shoppers are delighted to have this opportunity to buy all the multitudinous handicrafts of the Kingdom without leaving Bangkok.

Living, working and laughing with Thai people, and spending very frequent visits throughout the Kingdom, I have seen the results of this cultural attribute of Thai people – patience. This patience, combined with the ever-present Thai smile (not necessarily because the person feels happy, but because they want you to feel happy), dominates every aspect of Thai life.

No, of course I'm not patient – I just try harder!

Go for It!

PETER MCGRATH

Like most Australians I got caught up in the atmosphere of the Sydney Olympics and thoroughly enjoyed the performances of the athletes. When the Paralympics came along, I decided to take the opportunity to keep this exciting atmosphere alive and attend these games.

I had limited knowledge of the Paralympics and the various categories of the athletes. I went to a variety of events and was impressed by the accomplishments of all competing, but there was one athlete in particular who touched me.

I was watching the swimmers prepare themselves for a heat in a 100 metre amputee race. A number of athletes needed to be assisted from their wheelchairs into the pool.

In this race was a young female who had no arms or legs. I remember wondering how she was expecting to compete. But when the gun went off I was amazed to see this young lady swimming in a snake-like motion. I don't recall which country she came from but if you had heard the roar from the crowd when she finished the race you would have thought it was an Australian winning a gold medal.

For the record she finished third in the heat but as she was assisted out of the pool I was drawn to her face. It was wreathed with a huge smile.

Thinking of the difficulties in life that this young lady had to overcome helps put life's problems in perspective. Yet many people, whose difficulties in life are minor in comparison to this athlete, are prepared to give up so easily. Here was someone who had made the most of her opportunities and as such was now representing her country.

This unknown athlete showed me what inspiration was. Now any time I feel that I can't complete something and have the urge to give up, I recall what she was able to achieve. Inspiration can come from the most unlikely of sources.

When Florence Met the Queen

As told by Florence to Dr Janet Hall

Florence Houghton is a public speaker, seasoned traveller and remarkable human being. Now aged ninety-five, she is still 'adding life to years' in taking advantage of experiences that most young people would find daunting. These include parachuting, flying in hot-air balloons, doing aerodynamics in RAAF World War II planes and driving with Peter Brock in his racing car at 200 kilometres per hour.

Florence has always been a fan of Queen Elizabeth and here she recalls her lucky break in life when she was seventy-eight and actually met Her Majesty.

In 1983 I was staying in England. I wanted to see as much of the country as I could, but since I was on a pension, I had to do things on the cheap. I bought a little book called *Away from It All – 135 Retreat Houses and Monastic Buildings to Stay In* by Geoffrey Gerard. However, my plans to stay in the cheapest accommodation

I could find were quickly changed because of a chance meeting.

I happened to meet Mr Peter Wright, chief almoner for the Queen, who was in charge of giving money to the poor on Maundy Thursday. He suggested that I travel to Exeter where I might have a chance to see the Queen.

I took the train to Exeter and I was lucky to find a lovely bed and breakfast with white curtains and a red geranium in the window. It was quite expensive on my meagre budget but I was determined to see Her Majesty. To cut costs, when I was given a big breakfast I ate only the egg and tomato in the morning and I saved the sausage and bacon to get me through the day.

I was disappointed on the first day to find that I was not allowed into Exeter Cathedral because they were preparing for the next day's royal ceremony. However, I did manage to see into the guildhall where the Queen was to have lunch. The walls and ceiling had been decked in hessian which was completely covered by a superb collection of flowers from the typical English garden. I was amazed and delighted. No painting could have exceeded the beauty of that floral spectacular.

Next day I stood behind the barrier with the rest of the crowd and saw the Queen and Prince Philip getting out of their maroon limousine. On either side of the path where they walked were schoolboys in short knickers. They were holding bouquets of daffodils shaped in the letters of the Queen's name.

The Queen disappeared for a while – perhaps she went to the Vicar's house for a cup of tea or to spend a penny – and I kept waiting, hoping to get another glimpse of her.

She eventually reappeared and began to walk past the crowds to chat with a lucky person or accept a posy. I madly waved my flag of the Union Jack and called out, 'Your Majesty, Your Majesty.' To my delight she came over to me and said, 'You must be from Australia.' (She had recognised my accent.) She offered me her gloved hand and held my hand for the whole time of our wonderful conversation. She asked me what part of Australia I lived in, and when I told her that I lived in Melbourne she said, 'My son, Prince Charles, and his wife, Princess Diana, are visiting there now.' I replied, 'Yes, I know, Your Majesty. I moved out to make room for them.'

Well, the Queen threw her head back and laughed out loud.

She then asked me where I was staying in England. When I said that I was hoping to use the little book to find my accommodation in ecclesiastical places, she turned to her lady-in-waiting and asked her to purchase her a copy. The Queen then wished me a blessed and Holy Easter and a safe return to Australia.

Next port of call for me was Paddington but when I knocked on the door of the retreat house where I intended to stay the nuns said that they had no vacancy. Kindly, they offered me tea and helped me find another option. They found me a place where the nuns were committed to be in complete silence until Easter Monday. When I arrived, they wrote on a blackboard to ask me if I had had my supper.

I actually enjoyed the silence on Good Friday as I had a well-earned rest after the excitement of meeting the Queen. On Easter Saturday, the nuns shared a big fruitcake and as they cut it big chunks of almonds fell out. This was the only time the silence was broken. One of the nuns whispered, 'I'll have the fallen almond bits.'

The nuns were from the order of the Community Resurrection of Our Lord and I was delighted on the Monday when they shared Easter presents. There were four tiny eggs and a card on my plate. The card had been recycled from an old card; it had a purple tassel and a purple Iris painted on it. I have long lost the card but I never forgot the prayer that was on it.

Look to this day for it is life
The very light of life
For yesterday is already a dream
And tomorrow is only a vision

But today well lived
Makes every yesterday a dream of happiness
And every tomorrow a vision of hope.

I've never forgotten it and I always think how true it is.

Eventually, when I returned to Australia, I wrote to the Queen and told her that I so enjoyed meeting her and that I had returned safely to Australia. Her lady-in-waiting wrote back and said that the Queen remembered me and wished me well. I also wrote a thank you note to Peter Wright and told him how I had met the Queen thanks to his suggestion. He wrote back and said, 'London will never be the same without you, Florence.'

Florence finishes her story with a gleam in her eye: 'How's that! Haven't I have been the luckiest person ever!'

Note
Florence passed away suddenly in April 2001. Her ashes were scattered from a RAAF helicopter over Port Philip Bay. Florence would have loved to have known that she would make her last adventurous flight like that!

Leading the Way

JOHN WILLIAMS

'In the face of what I thought was extreme suffering and injustice, the Papunya people seemed to have a positive view of life. They played games, sang songs, painted pictures; there was a real sense of soul in their relationships and community. It was like all the stuff we have, all the materialism was stripped away and the really important things were left. And yet there is enormous tragedy in their lives: their living conditions and their physical condition are terrible. It seems that all people need to enrich their souls, no matter what their material circumstances. They need to build an enriching culture to survive, but this doesn't make injustice and exploitation acceptable.'

These were the words of Helen Scotford talking about her visit in 1999 to the Aboriginal community in Papunya, Central Australia, where there is a World Vision health care program.

Helen is an associate youth minister at St Stephens Church in

Belrose, a position in which she brings creative arts into worship, evangelism and community programs. Helen, aged twenty-two, says she is endeavouring to discover how creative arts can break through people's insularity, so that they can feel the injustice in our society, and be moved to do something about it. She believes that creative expression is a vehicle to heal people's emotional wounds.

This has been Helen's personal experience. Her process of healing has come through her creative expression, and the healing has brought strength, sensitivity and determination for her. Helen recalls her pain from around the age of fifteen. She had been actively involved at school in interschool Christian fellowship, leading prayer groups and using drama, dance, poetry and song in worship. Helen had had dancing and music lessons from the age of five, and she brought all these talents to the expression of her Christian faith.

But it got her into trouble. She was labelled a fanatic, her parents thought her priorities were all wrong. She was neglecting her academic studies for her faith, and following her heart, not her head. Instead of being encouraged and supported, she faced strong opposition. She felt devalued and invalidated. After two years of challenges Helen, in Year 12 at school, began to feel and see her pain. She was trapped and she had to escape.

It was after she arrived at St Stephens in that same year that Helen found the safe place for her healing to begin. Helen found the freedom to worship without being constrained; it was safe to cry, people prayed with her, she had loving friends and carers. It was the beginning of her transformation.

Early the next year Helen was suffering from depression, but she didn't know it. She went for two weeks without sleep, and then one morning around 3 a.m. her soul cried out and she wrote a song, which she called 'Faith'.

Through the darkness of night
I reach to grab your hand
When there's nothing left to hold onto
For I'm holding to your promise
That some day you'll return
And the pain will be no more

For you are my strength
When all my strength is gone
You give me joy when my feelings have run dry
You breathe new life right through me
Like a mighty rushing wind
For still, you are God.

And she slept. She had let go, realising that no matter what she experienced or felt, 'Still, you are God'. This is the beginning of faith. The song 'Faith' was included on a worship CD which St Stephens produced in 1997. It is a beautiful and moving song, with wonderful lyrics and music, and has been a source of comfort to many people.

Helen had started university in 1997, studying to become a social worker, but she couldn't cope. Her depression had led to physical illness and debilitation, and she had little energy. At the end of the year, she spent several months in France. Her mother had given her the opportunity to do an advanced course in French, which Helen speaks fluently. While she was away Helen was able to take time out to reflect and experience some healing. She also wrote another song called 'Compassion', which truly reflects her values. One verse says:

Send us out with the love that flows from you,
Open my eyes to see the need you can fill,
Break my heart with the pain they're going through,
Lord, give us compassion for the lost.

Strong words for a nineteen-year-old, the words of someone who feels deeply, very deeply. They are the words of a person who feels the pain of this world and wants to respond to that pain with all the love she has, with all the love she receives from God.

In 1998, Helen returned to her studies at university, but again she struggled with ill health, depression and lack of motivation. She needed to be 'hands on' doing real social work, in a God-inspired way, so she discontinued her course.

In 1999 Helen turned to ministry work in the church. She started as a youth leader, without pay, supporting herself by casual work in a coffee shop. During the year she attended a conference in Canberra, and heard the Quest Australia vision of 'filling the streets of Sydney with creative arts during the Olympic Games'. Inspired by this vision, Helen started a worship dance group, called X-treme Dance, which went on to win several awards. The dance group was also an expression of Helen's dream, and by the time of the Olympics in September 2000, they had the confidence and commitment to bring worship dance to the streets and plazas of Sydney.

It was in 1999 that Helen joined a friend, Sarah Dunbar, who had arranged a mission trip to the Aboriginal community at Papunya. It was a mission to meet and understand and love these indigenous people, an act of reconciliation. The trip led to an evening of creative arts in Sydney called 'Dance upon Injustice'. It was held under the auspices of World Vision Indigenous Programs. Helen and Sarah and others produced an evening telling the story of the Papunya people and the injustices that they had suffered.

Helen has also developed a team of young men and women to use drama as a means of communicating the gospel message. She is willing to experiment, to risk, and to reach out to people, both inside and outside the church, to bring them the message of God's love. Her youth leadership is bringing young people closer to God.

Helen shows us a way to change the world. It starts with faith in the God who made us all, it grows in the experience of God's love for us, and it comes into the world in an expression of creativity which is truthful and beautiful.

Youth leader, song writer, singer, dancer, dramatist, social activist – these are all 'labels' that could be used to describe this young woman. But only when you see someone who deeply and passionately loves God do you see the real Helen.

This year, Helen is planning to develop her skills by undertaking studies in creative ministries, and to broaden her ministry work to reach all ages in our society. The senior minister at St Stephens has appointed her as the creative arts coordinator, an innovative and bold initiative for a church. Helen has become stronger; her dream is becoming a reality.

Helen says she still doesn't really understand why she is so passionate about the use of creative arts to fight injustice. She believes it works in the spiritual realm, and brings about change for the better in people's souls.

How many other 'Helens' are there in Australia today? Young men and women, passionate about life, searching for ways to bring love into a loveless and godless society? Let us all hope and pray that our 'Helens' are supported, encouraged and loved, and perhaps then Australia will become a truly compassionate and just society.

You have healed my heart and set it free,
You gave me life through the One who died for me,
You fill my soul with a love that never ends
Lord, let your love flow through me.

Helen Scotford, 'Compassion'

Norm Smith: The Master Coach

RICHARD WARD

Norm Smith, the champion ex-Melbourne footballer, and multiple premiership-winning coach of the Demons, was coming to coach South Melbourne in the VFL competition.

As a thirty-year-old football-mad doctor with my own practice, and working as a medical officer for the South Melbourne Football Club, I was tremendously excited by this announcement, but I was also curious. Why was he coming?

Norm Smith had nothing to prove. He was the most successful coach in the modern football era. He was openly admired by all football followers, deeply loved by the supporters of his Melbourne Football Club and superficially disliked by the supporters of his opponents' clubs, especially Collingwood, who seemed to suffer most at the hands of his coaching brilliance. He had also nurtured Ron Barassi, who had already set a great example both on the playing field and in the coaching arena.

South Melbourne was a club of great tradition and an essential part of the working-class communities of Port Melbourne and South Melbourne. Their home ground was Lakeside Oval and they were commonly called the Swans. They came from a tough area and were affectionately referred to as 'the Bloods'. Their last premiership had been in 1933, when they won the flag with a team full of imports. Their last Grand Final was in 1945, when they were defeated by Carlton at the Prince's Oval (the MCG was being used by the armed forces) in a violent game remembered as the 'bloodbath' Grand Final. The club had been the breeding place for many brilliant individual and team-oriented players and Brownlow Medallists, unmatched by any other team, and yet they had not played in a Finals series for twenty-five years.

The players and staff were not sure what to expect from Norm Smith's coaching. It wasn't long before they were very surprised. One evening early in the season, when the players were getting ready for yet another training night on a damp ground, Norm stopped them, told them to have a shower and get dressed, because 'we're all going to the Chevron for a dinner dance'. Thirty minutes later a bus arrived with the wives and girlfriends of the players on board. Norm had individually contacted these women, sworn them to secrecy, and invited them to come along so that everyone could get to know everybody else. It was a wonderful night and Norm and his wife, Marj, were the centre of attention and activity, with Norm dancing with every woman in the room and having an ale with every man in the room. Norm loved his beer.

In the weeks that followed, one had the feeling that the superglue applied that night was starting to set and that the talented ingredients of this football club were blending into a strongly bonded team. The players responded to Norm's illustrious presence. Fred Way, a ruckman, drove his truck down from Berrigan in New South Wales to train twice a week, returning home immediately after each session. Russell Cook, also a ruckman, arranged time off from his police duties to attend training. John Sudholz, a full-forward, travelled from his farm, as did an exciting young half-forward flanker, Jim Prentice. Port Melbourne provided several young recruits, including Shane McKew and Gary Bryce, and there was the brilliant backdrop of Bobby Skilton, John Pitura, John Rantall, Peter Bedford, Reg Gleeson, Greg Lambert, Dave McLeish and Wayne Walsh. Norm was not the coach, he was part of the team, and belief grew that this team could be successful.

With Norm, only the best would do. In 1970 South Melbourne played Carlton at the Lakeside Oval and was leading by twelve goals early in the last quarter. One of the players made a foolish mistake on the backline, which allowed Carlton to score an easy goal. I was standing with some of the support staff on the boundary watching the game when I heard a very loud thud, then deathly silence, followed by the hasty departure of the runner from the benches to deliver a message to the offending player.

A couple of minutes later Norm tapped me on the shoulder and said, 'You better have a look at this, Doc,' and showed me the back of his right hand, where he had three deeply cut and bleeding knuckles. I looked at the assistant coach, who simply pointed his finger at the corrugated roof of the little tin box where the coaches and support staff sat. Norm had punched the roof, dinting it and loosening one of the holding-down nails. That was the only injury South Melbourne suffered that day.

As usual, after each home game, we'd all go down to the pub opposite the South Melbourne market. The players, coaching staff, support staff and die-hard supporters would go down to have a beer with Norm. He would talk to them all night as long as it was about his passion, football. He never refused to talk to anybody, friend or foe, about the game he loved. He loved the football supporters, regarding them as the backbone of the game, and deeply respected club allegiances.

One fine day when we were playing Collingwood at Victoria Park, Norm put on his grey plastic raincoat and then threw one to me. 'Put this on, Doc. You'll need it,' he said.

I replied, 'Norm, it's not raining,' to which he replied, 'Put it on, it will be soon.'

As we walked up the race after the players had entered the field, he said, 'Walk with me, but stay on the inside of the field and stay inside the boundary line.' I asked why I needed to do this on such a sunny day. He said, 'They hate me out here and they have every right to. Look what I did to them in the 1950s. Some of them will spit at me, but they're getting older and six feet is their range, so we'll walk inside the boundary line. Throw the raincoat away at the end of the day.' We then sat on the bench on the boundary line, and during the next two and a half hours I heard a constant tirade of profanity and life-threatening abuse that has remained in my memory ever since.

At the end of the day, as we walked from the field, without police protection, Norm told me, 'I'm still their enemy, but they don't dislike me nearly as much as before the game.' Their side had won.

The South Melbourne Football Club, coached by Norm Smith, made the Finals series that year. On 29 August 1970 we played St Kilda in the first Semi-final in front of a record crowd, in the vicinity of 109 000 people, at the MCG.

There were three distinct roars that day. The first roar was when St Kilda ran onto the arena. It was deafening and matched only by the second roar, which erupted when South Melbourne entered to contest their first Finals series for twenty-five years. As I walked onto the arena with Norm Smith a third and even greater roar erupted from the crowd. The football public was saluting the Master Coach.

We were the underdogs. It was to be champion Bobby Skilton's first appearance in a Finals series, and his last game of football. We were inexperienced in Finals campaigns and were relying heavily on skilful and courageous players to upset the physically stronger and more favoured St Kilda. We got to the lead just before half-time, but faded in the second half. In the final quarter Norm Smith told Keith Baskin, our super-quick, highly skilled, uncanny but unpredictable player, to do whatever he liked up forward: nothing ventured, nothing gained. The move was audacious, and successful for the first ten minutes, but the weight of experience saw St Kilda steady and creep away finally to a comfortable victory. Prophetically, Ron Barassi used this ploy to great effect three weeks later to win the 1970 flag!

Then it was time for the end-of-season football trip. I think every team in the VFL went to Surfers Paradise; certainly South Melbourne always did. We stayed at the Beachcomber Hotel in Cavill Avenue. It was a comfortable, old-fashioned hotel with large double rooms and relatively unbreakable fixtures, in close proximity to the very popular Surfers Paradise Beer Garden. Norm seemed to know everybody in Surfers and everybody seemed dedicated to getting Norm intoxicated. I roomed with him to make sure he got to bed safely and as healthily as possible.

On our second afternoon we were all gathered in the beer garden when a testosterone-induced altercation broke out between two of our players, who were brothers. Norm was furious. He got them by the ears and dragged them into the male toilet just off the drinking area. Both boys were bleeding from cut eyebrows. Fortunately there were two cubicles so both brothers had a seat. Norm stood there and gave them the best lecture I've ever heard any father give a son. He talked about the values of the club, about being proud of what they had achieved that year. He told them they owed the club a lot and it was about time they started to repay the debt. They were to apologise to each other in front of their team-mates and to the management for causing a fracas in the beer garden, and if any further trouble occurred, they would be sent back to Melbourne immediately. He then despatched me to get my surgical instruments and I sutured their lacerations, using the cubicles as my operating theatre. Fifteen minutes later, the two sobered brothers emerged from the toilets, apologised appropriately, and resumed their holiday. Norm never mentioned the incident again.

One night at approximately 2 a.m., I was asleep on my side of the large room when I heard the door open. The lights were off and in the glow from the hallway light I saw Norm enter. He was very unsteady on his feet and had obviously been heavily entertained by his many friends in Queensland. I heard a heavy squeak as he sat down on his bed and a clunk as he removed his shoes and dropped them on the floor. I said to myself, 'Well, at least he's at home and in one piece,' and rolled over to get back to sleep. About a minute later I felt the bedclothes of my bed being thrown back as Norm jumped in and covered himself up. I thought the tiny bed was going to break.

'Doc, are you awake?'

'I am now, Norm.'

'Good. Doc, I've got a question to ask you. Where the hell are we going to play Keith Baskin next year?' He then fell deeply asleep. I extricated myself from being crushed against the wall and went to sleep in his bed, fully convinced that I had now met somebody who ate, slept and dreamed football.

Meeting a Friend

FATHER LEO HILL

Death is always a great mystery for us. We have never died before and we don't know what our personal death will be like. Will I have time to prepare for it, to say my goodbyes surrounded by caring family and friends, or will I die alone, suddenly, as in a car accident? The future is hidden from our eyes and perhaps that's a good thing.

I would like to share with you my first experience with a person dying and how he faced up to his own passing. It was my father. He was sixty-seven and had never had a day's sickness in his life. In July 1963, he was diagnosed with bowel cancer. In those days, cancer was not just a word but a sentence.

He was operated on in Melbourne. The cancer had spread to the liver. There was no hope. He was sewn up and left to die in the care of his wife, family and friends, and in the final days in the devoted and professional care of the staff of the local hospital.

We were forbidden to tell him he had inoperable cancer. The doctor said, 'If they know, they become impossible to nurse and drop their bundle!' That was the attitude in those days. When I protested about not telling him, as I knew my father would like to prepare himself for death, sort out his business affairs and say his 'goodbyes', the doctor conceded, 'You can tell him if he asks!'

My father never asked the family or me. However, before he left hospital, he did ask Sister Angelinda who nursed him, 'I presume it's cancer. How long have I left?' The 'little angel' said, 'You guessed right. You have three to four months to live.'

We played cat and mouse for two months. I asked leading questions, but got no significant replies. He wanted to keep his secret to himself lest he hurt us with his sad news. In the end I wrote to him and told him he had cancer, and had two months left. He was now able to share his secret with his family and friends.

Back home, where he seemed to regain strength, he was soon attending mass each day at his parish church. The liturgical prayers took on a different meaning now: 'Grant us peace in this life, save us from final damnation, and count us among those you have chosen.' 'Keep us faithful to your teaching and never let us be parted from you . . . May the Body of Christ bring us to everlasting life.' It was amazing – new situations, new emphasis.

My Father continued his daily mass right up to a week before his death. Some mornings he drove the car up to the side door of the church and stayed there during mass. He was too weak to enter the church, and the priest brought him Communion as he sat and prayed in his car.

Instead of poring over the daily papers as he was wont to do, he turned his attention to the gospel stories and meditated on the life of Jesus. He said to his wife: 'Amy, you know how excited we were this time last year when I took you back home to Ireland? Well I am just as excited about going to heaven.

'To think, in a few weeks I'll be in heaven and be able to see Jesus face to face! I'm not afraid to die. I'm sad to be leaving you all behind. This is a lonely journey and a painful one, but I'm going to meet a friend.'

My father, Philip Hill, died peacefully and full of hope on 16 November 1963, and he was given one of the biggest funerals Colac had ever seen.

Biographies

JULIE ANTHONY | Julie Anthony holds a unique place in the heart of the Australian entertainment industry. Her long list of achievements on the concert stage, in musicals, cabaret and on television reflect a remarkable career spanning almost thirty years.

From a 600 hectare property in South Australia, she travelled to Sydney, then to London's West End for *A Star is Born*. This was followed by a period in the USA, where she performed with such great stars as Bill Cosby, Roy Clarke and Merv Griffiths.

In more recent years Julie helped establish 'Advance Australia Fair' as our national anthem, giving it the heart and soul it needed. Her recording became the definitive version.

It was Major General Peter Cosgrove who, in 2000, called Julie 'Australia's Sweetheart', and it was a very proud nation that saluted her when Julie delivered her unforgettable rendition of 'Advance Australia Fair' at the opening ceremony of the Sydney Olympic Games.

JULIE AUNGER | In the two years that she has lived at Garfield, Julie Aunger has been on a learning curve that has changed the way she sees reality. Today she works as a volunteer in her community and is secretary of the Howqua Landcare Group, whose members are dedicated to the improvement and maintenance of the Howqua Valley and Howqua River. Julie is also secretary of a small investment group whose members are women in the valley who are taking responsibility for their long-term financial security and have chosen to invest their monies in ethical companies.

Julie's door is always open to people and animals who need help. She is dedicating the rest of her life to her spiritual wellbeing and that of others.

ARI BADAINES | Ari Badaines PHD is a clinical psychologist who trained in the USA. He migrated to England in 1972. He practised there until 1985, when he moved to Sydney. He now has a psychology practice, teaches, consults with organisations and runs training groups in Sydney and Melbourne.

Each year Ari returns to Europe, where he facilitates a variety of training and experiential groups. Visiting his two daughters and three grandchildren, having fun, playing baseball and being mischievous are his ways of counterbalancing his serious side.

DAVID BARDAS | David Bardas was the head of the Sportsgirl Sportscraft Group for thirty-seven years. A lawyer by training, a businessman by necessity and now a poet by choice, David has written and published a book, *Clown Hall*, an insider's view of bureaucracy, and a set of business tools called the 'Success Pac'. He has been on the Melbourne City Council and was an original member of the 'Life Be In It' and 'Action in Melbourne' committees.

He is sixty-three, has a wife and six children, and is a passionate republican and supporter of reconciliation.

CAROL BATES | Carol Bates was born in England in 1945. Her family migrated to Australia when she was four years old and she spent her childhood in Mt Macedon.

Married for thirty-five years and with two adult sons, she is currently doing everything she has ever wanted to do, including studying natural therapies and writing a book on franchising. She would love to hear from franchisees who have encountered problems, and particularly from people contemplating franchising their business, so that she can use her expertise to help them avoid hidden pitfalls.

To contact Carol, phone or fax 03 9682 3553.

RAY BEATTY | Ray owns a marketing company called Beatty Marketing Solutions. An English journalist who spent three years hitch-hiking around the world, he arrived in Australia in 1970. He writes articles for magazines, sits on committees of the Melbourne PC Users Group and Melbourne Youth Music and is an incorrigible opera addict. Ray is married to image consultant Pam Abeling and has two children and two stepdaughters.

To contact Ray, email: raybea@melbpc.org.au or web: www.ebeatty.com

BRIAN BELL | When a change in perspective brought about by facing difficulties in life resulted in depression, the only relief Brian Bell could find from this was in the creative process of writing poetry. Within four years he had won the Gulgong Henry Lawson Award, and this was followed by the Will Ogilvie Prize, the John O'Brien Poetry Prize, the Bremer Valley Poetry Award and the first Bundanoon Reciter's Cup.

Today, Brian recites for Rotary and similar organisations – a far cry from his past life of accounting and computer programming.

ARTHUR BRAITHWAITE | Arthur Braithwaite was born in Melbourne in 1932. He joined the priesthood in 1959 with a group called Missionaries of the Sacred Heart, a worldwide religious society whose Australian base was established in Sydney in 1885. Its works extend from Japan to Tasmania, serving Aborigines, Papua New Guineans and Pacific Islanders. After spending twenty-five years in colleges, Arthur is now based in Sydney, involved in counselling work and chaplaincies. In recent years he has become involved with preparing engaged couples for married life or lifelong relationships. He also ministers marriages, and receives requests to conduct the christenings or naming days that inevitably follow.

To contact Arthur, phone 02 9181 5982 or email arthurbr@ozemail.com.au

SALLY BROWNE | Sally Browne is a small-business dynamo, fashion identity and futurist. She has received myriad awards for excellence in fashion design and outstanding business leadership.

During the 1970s and 1980s, Sally built a diverse multi-million-dollar fashion empire. Then, in the early 1990s she opened a lifestyle company and worked with scientists in Finland developing a Polar Mentor, the first heart-rate monitor to identify stress.

In the late 1990s Sally focused on researching future lifestyle and business trends and is currently a very popular keynote business speaker. She has four children, loves adventure and serves on many community and business committees.

SUE CARR | Sue Carr began her interior architecture practice, now the CARR Design Group, in 1971. She became known for her high standards of creative design with her work, winning design awards and being widely published in Australia and overseas.

Sue's completed projects demonstrate a capacity to push conventional boundaries: the Australian Stock Exchange, Citibank, Santos, Tabcorp, ANZ Securities and Hindal Corporation are just some of her clients. Projects undertaken recently include the Westin Hotel, City Square, Melbourne; the Mercure Hotel, Spring Street, Melbourne; the Hotel Causeway, Melbourne; the Park Royal, Parramatta; and the Wentworth Hotel, Sydney.

For recreation Sue enjoys theatre, books, music, travel, art and gardens.

She has a passion for her family, living life to the fullest, and making a difference in the design world.

Phillipa Challis | Phillipa Challis is a dynamic professional speaker and MC. During her presentations she passes on an expertise gathered from over thirty years in the public-relations and promotions industry. Her company, Get Noticed, provides keynote presentations and seminars in Australia and overseas that motivate individuals, corporations and organisations to raise their profile and increase their profits.

To contact Phillipa, phone 03 5221 4266 or email 1challis@tpgi.com.au

Sue Chapman-Popa | Sue Chapman-Popa, the youngest of five children, was born in Flint, Michigan, USA, in 1962.

She has spent most of her life outside the USA, particularly in Germany and Australia. An elite oarswoman, she has represented Australia at several events, including the Olympic Games and the Commonwealth Games, winning medals at both. Sue also works as a personal trainer.

Sue and her husband Ion have owned a retail business since 1991. They live in Melbourne and have two beautiful children, Ted and Rosie.

Yvonne Cholmondeley | Yvonne Cholmondeley was born in New Zealand. After a stint in the Royal Women's NZ Naval Service as a radio telegraphist, she married a Canterbury farmer.

With four children to educate, the family later relocated to a larger country area with an excellent high school. From then on Yvonne was able to turn her hand to crafts, such as spinning, weaving, floral art, sewing and writing. Being an avid listener to other people's experiences, she sometimes confounds herself with her memories, but on the other hand, she can't for the life of her remember where she put her specs!

Yvonne and her husband, Charles, have lived in Australia for twenty-two years to be near their children and grandchildren.

RON CLARKE | Ron Clarke set more official world running records by greater margins for the middle distances than any other athlete in the history of the sport, yet he did so while pursuing a full-time, highly responsible career in his profession as an accountant and raising a family of three children.

Ron has been happily married to Helen for forty-two years and has two grandchildren. He remains fully involved in life and recently conceived, designed and built the award-winning Couran Cove Resort on South Stradbroke Island and the nearby Runaway Bay Sports Centre.

Ron has recently published his tenth book, *Run Easy*.

MERLIE CLAYTON | Merlie Clayton was born in Gisborne, Victoria, in 1937, is married to Barry and has four children.

She has a passion for writing, and her published works include the children's book *Grandpa's Gone to Heaven*, numerous short stories and feature articles. She has also written several plays that have been performed.

Every event in Merlie's life has the potential to evolve as a story, and she has great fun embellishing a fact to make writing more interesting. Merlie likes to inspire others to write – to paint pictures with words – and is currently tutoring children and adults in creative writing at South Kingsville Community Centre.

PHYLLIS CRAWCOUR | Phyllis Crawcour is sixty-one, has been married to Michael for forty-two years and has three married sons and one beautiful grandson. In retirement, Phyllis and Michael purchased a country property and opened an extremely successful tea room and tourist shop. Unfortunately, breast cancer and chemotherapy treatment made it impossible for Phyllis to maintain the business and it closed. Two years later, she was sentenced to four and a half years' jail, of which she had to serve a minimum of three years.

ANN DAVIS | Ann Davis, a Sydney writer, has had articles, fiction and poetry published in a wide variety of newspapers, magazines and journals.

Her first collection of poetry, *Moths and Camels*, was published in 2001.

Ann was the deputy chair of the organising committee for the twenty-first World Congress of Poets, held in October 2001. As the mother of five daughters, she has ample material on which to base her 'fiction'.

KATHRYN DAVIS | Kathryn Davis has spent thirty years trying to find the meaning of life and has so far worked out how to operate a VCR. The second of Australian poet Ann Davis's five daughters, she is an expert on blaming other people and getting away with it.

Beloved by small children and stray dogs, she is thrilled to be published here for the first time.

DIANE DEEMING | Diane Deeming lives in the Adelaide foothills with her daughter, Maryanne. She operates a small home-based business specialising in major events and marketing. Diane enjoys interacting with her daughter and her teenage friends and loves theatre, writing, cooking and furniture restoration. She keeps fit at the gym, walks the dog, and plays an enthusiastic but abysmal game of golf.

MATTHEW DENNE | Born on Valentine's Day in 1980, Matthew Denne moved with his family from Sydney to Mount Hunter, about an hour's drive from Sydney, from there to Devonport, Tasmania, and then to Grafton, New South Wales. Later Matthew went to boarding school in Toowoomba, Queensland, while his family lived in Murgon. He is currently in Brisbane, where he is studying commerce at the University of Queensland and working full time for an accountancy firm.

BRENDA DIMMITT | Brenda commenced her working life in Melbourne at age sixteen, learning the booktrade, both retail and wholesale. Six years later, in 1969, she set out for England on a working holiday and, for the first five months, managed a small bookshop in London's Chancery Lane. However, lack of adequate income led her to seek a 'live-in' position where she found herself as nanny to the two young children of British actress Dorothy Tutin. After three years, Brenda returned to Australia and eventually took up nursing in 1975. For fifteen years she specialized as a urology nurse at the Austin Hospital Spinal Unit. She now enjoys semi-retirement and concentrates on her love of writing.

STEVE DUFFY | Born Stephen David Duffy in September 1951, Stephen was also known variously as Bilbo, Stevo, Duff and Duffy. From a large working-class family in inner-city Melbourne, Stephen started cooking at home at the age of eleven, later dabbling with university and teachers' college. In the early 1970s, Stephen got into cooking professionally in Sydney, travelled a bit overseas, then returned to Melbourne to work as a chef in several restaurants and pubs . . . and is still doing it!

Now with a wonderful partner and three sons, in retrospect he would have liked to have been an artist, builder and designer as well. Stephen jumped off a mountain for the first time (rope attached) only three years ago – but that was easy compared to what had come before.

BARRY EVERINGHAM | Barry Everingham is an internationally known broadcaster, author and journalist. He recently returned to Australia after working in New York where he was consulting for public relations clients. He was, in addition, providing comments for MSNBC and Extra! TV. Barry operates a niche public-relations consultancy in Melbourne.

EVELYN M. FIELD | Evelyn M. Field is a counselling psychologist in private practice. She sees children, adolescents and adults. She has developed a simple social survival skills model, the 'Secrets of Relating', and has presented her work locally and internationally.

Evelyn speaks professionally on bullying in the school and workplace. Her book *Bully Busting* was published by Finch in 1999. She is currently writing a book on dealing with bullying in the workplace.

Evelyn was an ambassador for National Friendship Day and is actively involved with the Australian Psychological Society.

To contact Evelyn, phone 03 9509 1414 or email efield@netspace.net.au

ELIZABETH FINLAY | For Queenslander Elizabeth Finlay, her love of health and fitness came easily. At eighteen she trained as a grooming schoolteacher. After marrying at twenty-one, she moved to London and established her own grooming business. In 1982 she became a writer on health, fitness and beauty while working as public relations coordinator for a chain of health clubs.

Living in Bermuda and married to Canadian John Finlay, she has two daughters, Lisa and Ellie Heine, and three stepdaughters. She is currently taking her second writing course and is midway through her first novel.

MARY FRYDENLUND | Born in Norway in 1946, Mary Frydenlund is the daughter of a war bride from England and a Norwegian. She worked at Norwegian Telecom in Oslo from 1964 until 1997. In 1970 she married Jan Arne and moved to Gjovik. Jan Arne is an architect, and daughter Ellen, born in 1972, was married in 1997.

Mary is now enjoying life as the grandmother of three-year-old Jan Kristian and baby Mina Sophie. Her hobbies are china-painting, rubber-stamping and mushroom-picking in autumn (she delivers mushrooms to the best restaurant in Gjovik!). She also loves knitting, reading, gardening, skiing and tennis – in fact, all the things she did not have time to do in the years she was working.

PROFESSOR JOHN FUNDER | John Funder was educated by the Jesuits and at Melbourne University, and has worked in medical research for thirty-five years. He has published over 400 scientific papers, and occasionally on other topics. These include *All Really Great Lies are Half True* (Science, 1979), a chapter in *More Memories of Melbourne University* (Century Hutchinson, 1985), *A Tale of Three Cities* (Steroids, 1994) and

'Melbourne Millefeuille' in the *Oxford Book of Australian Schooldays* (OUP, 1997).

NADA GLAVIC | Nada Glavic migrated to Australia from Croatia with her family at the age of six, settling in Geelong. Just as she was starting Year 11, she married and moved to Melbourne. She had her first son at seventeen and the second at twenty-one.

From then on, life experiences were Nada's education. She used to view her journey through life as something very painful, but she kept going. It is only looking back now that she sees it as liberating. Pain, she believes, is sometimes a blessing in disguise.

TOTTIE GOLDSMITH | Tottie was born into a showbiz family: her father, Brian, was the doyen of the Melbourne night-club industry and her aunt, Olivia Newton-John, provided early inspiration. As a teenager Tottie appeared in many television shows, which led to acting roles in the ABC series *Harvey McHugh,* the Paramount production of *Mission Impossible*, the Nine Network's *Law of the Land* and Grundy's *Embassy.*

Upon leaving 'The Chantoozies', the band of which she was a founding member, Tottie embarked on a solo career, singing and studying acting in America. In 1996 Tottie signed on as host of Channel 10's controversial series *Sex/Life.* During this time she also headlined Melbourne's top-rating breakfast program on TTFM. In 1998 Tottie played Janet in *The New Rocky Horror Show* at Sydney's Star City. It was a role which offered Tottie the chance to display her many talents – a culmination of all her acting, singing and dancing experience. Tottie continues to be a big part of Australia's entertainment industry with many exciting forthcoming challenges on stage and in front of the camera.

DEBORAH GRAY | Deborah Gray is mother to a wonderful teenage son and a particularly unattractive tom cat. Her public relations business and various radio gigs keep her out of trouble and on the edge. Her hobbies include drinking French champagne, eating junk food, jogging and Jenny Craig. And what of the future? She still hasn't decided what she'll do when she grows up!

ELLEN GREEN | Ellen Green trained as a primary-school teacher, specialising in infant method. She spent the last twenty years of her working life in teachers' colleges as a lecturer and school-experience officer. She took early retirement and has been involved in sharing her experiences and her expertise with others. She does volunteer work in role-playing for medical students through the Alzheimer's Association.

BRENDAN GULLIFER | After almost a decade as a journalist in Australia and Asia, Brendan Gullifer became the Australian commercial representative for the UK-based business magazine *The Economist*. In 1988 he was convener of the major Australian trade and investment conference, The Australia Summit. In 2000 Brendan was managing director, Australia/New Zealand, for PressPoint, a US publishing company with strong involvement in the Sydney 2000 Olympic Games. Brendan is an inveterate traveller, former marathon runner, motorcyclist and horse-rider. He has a passion for technology, biographies and world affairs.

Brendan is married to Robyn and has three children, three cats and a dog. He now works as a real-estate agent with Collins Simms and lives in Melbourne.

ATHOL GUY | Athol Guy spent forty years in the communications and music industries. He still enjoys every moment of public contact, whether on behalf of a short list of prestige clients or musically with his best friends, The Seekers. His eight years as a member of State parliament (1971–1979) was his 'degree in Humanity'.

'Life is all about the inexact science of personal relationships,' says Athol. 'Every story worth telling should reveal a little more of the ultimate puzzle.'

IAN HAIGH | Ian Haigh has spent the last ten years in the welfare sector with development and fundraising responsibilities. He has worked with the Smith Family and Odyssey House Victoria and is currently working with the Spastic Society of Victoria.

For many years he worked as a journalist in newspapers and television and later in public relations in the corporate area and as a private consultant.

DR JANET HALL | Dr Janet Hall is a psychologist in private practice in Richmond, Melbourne. She specialises in stress management, success coaching and family and relationship therapy. She is the author of six books on family issues, including *Fight-free Families*, *Fear-free Children* and *Sex-wise Teens*. Jan co-authored the software program 'Goalmaker', which helps you to set goals and manage your progress to success.

Jan has produced seventeen audio tapes on sexual issues ranging from sex therapy with adjunctive hypnosis to sexual fantasies and strategies for 'sparking up' your sex life.

To contact Jan, write to 69 Erin Street, Richmond, Victoria 3121, phone 03 9429 1677, fax 03 9429 7822, email hall@goalmaker.com or visit her websites www.sex-therapy.com.au and www.goalmaker.com/asc

MARY ANNE HARTLEY | Mary Anne Hartley is a Melbourne barrister and company director. She began her professional career as a psychologist, and was a partner in a national law firm before joining the Bar in 1977. She shares her domestic life with Althea, her teenage daughter, and Joseph, whose love of football means daily devotion to watching the game – live on TV and even on the Internet.

FATHER LEO HILL | Father Leo Hill MSC was born in Camperdown, Victoria, in 1932, the youngest of eight children. Leo's family moved to Colac in 1942. In 1947 he left home to begin his studies for the priesthood at the Juniorate for the Missionaries of the Sacred Heart at Douglas Park.

He was ordained in St Patrick's Cathedral, Melbourne, in 1959, and has worked in parishes throughout Australia. Leo also gave missions and retreats for ten years. He is now engaged in parish supply work for the Sacred Heart Monastery in Kensington, New South Wales.

CHARLIE HOGG | Charlie Hogg grew up in Melbourne and began a degree in architecture at Melbourne University. He did not complete the course and after extensive travel began studying with the Brahma Kumaris World Spiritual University in London. Charlie now co-ordinates thirty Brahma Kumaris Meditation Centres around Australia. He has visited more than forty countries around the world, speaking about spirituality and the benefits of meditation. He is based at the Brahma Kumaris Centre for Spiritual Learning at Leura in the Blue Mountains.

JAMES HORSMAN | James went back to school and passed Year 11. He has now moved back to Melbourne and still hasn't gone back to drugs, nor does he want to. He lost a few mates because he didn't want to do drugs anymore, but at the same time he has made more mates because he doesn't do drugs. The only thing he does now is smoke cigarettes and drink a fair bit of beer when he goes pubbing. He got his life on track when he went to stay with Donald. His life is still on track 'and that's the way it will stay'.

DANIEL JOHNSON | Daniel Johnson is the co-author of two previous books with Sue Calwell: *There's More to Life than Sex and Money* and *There's So Much More to Life than Sex and Money*. He has also written nearly a dozen other books on customer service and personal motivation. He is a devoted family man and lives with his wife and four children in the beautiful ski resort town of Breckenridge, Colorado. He is the founder and owner of Resort Loyalty, Inc., a company that specialises in improving guest service in resort communities. As Daniel always says, 'Love life!'

To contact Daniel, phone +1 970 547 4435, fax +1 970 547 9886 or visit the website www.resortloyalty.com

JULIA KAY | Julia Kay is the mother of two terrific teenagers whom she brings up single-handedly. They are the light and challenge of her life. In her spare time she is a writer, journalist, lecturer and teacher, movement therapist and educational consultant.

JOHN KNOWLES | John Warner Knowles, at sixty-two years of age, is a director of the Knowles Group of Companies and Australian Retirement Communities Pty. Ltd. He lives in Brighton and is divorced but still living with his wife (people do funny things). He has two beautiful daughters, Amber and recently married Camilla.

GLORIA KROPE | Gloria Krope has forged a prominent and successful career in event management and public relations since being crowned Miss Australia in 1978. She helped launch Melbourne's Regent Hotel and the Hayman Island Resort in the 1980s and was widely respected for her outstanding work with the Liberal Party as Executive Director of The 500 Club throughout the 1990s. She remains in demand as one of the country's most talented special events consultants. Gloria lives in Melbourne with her two poodles, Bijoux and Bosie, and spends her spare time travelling to exotic locales to indulge her passion for scuba diving.

GREGORY LANDSMAN | Gregory Landsman is a world-renowned speaker working with Speakers Network International and the author of the highly acclaimed book *The Balance of Beauty Explodes the Body Myth*.

In all his work, Gregory explores the link between looks and love and their inevitable impacts on our relationships and sex lives. He is acknowledged as a leading authority in the areas of relationships, love and body dissatisfaction.

To contact Speakers Network International, phone 02 9953 3399 or email info@speakers.com

GORDON LINDSAY | Gordon Lindsay loves all things mechanical: his real-estate purchases have always been 'garage with house attached' rather than the other way around. When not involved in the engineering business, he is an actor and scriptwriter – an unlikely combination. A believer in fate, he constantly marvels at how things fall into place. As a traveller through life, he is fascinated by the diversity and similarity of cultures and beliefs.

David is currently acting as a consultant and writing a feature film. And he drives, races and rallies his beloved Lagonda at every opportunity.

JILL LOVETT | Born and raised in Sydney, Jill Lovett attended Sydney Girls High School, then worked as a secretary at the University of New South Wales before marrying at the age of twenty-one. She and her husband became the parents of six children: four boys and two girls, in that order.

In 1984 Jill began studying at the University of New England, where she graduated with a Bachelor of Arts in 1990. Following her divorce in 1997, Jill continued post-graduate study at UNE, graduating with a Master of Letters in English in 1999.

Today Jill is also a grandmother of twelve.

JUDY MCARTHUR | Judy McArthur trained as a kindergarten teacher in Melbourne and in later years taught children with special needs, whom she enjoyed integrating into her centre.

When her husband was diagnosed, at fifty-seven, with early-onset dementia, she persevered for months with the Alzheimer's Association of Victoria to set up a support group for other sufferers and their carers. It started as The Young Ones, with Judy as co-founder, and provides a day program as well as social activities and a carers' group. It now also embraces people newly diagnosed and in the early stages of Alzheimer's, and this group is known as The Early Timers.

PETER MCGRATH | Motivated by the story that appears in this book, Peter McGrath left a successful career that had taken him around Australia and to a variety of overseas destinations to form his own business. Please Returnme was created to assist in the return of lost keys to their owners.

To contact Peter, phone 1800 637 180 or visit the website www.pleasereturnme.com.au

JAN MCGUINNESS | Jan's background is in journalism and TV production. She has been a senior writer and editor with the *Age*, the *Times on Sunday* and *The Bulletin*, and a news and current affairs reporter and producer with the ABC in early eighties. Jan now writes for the *Sunday Age* and has a column in the *Melbourne Weekly* and has set up a company to develop web sites as management tools, selling this concept successfully into top corporations and banks.

EDDIE MCGUIRE | Born in Melbourne in 1964 and educated at Christian Brothers College, Eddie McGuire began his media career in 1978 as a football statistician with the *Herald* newspaper. He has been a cricket writer for Australian Associated Press, a sports journalist, a presenter for Channel 10, and a media writer for the *Sunday Observer* and the *Sunday Herald Sun*.

Eddie has also written two bestsellers: *Pants – the Darren Millane Story* and *Footy Show Screamers*, and presents 'The Footy Show' and 'Who Wants to be a Millionaire' for the Nine Network. A devoted Collingwood fan since childhood, Eddie became the president of the club in September 1998.

Away from his professional commitments, Eddie spends time with his wife, Carla, and enjoys running, playing tennis and watching all spectator sports. In December 2000, Eddie and Carla welcomed their first child, Joseph.

WAL MAGGS | Wal Maggs lives with his wife, Beth, in the Lockyer Valley, 100 kilometres west of Brisbane. He is a retired schoolteacher with a keen interest in writing. He has had five books and many articles published. He loves the country life and visiting his seventeen grandchildren.

DOUG MALOUF | Doug Malouf is one of Australia's most highly awarded corporate communicators. He is the only Australian accepted to present keynote presentations for the past ten years at the world's most prestigious forum: the American Society for Training and Development.

In 1966 he was nominated Speaker of the Year by the National Speakers Association – New South Wales chapter. He is foundation vice-president of the National Speakers of Australia, and a fellow of the Australian Marketing Institute, the Institute of Management and the Real Estate Institute.

Doug believes his greatest accolade is to be invited to address the same client again. His phenomenal record of return engagements is testimony to the impact of his presentations.

To contact Doug Malouf, phone 02 9360 5111 or fax 02 9360 5199.

BARRY MARKOFF | Barry Markoff is the managing director of ICMI (formerly ICM), Australia's largest speakers and entertainers bureau. His organisation has seven offices nationwide and is a multiple winner of the Australian Marketing Award for Excellence. In recent times ICM was appointed under licence by the Australian Olympic Committee to run Olympic Communicators, the official Olympic Speakers Bureau.

Markoff, who has a Masters degree from the University of Southern California, has received the Award of Merit from the Victorian Amateur Football Association, is the author of *The Road to A Grade* and has represented Australia in Masters Squash.

SUSIE MARONEY | Susie Maroney OAM has been awarded many times for her sports achievements and she holds at least six world records, including Youngest and Fastest Australian to Swim the English Channel (at age fifteen). She completed the Round Manhattan Island swim at seventeen and was the first person to successfully complete the swim from Havana, Cuba, to Key West, USA. In 1998 she completed the longest swim ever: from Mexico to Cuba.

Susie has received an OAM, a Variety Club Sportswoman of the Year award, a Young Achiever of the Year award (twice!) and many other honours. However, it is for her incredible commitment to community service that Susie will be best remembered by those many organisations and people she has touched and assisted.

COLLEEN MELDRUM | Colleen Meldrum grew up on a property in country Tasmania with her parents and one brother. After being schooled in Tasmania she moved to Sydney where she worked for a large construction company and married a fellow Tasmanian and had two children. Following the break-up of her first marriage, she met and married Richard Meldrum, a leading Melbourne architect.

She became extremely involved with several charities, including the Lord Mayor's Fund, the Queen Elizabeth Centre, St Vincent's Private Hospital, Diabetes support groups, the Melbourne City Mission and College of the Arts, and has worked with the Bone Marrow Institute for the past four years. She now lives with Richard in East Melbourne.

SIMON MOLESWORTH | Simon Molesworth has simultaneously pursued three careers, one in law, a second in environmental planning and a third in cultural heritage. He is the President of the National Trust of Australia (Victoria) and was from December 1986 to December 2000 the Trust's Chairman. From 1987–1992 he was a Commissioner of the Australian Heritage Commission, and as one of seven commissioners, was responsible for identifying and advising the Commonwealth Government on Australia's National Estate.

As a practising barrister he was appointed in 1995 as one of Her Majesty's Counsel, specialising in environmental, planning, local government, heritage and natural resource law. In 1989 he was awarded the Australian Environmental Law Award for being a person who 'Made an outstanding contribution to the development and understanding of environmental law in Australia'.

In October 1995 Simon Molesworth became the National President of the Environment Institute of Australia, the national professional association environmental practitioners. In November 1999 he was awarded an Honorary Fellowship of the Royal Australian Planning Institute and in May 2000 was made a Fellow of the Victorian Planning and Environmental Law Association.

A.R. MORRISON | A.R. Morrison was born in Dubbo, NSW, in 1935 and brought up on Buckiinguy Station near Nyngan. He has spent a lifetime in the sheep and wool industry, variously located in Western Queensland, Sydney and the Riverina region of NSW. For nearly thirty years he has been associated with Merino Stud Breeders – F.S. Falkiner & Sons Pty Ltd, located near Deniliquin. It is Australia's largest sheep stud operation, running over 100 000 sheep on around 300 000 hectares and home of the Boonoke and Wanganella studs formed in 1861. These two studs produced the foundation stock of the Peppin bloodline, from which 80 per cent of Australia's Merino sheep are descended.

A.R. Morrison was chief executive of the F.S. Falkiner Company from 1978 until 2000, which was the period during which it was owned by News Limited. He then retired to live in Melbourne. He was also Chairman of the International Wool Secretariat, later R. & D. Woolmark Company, from 1996 to 1998.

Married twice, he has two sons, one daughter and six grandchildren.

GEOFF MUIRDEN | Geoff Muirden is a man who seeks the truth. He wants to embrace a philosophy that builds truth about God and the world into our lives and makes life on Earth better for others and ourselves so that we can all contribute our best.

NATASHA OBEROI | Natasha Oberoi was born in India in 1963. She was educated in England at Hatherop Castle, Gloucestershire, and Edward Greens, Oxford. Natasha studied French at the Institue de Française in

Villefranche sur Mer in the south of France for one year, prior to attending university in California.

She received a Business and Economics degree from Peppendine University in Malibu, California, and went on to get her Certified Management Accounting degree, for which she was awarded the silver medal for the second highest degree.

Ms Oberoi moved to Melbourne in 1992 and worked for the family business at The Windsor Hotel. She currently resides in Melbourne.

DAVID PALUMBO | David Palumbo was born in Norfolk, Virginia, USA, in 1947. After marrying at twenty-three and having a son, he and his family moved to Washington DC, where he began an apprenticeship in house painting and started flight school, ultimately becoming a flight instructor. He divorced in 1980 and moved to Las Vegas in 1982, where he started a paint contracting business.

David met Olga Tomic through an Internet service designed to help people find partners. After two years of travelling backwards and forwards between Australia and America, he sold his business and moved to Melbourne to live with Olga. After eleven months, he returned to Vegas, and Olga followed shortly afterwards. They both now live in Vegas, where they run an Internet company.

MARGARET PORRITT | Margaret Porritt, founder and managing director of Feathers fashion stores since 1972, has built a successful business on her true belief in customer service, adapting to change and listening to her customers' needs.

Originally an apprentice milliner, Margaret has also worked for Norman Hartnell (London) and Sportsgirl. She won the 1998 Telstra Business Owner Award and, in recognition of her company's high standards of service, the 1999 Metropolitan Fair Trader of the Year Award. In 1999 she was inducted into the Business Women's Hall of Fame. She is a current Australian Retailers Association Victorian Division Councillor and ARA National Councillor.

DR COLETTE RAYMENT | Dr Colette Rayment is an honorary research associate within the Department of Religion, University of Sydney, where she is president of the Society for Religion, Literature and the Arts.

She is a former artistic director of the Australian Theatre for Young People and now writes on the interdependence of religion and literature. Her book *The Shapes of Glory: The Writings of Peter Steele* was published by Spectrum Publications in Melbourne in 2000. She has five sons.

GINA RENNIE | Gina Rennie has exhibited as an artist under the name Gina Peck, starting at the age of five and going on to win prizes in the National Sun Youth Awards and the Greenhills Art Show.

She has had thirteen solo exhibitions and been part of numerous group shows in Australia and overseas. In 1982 she was invited to represent Australia in the Grand Prix D'Art in Monte Carlo. She is also featured in the *Dictionary of Women Artists*, by Max Germaine. Gina holds degrees from Monash and Melbourne universities and has worked as a counsellor for many years.

She believes that she is privileged to have four beautiful children who bring her constant joy and inspiration and with whom she has many fabulous adventures.

ANNIE ROBERTS | Annie Roberts was born in England and immigrated to Australia when she was seven. She attended primary and high school on the Central Coast of Eastern Australia. She has worked in a boy's detention centre, in schools and on a ship. She thrives on travel and has always had an incurable travel bug.

Annie is currently a program coordinator at Lake Ainsworth Sport and Recreation Centre, where she organises and teaches outdoor education programs for children.

Annie writes mainly as a healing tool but also to record emotions experienced and expressed at a particular time. She has recently had a poem selected to appear in a forthcoming publication.

Carol Rojo | Carol Rojo lives in the Tarra Valley just near the Tarra-Bulga National Park. She moved to the country twenty years ago to bring up her three children in a clean, safe environment. Now that her children are grown up, she has returned to work part-time and is looking forward to living her life to the full.

Cameron Schwab | Football is in Cameron Schwab's blood. His father, Alan, was one of the leading administrators in the game for over thirty years, his uncle Frank was a Grand Final umpire, and his cousin Peter is a Premiership player with Hawthorn and now Senior Coach of that club.

Cameron was educated at Camberwell Grammar School. He began his working life as a cadet administrator with the Melbourne Football Club in 1982 at the age of eighteen and later became Melbourne's recruiting manager. In 1988, he was appointed general manager of the Richmond Football Club.

Cameron left Richmond in 1994 to study a Master of Business Administration (MBA) and Master of Marketing at Melbourne University.

In 1997 he was appointed chief executive officer of the Melbourne Football Club. Cameron is now chief executive officer of AFL.com.au, the official Internet site of the AFL. He is also undertaking a Doctor of Business Administration (DBA).

Cameron is thirty-seven years old and has a two-year-old son, Lachlan.

Margaret Sheehan | At the time of Martin's accident, Margaret Sheehan was teaching at Donald Primary School. She went on leave to recover from the tragedy and devote her time to her husband, three children and the exchange student living with them at the time. She worked on the family farm, learned to paint in oils and studied grief counselling. After seventeen months she accepted a part-time position as a literacy tutor at a local high school. She finds every day challenging and rewarding, helping children to improve their literacy skills on a one-to-one basis. She is also establishing a 'Compassionate Friends Group' to provide support for other bereaved parents in the area.

JENNY SMYTH | Born in 1930, in the Depression years, Jenny Smyth had a somewhat haphazard and minimal formal education before starting school proper aged ten years. After spending time overseas, she returned to study arts at Melbourne University, to write reviews and plays, and to work for TSA Johnston creating art works.

With her marriage to Dacre, Jenny became a Naval wife, moving twenty-three times as she and her husband ventured around Australia and the world. In the process, they had four marvellous daughters, one of whom they sadly lost to breast cancer when she was forty-one. They also have a son residing overseas.

Now living in Melbourne, Dacre writes and paints while Jenny tends the edible and children's garden she has created and compiles a family history with a particular focus on her mother, who was born in the Yarra Valley in 1902.

OLGA TOMIC | Olga Tomic is forty-two, currently lives in Las Vegas and is co-owner of two separate businesses, one in Australia and one in America.

By the age of twenty-one she was married, and at twenty-six she had her first child, Ashley. Her second child, Jason, was born when she was twenty-nine and was diagnosed with ADHD at the age of two-and-a-half. By this stage Olga had separated from her husband and was living as a single mum, working full-time.

The following thirteen years were certainly challenging. As well as trying to raise two young children on her own, she resigned from her well-paid managerial position to start a new business in Australia.

In 1998 Olga met David Palumbo (an American) through an Internet dating company. After months and years of travel and expensive phone calls, David moved to Australia in January 2000. While he was applying for residency he was unable to work. They also both realised that business opportunities were better in America at the time, so they decided to move to America and run their company www.salesgalore.com, which is an Internet store.

To contact Olga, write to 4933 W Craig Road, PMB 254 Las Vegas, Nevada 8130, USA, phone +1 702 656 7770 or fax +1 702 656 6166.

LES TWENTYMAN | Les Twentyman OAM, a full-time street worker with Open Family (which he joined in 1977), has had a long and notable history of assisting disadvantaged young people. As a secondary-school teacher for ten years, Les identified many problems with disadvantaged young people. In 1989 he developed the Back to School program, which provides textbooks to homeless children to keep them in school. In 1986 he established the Care for Kids program, which has been adopted by 200 primary schools throughout Victoria. High-profile footballers visit primary schools and act as teachers' aides to encourage children in the classroom. Many of these children live in dysfunctional family circumstances in which education is given low priority. However, the footballers reinforce the importance of education and are viewed as positive role models.

Les has been honoured many times for his efforts and has established a number of innovative programs for excluded youth, most notably the Smorgon Twentieth Man Fund Youth Refuge in Sunshine, Victoria. The Youth Refuge now accommodates 200 young people a year.

In February 2000, Les was nominated by AMP to carry the Olympic Torch in Melbourne.

Les Twentyman has a new book *20 years of life on the Streets*, published by Hardie Grant.

ANTONIETTA VENTURA | Antonietta Ventura was born in Pescara, Central Italy, and came to Australia as an eight-year-old. She left school at fifteen and later resumed study as an adult, the highlight being her enrolment in a Bachelor of Arts at Melbourne University in 1980.

Antonietta has been a voluntary guide at the National Gallery of Victoria for the past ten years and has three adult children.

DR VACY VLAZNA | Dr Vacy Vlazna was born in Czechoslovakia and came to Australia as a child, with her refugee parents. She has a son and daughter and a grandchild on the way. The year 1994 was a milestone for Vacy: she completed a PhD on the mystic experience in the poetry of an American poet and, surprisingly (not the least to herself), became a fervent activist for East Timor, which she had never heard of before.

Vacy visited Timor twice during the Indonesian period (in November 1998 and April-May 1999), worked in UNAMET and was evacuated (shamefully having let the Timorese down) from the UN compound. She returned to work in UNTAET in April 2000.

At present she is a district field officer in Same Subdistrict, the jewel of Timor Loro Sae. 'The Timorese,' she says, 'have captured my soul. Being in Timor is a profound spiritual experience.'

SOPHIE WAJSMAN | Sophie came to Australia from Belgium as a three-year-old with her parents, who had survived the Holocaust. She has had a number of life and career changes. She moved with her husband, Steve, to the Mallee for life on a cattle station. They have a son, Jake. Sophie saw the best of life in the bush and the worst of it when drought and the rural recession hit. When her husband became a Member of Parliament, the family moved back to Melbourne.

Sophie has been a teacher, counsellor, youth worker, consumer worker and marketing consultant. She is available for speaking engagements and can be contacted at halben@ihug.com.au

JAYE WALTON | In 1990, when Jaye Walton considered herself to be retired from a multi-media career stretching over twenty years of television, filming, writing and radio work, she was given the opportunity of assisting in the re-establishment of the Oncological Society of Thailand. It was a challenge she had to accept. She had already been the honorary consul general of Thailand in South Australia and the Northern Territory since 1979; she knew some of Thailand's influential citizens; and she had some experience in charity work and fundraising. (Her Majesty Queen Sirikit graciously became the royal patron of the Oncological Society of Thailand.)

Jaye lived in Thailand from 1990 to 1992, together with her husband and his mother. Since then she has continually travelled between Australia and Thailand, using her media experience to help Thailand and Thai people and to strengthen international relations between the two countries.

CAROLINE WARD | Caroline Ward is the CEO of About People, the Australian-based transition-management firm famous for its creative and humanitarian approach to change management. Blue-chip companies and government departments rely on Caroline to design innovative and effective interventions to enable their people to move to new, more productive, more fulfilling ways of working.

Caroline is the founder of Women of Spirit, a global women's network, and her name has become synonymous with the international women's leadership program The Four Faces of Women. She is a professional speaker, a published writer and a Raja yogi, and spends much of her time trying to maintain balance in life.

To contact Caroline, phone 03 9686 0366, fax 03 9686 0566 or email aboutpeople@aboutpeople.com.au

DR RICHARD WARD | Dr Richard Ward graduated in 1963 and started practising sports medicine in 1967. He was a medico for four Victorian Football League clubs: South Melbourne from 1968 to 1974, Carlton from 1978 to 1983, Richmond from 1983 to 1985 and St Kilda from 1985 to 1987.

Gai Waterhouse | Gai Waterhouse is the daughter of the legendary horsetrainer T.J. Smith. After a prolonged battle with officialdom, Gai was granted her licence to train thoroughbreds in January 1992 and has achieved monumental success at the highest level. Gai has finished in the first three on the Sydney trainers' premiership for the past seven years, winning the title in 1997, when she became only the third trainer in history to train more than 100 metropolitan winners in a season, ten Group One winners among them.

Gai is highly sought after as a public speaker and heads numerous charity committees. Her client list reads like a 'who's who' of business, in Sydney, interstate and overseas.

In 2000, Gai was named Telstra Businesswoman of the Year (NSW), and the National Trust has classified her as a 'living treasure'.

Leon Wiegard | Leon Wiegard played water polo at the Tokyo Olympic Games in 1964 and was vice captain of the water polo team in Munich in 1972. He was the long-term president of the Fitzroy Football Club (AFL) and is president of the Olympians Club of Victoria.

Maureen Weiner | Maureen Weiner was born in Bulawayo, Zimbabwe, and moved to Cape Town, South Africa, where she qualified in medical technology, specialising in blood transfusion. In 1981 she and her husband, Allan, migrated to Australia, where they established The Granary, a vegetarian restaurant, which they ran for ten years.

Maureen then studied bodywork with a special interest in massage and Reiki and today works as a massage therapist. She has written and self-published a book called *Simply Soul*. Maureen lives with her husband and three children, Dylan, Tali and Jake, in Perth, Western Australia.

To contact Maureen, email paz@iinet.net.au

DAVID WESTON | David Weston has enjoyed a thirty-year passionate affair with the tourism and hospitality industry. He has held positions with TAA (now Qantas), Wrest Point Casino, the Tasmanian Convention and Visitors Bureau and Parks Victoria. Currently he is chief executive of Australia's longest-established tourism and hospitality training college, William Angliss Institute.

Like all passionate people, David has a strong belief in contributing to community and industry organisations. At various times he has been on ministerial advisory councils, chaired industry associations and been involved in promoting festivals in his favourite city, Melbourne.

David is often outspoken, is strong-willed and espouses his views with conviction; anyone who interacts with him knows what he stands for and where his passion lies.

'My greatest achievement is to have played and continue to play a role in the development of tourism in Australia, an industry which builds on our greatest strengths, our natural environment and our people.'

SUE WILKINSON | After a very non-eventful education in the outer Melbourne suburb of Watsonia, Sue Wilkinson found herself a horrible job in a sandwich bar and worked her way through teachers' college. She worked in a special school at an old-style institution for four years, enjoying every moment, and while teaching completed a Graduate Diploma in Special Education.

She now teaches life skills to the intellectually disabled at Ascot Vale Special School and has gained a Bachelor of Education in the Hearing-Impaired.

While studying and teaching Sue met Anthony, whom she later married and who taught her all she knows about art. She began painting after she turned thirty, and had several successful exhibitions, before Sue and her husband started a family. Henry was born in 1998, but died when he was thirteen days old. Mabel, his sister, was born on Boxing Day in 1999. Sue is currently pregnant with her third child.

John Williams | John Williams is an executive in the power industry, specialising in strategy and business development. He has provided strategic and leadership advice to power companies in Australia, China, Vietnam, India and Japan.

He is actively involved in the church, with a strong interest in small group ministry and the mentoring of young men and women. John seeks to integrate his spiritual knowledge from the church and his strategic management knowledge from business for the benefit of his work in both spheres. He is exploring the practice and application of the Christian faith in the workplace, in business, and in all aspects of life

John is married to Jenny and they have three sons, Gregory (married to Susan), Christopher and Michael. He lives in French's Forest in Sydney.

Professor Carl Wood | Professor Carl Wood was the foundation professor of the Department of Obstetrics and Gynaecology at Monash University. In 1973 his research team achieved the world's first clinical IVF pregnancy, in Melbourne. While that pregnancy did not progress beyond a few days, in 1980 his team was responsible for the birth of Australia's first IVF baby.

In 1998–99 Professor Wood became director of the Melbourne Fibroid Clinic and director of the Endometriosis Care Centre of Australia. He is currently conducting research into endometriosis.

Professor Wood has lectured around the world on such subjects as infertility, in-vitro fertilisation and premature births and, more recently, gynaecological endoscopy. He has co-authored more than twenty-three books, fifty-eight book chapters and 394 journal articles.